UNHOLY GROUND

John Brady

ARROW BOOKS

Arrow Books Limited
20 Vauxhall Bridge Road, London SW1V 2SA

An imprint of Random Century Group

London Melbourne Sydney Auckland
Johannesburg and agencies throughout
the world

First published in Great Britain in hardback
by Constable & Company Ltd 1989
Arrow edition 1990

Printed and bound in Great Britain by
Courier International Ltd, Tiptree, Essex

ISBN 0 09 978140 9

To Hanna

Strength and love,
Trust and patience

CHAPTER 1

Whoever had held the nylon rope around Combs' neck, whoever had shoved a knee between Combs' shoulder-blades as the life was choked out of him, needn't have been a Hercules. Combs was seventy-three, a decrepit seventy-three. He had thrashed briefly and died. His swollen face and bulging, yellowed eyes greeted Mrs Hartigan, his housekeeper, on Sunday as she was on her way home from evening Mass.

She had walked up to the open door, halloing as she went. Would Mr Combs be wanting dinners during the week or . . . ? No, he wouldn't, she saw then. The kitchen was frosted. She closed her eyes then unbelieving. Mrs Hartigan stood in the doorway, feeling the weight of her own body press gently on her hips, her feet rooted to the floor. Her back ached familiarly, almost a comfort to her now. She wanted to sit down. Birds chortled and fussed in the hedge by the window. The tap dripped slowly, a dull, irregular pat on enamel. The frost was spread over a floor littered with broken crockery, tins and shattered jars, utensils and packages from the cupboards. Through a confusing blend of smells, the kitchen still held that stale

1

bachelor smell she recognised. It was now mixed with the stench of the old man's indignity in death.

The hand resting on the doorhandle was her own, she realised after some time, and this brought her back. She looked out the doorway at the fields beyond. A flock of starlings clouded overhead. The birds landed together under a hedge. Within seconds they were in the air again, swarming. Mrs Hartigan asked herself if this could really be happening. The kitchen like a room unopened for centuries, the dust . . . but more like snow . . . white, angel, Christmas, dead . . . her thoughts ran again: *it's like a tomb, for all the world. . . .*

Something terrible had happened. She backed away from the door, only then feeling the ice grasp her heart. *Is there a murderer here still maybe?* Her heart fluttered. She thought of the phone in the hall, beyond the kitchen. Couldn't go in, no. Spots formed and burst slowly in her vision as she dithered by the door. A lark sang high, unseen, at the end of the day. Mrs Hartigan whispered a prayer, asking God to get her down to the end of the lane alive.

That same Sunday evening, Minogue's gaze was drifting down a row of trees lining a narrow country lane. His eyes wandered over the trees to the Dublin Mountains beyond. One straggly, mustard cloud remained over Two Rock Mountain. To the east, over Killiney Bay, the sky had already darkened. The air was very still, waiting for the first stars. Minogue looked for a moon but found none. A necklace of lights blinked under Killiney Hill. Eight miles out into Dublin Bay, the Kish lighthouse beamed foolishly.

The air was full and moist. Scoutch grass bushed out onto the road. Next to a stile built into the wall opposite, nettles and dock plants reached up to the brambles swelling out from the wall. He gazed at the

2

ruins of the church which lay fifty feet beyond his car, the Romanesque arch there, the gravestones choked with grass. Minogue was spending an hour of his Sunday evening sitting at the base of a cross in Tully, County Dublin. The cross, eleven centuries old, was anchored in a massive granite block itself mounted seven feet up off the road on a bulwark of limestone rocks. The stone, warmed from the day, had no sharp edges to it. When Minogue ran his palm across the warm granite, his thoughts let go at last and he found himself ten minutes later, still stroking the stone but wondering why he couldn't see so clearly now.

Before he climbed down, Minogue stood by the cross and stretched. He turned to look at the ring of mountains. The circulation eased in his legs and he turned to back down the steep steps. Descending, he inadvertently laid his hand on dried bird droppings. He thought he heard a bird chortle in the gloom of the brambles to his right. Wasn't that what they called pathetic fallacy? Down now, he wiped his hand on the back of his weekend trousers.

He smiled when he thought of Jimmy Kilmartin, an Inspector in the Gardai and a pal, and how Kilmartin might envy the birds' ways. Starting Monday, Minogue was to stand in for Kilmartin. Jimmy had finally had to have an operation on his bowel; otherwise, as he confided sheepishly to Minogue, he'd be properly banjacksed for the rest of his days. Minogue had resisted telling him that it might be wise to have the operation now rather than be caught between two stools in later years.

For devilment, Minogue drove back toward Cabinteely and the Bray Road. He drove with only his sidelights on. The road from Tully was now a dark green tunnel, wide enough for but one car. There were very few houses on the road. Minogue slowed to

3

look at a horse which surprised him on a bend. The horse stood motionless in a gap made by the gate in the gloom with the western sky behind. Not for the first time in his life, Minogue felt that there could be no better animal than a horse.

Minogue sighed as he turned onto Brennanstown Road. A half-mile from Cabinteely, it was lined with the houses of the fat-bellied country boys who were retiring behind the burglar alarms and the Tudor mansions here, now that they had gutted Dublin with their office blocks and ghettos. Minogue had heard moaning from Gardai in Cabinteely station about needing more staff to handle the telephone calls. The grandees up on the Brennanstown Road were seeing intruders everywhere. They were worried about their houses being violated while they were holidaying in Miami or Nice. Grubby hands fingering the locks on their gates, pawing their Jags, maybe even looking in the window as they watched television. Couldn't the Gardai mount extra patrols in the area? Minogue had retained enough of the folk memory of the Famine from his native County Clare — where families, farming fields of rock, yielded up life and even merriment — to believe these intruders could be ghosts of their dark fathers.

The traffic-lights in Cabinteely were red. As often happened to him in his waking life, Minogue was reluctantly coming out from a minor road onto a busy one. He was obliged to yield, to wait and watch a stream of cars speeding along the highway. He slouched in his seat, wondering. Of an evening at Tully Cross, he had imagined druids with their followers looking out on the present from the darkness gathering under the trees. And what of the O'Tooles and the O'Byrnes who later raided from the hills, snapping at the edges of the English Pale? What would they make of the place now?

4

Minogue's light turned green and he pulled away from the white line. Tires howled on the road nearby. A crowd of young lads in a BMW deciding at the last minute not to crash a red light. Minogue pulled around them slowly. Three of them, laughing; dressed and coiffed to the nines, rich snots on the way into Dublin, by the cut of them. A cigarette flicked out the window bounced on the roadway, sparking the gloom. Minogue steered his arthritic Fiat onto the new Bray Road. Before he let go of his acid thoughts, he resolved to side with the raiding O'Tooles and the vanquished druids. The gombeen sons could have their BMWs: he would have his pagan stones.

Detective Garda Seamus Hoey telephoned Minogue's home at six fifteen Sunday evening.

"C-O-M-B-S, like you'd comb your hair?" Minogue asked.

"Yes, sir," Hoey replied.

Minogue asked if the scenes-of-the-crime technicians from the Garda Technical Bureau had started the first sweep of the murder-site. Hoey said that they had. The victim's body had already been removed to Loughlinstown Hospital, pending autopsy in James' Hospital. Minogue's eyes followed the pendulum on the heirloom clock hanging in the hall while he listened to Hoey.

During a pause while he heard Hoey turning a page, Minogue said, "Strangled only? Nothing before or after?"

"No, sir. A quick job. No other injuries apparent. Yet."

Minogue waited for Hoey to say more. He heard another page rustle.

"Anything jump out at you, Shea?"

Hoey hesitated before replying. He had been on the Murder Squad for nearly four years, Minogue remembered, but still held the entry rank of Detective Garda. It was said that Shea Hoey didn't care to chase promotion because he had his own way in the hierarchy of the Squad. He had run several investigations, Minogue knew, but Hoey showed no rancour at having Inspector Kilmartin's name go on the press releases and reports.

"No," Hoey said at last. "It's early days yet. The house is a real mess. Soon as we sort out a bit of the stuff scattered around, we might get a move on. . . ."

"Robbery in progress?" Minogue tried.

"Has all the signs."

"Weapon on the site, is there?"

"Not yet located, sir."

"Have you a suspect at hand, Shea?"

" 'Fraid not, sir. I'm thinking it has to be local, though. If it's a robbery, like. To know the place was worth doing."

"Give me directions so." Minogue fumbled for a pencil.

Minogue wondered how he had missed any signs of Combs being strangled on that Sunday evening. That wondering was a conceit, he allowed, because Combs' house was near Kilternan. It was close as a crow flies to where Minogue had kept company with his stones, but Kilternan was below the high ground around Tully. Being a daylight rationalist, Minogue knew that he couldn't have expected divinations of what was happening over the hill from where he himself had put the July Saturday away. No stars over Combs' house, no banshee wails, no ghostly luminance.

It was a quarter to eight before Minogue found the house. The floodlights had raised a halo around it against the dark mass of the hills behind. He had driven through Dundrum to Sandyford and followed the signs for the Scalp. The road could now be called the Enniskerry Road. It corkscrewed its way through Stepaside and widened again before it reached Kilternan. The Scalp, a cleft in the hills which marked the border between Counties Dublin and Wicklow, was still three miles from where Minogue finally stopped.

Hoey had told him to take the turn up to Glencullen but to stop off to the right where he'd meet the first bad bend in the road. Combs' house was up the lane there. The hills above Kilternan were forested with spruce and pine, Minogue remembered, and high up over Glencullen, some miles into the mountains, the mountainsides were bog, carpeted with heather and ferns.

He parked between an unmarked police van and a Toyota Corolla squad-car. Twenty yards further up the road was another car, a Renault, illuminated by stalk lamps which Minogue recognised as forensic site equipment. A generator puttered in the near distance. He stopped by the Toyota. Smoke issued from the open window of the squad-car. The yellow interior light showed two Gardai pushed back in their seats.

"Minogue," he said to the two figures in the Toyota. "Off the Murder Squad. Are ye the first shift looking after the site until morning, is it?"

The driver, a young Garda with a puffy face patterned by acne scars, nodded.

"That's us, sir. We're due a relief about eleven."

Minogue stared up at the faintly milky sky behind the mountains before walking slowly toward the Renault. A scenes-of-the-crime technician squatted on the ditch side of the car. His tongue moved slowly across his bottom lip, his eyebrows silver in the lamp's glare. Minogue had forgotten the technician's name.

"Whose car?"

7

"Victim's," said the technician without looking up from the plastic bags he was sealing. He paused then and squinted up at Minogue, blinking. Widow's peak, bird eyes, Minogue thought: Rogers? McMahon? An old hand anyway.

"Have I safe passage up the lane here, er . . . ?"

"Jim Rogers. Stay to the left of the tape there. Can you see it?"

Minogue drew out a penlight from his jacket pocket. The battery was dead. Rogers turned the lamp toward the laneway. Minogue's eyes followed the taut yellow tape running to the house.

"We've done the lane once. We'll do it proper in the morning. The conditions are bad. Tire treads is all so far. It's all stones around here. Peeping up through the grass even."

Minogue started up the lane. He smelled the heather from the hills. He passed a gap in the hedge, stone posts anchoring a gate. A horse shook its head over the gate at him. Minogue started. The horse moved off the limit of a rope tethered to the gate.

"Don't be trying to frighten me like that, mister," he muttered after the horse. He stopped and looked back down the lane, his heart still pounding from the fright. The night was heavy and still around him. He wondered if the deadness in the air was here all the time.

Hoey was wearing a polo shirt under his jacket. He raised his eyebrows in greeting. Hoey's face was too long — mark of the Irish — the eyes too gentle, set in ruddy features: farmer's boy, a face peering over stone-walled Galway fields. The stakes and plastic ribbons had been erected all around the house. Minogue heard another generator grumbling out of sight. One of the lamps lit up the whole gable end of the house like a film set. Hoey stood behind Minogue

8

in the doorway, both looking over the whitened destruction of the kitchen.

"Did that stuff help us at all, Shea?"

"The flour, with footprints? No. Some settled on the body. So the killer went on wrecking the place after killing the old man. The bag of flour burst over there against the wall."

"Well. Who's here?"

"There's myself, of course. Pat Keating's inside. Two scenes-of-the-crime lads still upstairs," Hoey replied. "The local station is Stepaside. We have two of their district detectives helping us. They're out on interviews right this very minute."

Minogue nodded and stepped back from the doorway.

"Jimmy Kilmartin says how-do, by the way."

"And how's he doing, then?" Hoey asked.

"He's good, Shea. Up and about in a few days. I might go and see him tonight if I have the time later."

"Great. Great," said Hoey. The enthusiasm was fulsome enough for Minogue to glance over. Keating came around behind them. Minogue looked at the Polaroid dangling from his neck.

"Have the photo men been through already, Pat?" Minogue asked.

"Yes, sir. I've run off about thirty myself. Prior to removal. I got close-ups of the neck marks as well."

"Any tracks or traces close to the house here yet?" Minogue asked.

"Not yet," said Hoey.

"Hmm. How did the killer gain entry?" Minogue asked.

"Your man usually left the back door unlocked, says the housekeeper," Keating answered.

Great. Minogue almost voiced his cynicism aloud. He looked to the outside wall. The house was

9

stone-built, plastered and painted off-white. The windows looked new, and the gutters and the sills were in good condition.

"A few things strike me, though," Hoey began in a meditative tone.

"Fire away, Shea."

"Burglary gone wrong, that's easy enough to think. The old man is out, comes back to the house and interrupts a robbery. The killer might even have put the squeeze on him before killing him, to tell him where any money and so on might be hid. Odd thing is the destruction that carried on after the man was killed. The flour and bits of plates on the body tells us that easy enough. Cool one, the killer. Went around pulling out kitchen cupboards full of stuff."

"Disgusted maybe," Keating interjected. "The old man has no stash, but the killer either doesn't believe him or kills him to cover himself. Maybe a local all right, known by sight to the victim. Real animal work."

Hoey shrugged.

"There's fellas out there will go that far, I can tell you," he said. "Remember that juvenile, Rice, the lad who took a neighbour's housekeeping money and cut her throat to cover himself?"

Minogue remembered, all right. It was just before Keating's time on the Squad. Kilmartin had cursed psychiatrists and social workers for weeks after the diminished capacity ruling. Fintan Rice was a heroin addict at fifteen, a murderer at sixteen, an inmate in a prison psychiatric ward at seventeen. Dublin's Fair City . . .

"Fit of rage," said Hoey. "Like a ritual thing if the killer is a nutcase entirely."

"Defilement," Minogue muttered.

"Like in a church?" asked Keating.

10

"Wholesale wrecking of the place after the act. There's the other good angle. An acquaintance of the victim, a row getting out of hand. Maybe a mental case around here and something set him off."

Minogue thought it unlikely. In an explosive rage, nothing so neat as strangling with a rope would have occurred, especially without signs of resistance. His mind skipped erratically. Sex? Bachelor, old bachelor ... maybe of the "other" persuasion? Need background. Money? How much was the old man worth? If known to the victim, the killer could have surprised him handily enough ... back turned for a moment, the killer has his opportunity. Resources? Rope.

"The string or rope, Shea. That the kind of thing you'd find lying around handy in this man's house?"

"Good one," Hoey allowed. "That's where I go off a bit on tangents. A premeditated murder, a killer with the instrument ready in his pocket or whatever. The victim doesn't look to have been a handyman at all. His housekeeper says he never did repair stuff about the house but had tradesmen do it. We better dig up a solid motive for premeditated, more than a robbery trick. . . ."

"How long did you get with her?" asked Minogue.

"Mrs Hartigan? Three-quarters of an hour, sir. She's a bit out of it."

Keating edged up to the doorway and looked at the carnage in the kitchen again.

"Lunatic," he said.

"Money," Minogue echoed. "Tip-off from someone who knew or thought the old man kept money in the house. . . . Expected to find money and didn't. I wonder about that. Or came with the intentions to kill. . . . You told the Stepaside lads doing the local interviews to look for psychiatric cases around here?"

11

"Didn't have to. They copped on straightaway. They're on deliverymen, postmen, too. Any repairmen fixing the house. You know, Combs must have been out," Hoey said. "The smashing and breaking would have raised an awful racket. Like I say, there was some stuff under the body, so the job was underway when he came home. Even if it was a solo job, he'd have seen the car lights and known to get out cause the victim was coming home."

"Drove, I suppose," said Minogue. "Hardly out for a walk in the dark. And if the robber saw the old man's car, he wouldn't have started his job at all. Okay, so. Would he have seen the car lights at the end of the lane, where the victim's car was found?"

"Likely, sir," Keating argued. "This is an isolated spot, after all."

"Why didn't the victim drive up the lane and park by the house?"

Hoey shrugged.

"Turning space is a bit tight around the door here, sir. . . . I don't know."

"All right," Minogue sighed, shaking himself out of his speculation. "Enough of this headbanging. Let's start on filling in the blanks on this poor devil. See if we can place him for this past few days. I better start me prowl. Give us that Polaroid, Pat. Just in case."

Minogue entered the house. He tiptoed over the clear plastic sheets which the tehnicians had spread on the floor. Minogue's steps found a creaking runner as he went up the stairs. There was a strong smell of whisky, stronger as he ascended the stairs. There was little furniture in the hall, nothing that didn't have a daily utility. A hamper for dirty laundry had been over-turned. A coat and umbrella stand had been toppled. The coats scattered on the floor looked like human

12

scarecrow figures to Minogue as he glanced down over the banisters at the carnage below. The landing was narrow and dark, with no natural light but what an open door lent from one of the rooms. The technician walked heavily to the door.

"Is that you, Hoey, ya bollocks?" he said.

Minogue turned as the technician stepped over the threshold and into the landing.

"I'm not Hoey, I'm somebody else," Minogue said.

The stricken technician froze, the horsehair brush dangling from his plastic-gloved fingers.

"Oh, I thought it was — "

Minogue's feet sounded on the polished wooden floor. The smell of whisky was overpowering now. A skylight had been cut into the roof over this room. Although the room was small, there was a space enough for a drafting table and an easel. Paper had been swept into a heap on the floor. Pencils and small paintbrushes were scattered all over the room. Minogue heard whispering from the hallway. He heard his own name mentioned, and he wasn't at all displeased at the alarm with which it was hissed out.

"Are ye done in here?" Minogue called out.

"Nearly, sir. Nearly," an earnest voice replied. Built-in shelves flanked both sides of the chimney-breast. The fireplace itself had been walled in and covered up by an electric heater. Pieces from the shattered whisky bottles had reached every corner of the room. Scores of books had been knocked off the shelves, gathering in a heap by an overturned chair. Minogue glanced at some of the titles. Ancient monuments of the Irish countryside, a Spanish-English dictionary, books by Gerald Durrell about animals. A sink had been fitted into the wall next to the window. The walls themselves were covered in drawings. The drawings didn't look showy to Minogue — rather they seemed to be attempts to better draw a subject, pointers to improve the next version.

"Yes, we're all done in here, sir. And then there's daylight tomorrow and — "

"And ye'll be back with a vengeance," said Minogue. He turned to the two faces in the doorway. Grown schoolboy faces awaiting reprimand.

"And excuse the language, if you don't mind, sir. It's just that we know him and we do be slagging him. You know how it is."

Minogue put on his best version of a mollified teacher's face.

"To be sure, lads. Tell me, how long more here tonight?"

"Half an hour about. It's an awful sight, isn't it?"

Minogue nodded and turned to examine the room again. Drawers of clothes had been upended on the floor. He tiptoed around the clothes and stood by the window. It faced east so far as he could tell. He walked closer and looked out. A scattered sprinkle of lights from other houses tucked under the mountains.

There was nothing on the easel. What would be worth painting from this window? He hunkered down by the sheets of drawing paper which had been swept violently to the floor. Straightening one, Minogue felt a tremor of recognition. He stood back and studied the pencil drawing. The work showed practice and mastered technique on what Minogue would have said was a very difficult project. Though these concentric patterns could be found on other ceremonial stones from Ireland's prehistory, Minogue was certain that the stone and patterns in this drawings were from the ruins of Tully church. Minogue's hands remembered the warm, smooth granite of Tully. Succour. Was it that which attracted Combs there?

Minogue had been drawn to Tully and its stones by his sense that it had been built, like so many other churches, on a site of druidic worship. Several fields away was a tumulus, the burial site of a chieftain, which predated the upstart saints Patrick and Bride by a millennium. Less than a mile over the fields was one of the best-preserved dolmens in the country, ranking even with those stark masses of the ridges of The Burren in County Clare.

He flattened out other sketches from the heap of paper. There were charcoal sketches of stones with whorls worked into them, symbols of sun and moon. Beneath the sketches were pencil drawings of a dolmen, the huge menacing boulder on its three stone legs.

"Mr Combs was English?" Minogue called out.

"I believe so, sir," said the technician, a brick-red-faced young man with the beginnings of a porter-belly. He had the heavy blond eyebrows of Norse descendants in County Wexford.

"Yes, sir. They have his passport and everything taken away in the bags, but he was definitely from across the water."

Minogue turned toward the window again. When he didn't hear the two moving, he turned back to them. They couldn't help his puzzlement any more than he could himself.

"Thanks very much, lads."

He prowled the other rooms upstairs. A bedroom that Combs must have used, with the clothes torn off the bed. The mattress had been slashed on both sides. Looking for money in there...? A bathroom with new fixtures. The medicine box had been emptied out, too. Next door was an empty room the size of a box-room. The old man had been economical to the point of asceticism with furnishings. Minogue kept expecting to open a door on a room that would be

15

cluttered with the stuff which should fill houses. There was none. He couldn't decide if the sense of incompleteness here was a sign of transience or a permanent feature of an austere life. If this was it, Minogue thought, then the old man had led a lonely life.

Downstairs again, Minogue spied Hoey sitting on the kitchen doorstep. He was lighting a cigarette. Minogue looked into the kitchen. Almost like snow. Eerie. A fly was trapped between the curtain and the glass. It buzzed noisily, throwing itself against the glass, then rested. The outline on the linoleum tiles was the shape of a body lain on its side with the knees drawn up a bit, arms into the chest. A flash and the motorised ejection whirr of the Polaroid startled Minogue. He had been leaning on the button. Iijit . . .

The living-room had boasted no knick-knacks, it seemed. Books borrowed from the public library still lay atop a low table, the chaos on the floor all about it. There were no plants in the room, no pictures on the walls. Two ashtrays, both clean: copies of the *Irish Times*; magazines scattered on the floor. A colour telly with rabbit ears had been toppled, the screen cracked. The gravid atmosphere of the house begin to weigh on Minogue. He sat down on the doorstep next to Hoey.

"Who do we have available as of tomorrow morning, Shea?"

"There's you and me, sir. Pat Keating, of course. The two detectives from Stepaside; I know one of them — Driscoll. There's two Gardai from Stepaside taking statements and feeding them to Driscoll for us. I phoned in to get a crop of likelies off the Criminal Record Office. . . . Johnnie Carey is back in court tomorrow again and it might be for most of the week. The pub stabbing back in March. The defence threw a surprise in last Friday and they're rubbing Johnnie

16

hard on how he got the confession. He's lost to us for the week, I'd say."

Hoey drew on the cigarette. Minogue had a sudden lust for a cigarette himself. Keating stepped around the seated policemen.

"Well, the percentages so far," Keating began with a yawn, "tell me he was killed right in the kitchen. I was talking to the lads who went through the kitchen. . . . "

Minogue's attention was taken by the lurid light from the spots flaring against the gable wall. A uniformed Garda walked gingerly by them, nodding.

" . . . Nothing to suggest a struggle in or near the door. Not dragged in either."

"Heavy class of man anyhow," Hoey added.

"Can we place him at all yet, for the Saturday?" asked Minogue.

"Driscoll and the Stepaside lads are chipping away there, sir," Hoey reminded him. "They know the area. Never knew this Combs, though. A reclam — . . . a recl —"

"A recluse," Minogue said.

"That's it. A loner. Mrs Hartigan says he took a jar in the pub all right. He wasn't a total hermit."

"In a bit of a state, I suppose. Is she at home now?" Minogue went on. Hoey flicked open his notebook.

"Here's her number. The house is about half a mile back the road."

Minogue rose and yawned. Hoey stood then. Keating stared off at some point in the darkness beyond the oasis of light. Minogue followed Hoey down the lane. Hoey yawned again as he got into Minogue's Fiat, holding his notebook to his mouth. Keating took the radio-car which he and Hoey had driven out from Dublin.

17

"So the Killer is back on his feet," Hoey whispered through a yawn. Minogue spied Hoey's embarrassment with a glance. Kilmartin's nickname had slipped out. He smiled faintly at Hoey in the green glow of the dash light. Hoey rubbed his nose and switched on the interior light. He looked through his notes of his interview with Mrs Hartigan. Minogue drove off into the night. Kilmartin, Killer, he mused. Hoey absent-mindedly lit another cigarette. Hardly anyone has nicknames anymore, Minogue realised. What was that a sign of? Progress?

The nickname originated with quips which dated back to the renaming of the Murder Squad. Unlike its like-named counterpart in London, from which the name and the organisational structure had been derived, the Squad's name had gone under to the dictates of more hygienic prose. That prose had drifted in on airwaves and print from the American century which had lain offshore until the late 1950s. Irish people were now expected to rationalise their lives. They should now express opinions about the balance of payments and to use words from the new religion, words like *fulfillment, relationship, interaction.* . . .

The Murder Squad had emerged from this confusion as the Investigation Section. It formed a branch of the Technical Bureau, itself a branch of the Central Detective Unit. The CDU's new headquarters was based close to the City Centre in Harcourt Square, and CDU detectives rubbed shoulders with the other glamour boys of the Security Section, the Special Branch and the Serious Crime Squad. Austrian-made folding submachine-pistols, souped-up pursuit cars, computerised radio and telephone links, border shoot-outs . . . the whole shemozzle, as Kilmartin was wont to remark caustically over a Friday afternoon pint to Minogue. Television policemen, he called them.

The Murder Squad's transfer from the claustrophobia of Dublin Castle had brought it to St John's Road, close to Garda Headquarters in The Phoenix Park. Detectives working on the Murder Squad didn't mind a bit of glamour themselves. When other Gardai would ask them what it was like to work in the Investigation Section, they were told that it was murder, handily consonant with the nickname of the head of the section — the Killer himself, Kilmartin. The conceit around Kilmartin's nickname added to the Squad's reputation as being driven, meticulous and successful.

Less out of delicacy than sympathy, Minogue did not air his view that Jimmy Kilmartin was such a tiger abroad because he was a kitten at home.

CHAPTER 2

Mrs Hartigan's husband hovered uneasily by the door to the parlour. The Hartigan's house was a County Council labourer's cottage, scrupulously clean and suffused with the smell of a mixed grill. Framed photographs of weddings and children were marshalled on a dresser next to the door. Mrs Hartigan perched in the corner of a thickly stuffed sofa. A restless poodle lay across her oblivious feet. Two patches of colour stood out on her pallid cheeks. Her eyes were ringed red. Below the eyes her face seemed to sag. Like a stroke-victim, Minogue thought. Hoey sat next to a new television set while Minogue fell back into a tired spring armchair.

"To be sure, Mr Hartigan," Minogue looked up at the grizzled pensioner in the doorway. "Rest assured that your good wife will suffer no duress."

Hartigan scratched skeptically at a leathery ear.

"The doctor says she should be taking it cushy. She has blood pressure."

"Mr Hartigan. Our best opportunity for catching the person who committed this crime is with quick work. As much information as we can gather, as quickly as we can gather it."

"It's wicked," Mrs Hartigan interrupted. Her fixed stare hadn't shifted from the fireplace. "To do that . . . and the mess. It was like . . . I don't know what."

Hartigan withdrew, closing the door soundlessly. Minogue didn't care that he might be eavesdropping from the hall. Hoey flipped open his notebook to a fresh page.

"I spoke to this nice young man, didn't I?" Mrs Hartigan said drearily.

"You did, ma'am," Hoey said. "A little more might be the key. We won't tax you with repeating things, though, so we won't."

Minogue gathered himself at the back of the chair.

"Now, Mrs Hartigan, I know you didn't see Mr Combs since last Friday. But do you know what he did on his weekends? In general, like. A Saturday."

"Well. I told this nice man here that Mr Combs took a drink. He liked a drink. That's not to say. . . . But Joseph, my husband, saw him the odd time in the pub. Up in Fox's pub."

"Did he entertain visitors?"

"No, he didn't. I don't know what he did the days he'd go into Dublin, though. Or on his little trips out for his drawing and painting. Did I tell you that he liked the horses?"

Hoey nodded.

"The races. Leopardstown, for a flutter. He used to say that — 'for a flutter.' Oh," she sighed as she shifted in the sofa, "he had expressions I never heard of before. Sometimes he would have me in fits. Putting on the talk, you know. Sometimes after a little sup of drink he'd be very funny."

Mrs Hartigan seemed to catch herself. She frowned as she looked up over at Minogue.

"I'm not saying that Mr Combs was a, you know . . . "

"A heavy drinker?"

21

"Yes."

Her expression changed abruptly into a withered smile.

"I don't think he gave people a chance to know him, to like him. Talk to Joseph there and he'll tell you. He was always asking me what Mr Combs was like. People didn't know him. He could be terrible funny. Charming and gentle . . . "

She looked toward Hoey but her eyes did not focus. The poodle's legs twitched. It bared its teeth in sleep.

"Yes," she murmured. "A terrible ordinary man, if people only knew. Odd, certainly, but what of it? I remember him one day he had me in fits of laughing; he heard something on the radio and he turned it up loud. I came in from the kitchen to see what the commotion was and there he was, a glass of whisky in his hand, sort of dancing around the room. Some chorus, a man's chorus from Russia. They were singing 'It's a Long Way to Tipperary' in Russian. Their language, you see. He thought that was priceless. He once told me that I was a socialist but I didn't know it. But not in a nasty way, more a bit of tickling and fun. An educated man, you see. Never had to say it, you just knew it."

Hoey caught Minogue's eye.

"I'll tell you something now," Mrs Hartigan went on without prompting. "I forgot he was an Englishman half the time. Such a nice way about him when he wanted to be. . . . "

"Was he less than nice by times?" Minogue asked.

"Oh, I don't mean anything like that. I must say, I don't blame him a bit for being fond of a drop."

"You met none of his family or relatives," Minogue tried.

Mrs Hartigan shook her head.

22

"He didn't have any, he told me. But he had friends, I suppose. I don't know. I never saw any in the house at all."

Minogue counted to three before addressing her again.

"Mrs Hartigan, was Mr Combs homosexual?"

"Do you mean about women, that he never married . . . ?" her question tapered off.

"A man who's not attracted to women, but to men," said Minogue. "Have you ever . . . ?"

"Of course I have. It's on the television all the time," she murmured. "But I can tell you policemen, because I know you want to do right by Mr Combs. Yes. I wondered sometimes if he was — "

She looked up again and swivelled her eyes slowly toward Hoey.

"But I never seen one thing to suggest to me that he was one of them. I can tell you that for certain. People'll always talk, make up stories in their imagination. But I suppose I wouldn't know what to look for, I mean how would a body know? A woman of my age especially?"

Hoey cleared his throat. Mrs Hartigan's expression looked to be caught between a smile and mordant gravity.

"Certain types of books and such? Pictures and things, perhaps? A manner of speaking about people?" he said.

Mrs Hartigan's face contracted into a frown.

"No such thing as I ever came across. Oh no. He wasn't nervous around a woman the way a lot of men are, even married men are. He knew how to make you laugh when he wanted to. And it's not like we don't know about such matters as regards sex and so on, you know, what with the telly and everything."

23

"Did he mention any places he liked to go to in Dublin, Mrs Hartigan?" Minogue asked.

"No, he didn't, as a matter of fact. It was like I was explaining to this nice young man here the first time this evening . . . "

Hoey sat back in his chair. Minogue waited out her ramble.

"Nearly two years you did the housekeeping for him?"

"That's right."

She dabbed at the corner of an eye, heaved a sigh and went on in a lower voice.

"It's hard and you being old and having nobody. You lose interest, I think. Even if you have your hobbies and a bit of reading. You need the contact. But he didn't, not much anyway. Or not as much as we're used to here. Mr Combs was interested in the place here, though; he was often flummoxed by some things here, I remember. Him asking me about the politics and the way the country is run. He'd smile and shake his head when I told him. I think he liked it here."

Minogue waited out her derailed train of thought. As though roused from sleep, she started and looked glassily from Minogue to Hoey.

"Here I am rambling along. Maybe it's not what you want to hear."

"You're doing grand," Minogue whispered. "But look, can you go back in your mind to recalling any visitors. Anybody he talked about?"

She cast her eyes to the ceiling and held her gaze there.

"I know you asked me that before, this young man with you. Try as I can, isn't it odd? He didn't seem to need people, like individual people. He liked to know about people in general, he said. Human nature. I remember him saying to me once . . . it stuck in my mind. He liked it here, you know. 'A pity I didn't come here when I was a lot younger' says he to me once. For all I know he kept up his friends back in England with his letter-writing and so on."

"Any phone calls that you remember as being peculiar?"

"No. No. An old-style type of a man, always writing letters and educating himself. That's what I thought of him. A cultured gentleman, I always said to Joseph."

"Letters to . . . ?"

Mrs Hartigan's eyes focussed suddenly on Minogue.

"I never in my life read another body's letters or the like."

"I beg your pardon, Mrs Hartigan. I merely meant if you had seen the outside of the envelope. A name, an address."

Mrs Hartigan shook her head curtly. Minogue diverted.

"Something a little different now for a moment, Mrs Hartigan, if you please. Did you ever think or believe that anybody was snooping about the place, maybe sizing the place up for burglary? For instance, did you have anyone coming to the door looking for directions or that class of thing?"

"Oh," she sighed, "I'd have to think about that one. Me mind is very slow now. The doctor told me I'd feel like lying down . . . let me think."

Minogue stretched his legs out straight while he waited.

"Joe," Mrs Hartigan called out. "Joe."

Joseph Hartigan slid into the parlour.

"Are yous finished?" he asked.

"Joe. A sup of tea. I can't think at the moment. And these gentlemen, too . . . "

Minogue looked at Hoey. A tight smile of yielding and Hoey nodded.

"Yes, please," said Minogue.

Until the forensic work began to trickle in, Mrs Hartigan was the best help they had.

Jimmy Kilmartin, Inspector Kilmartin, had lots of comforts around his hospital room but no visitors until Minogue arrived. Minogue noted the stack of Sunday papers and magazines, the bottles of Lucozade, tissues, slippers side-by-side under the bed and a radio with headphones. Kilmartin's room had a colour telly on a stand in the corner, too.

"They let you in, bejases," Kilmartin marvelled. "It's nigh on eleven o'clock." He made an effort to sit upright in the bed.

"I had them check from the desk to see if you were still awake," Minogue replied as he eyed the colour television.

"Nice place to be ailing, James."

Kilmartin snorted.

"Ailing, is it? I never felt better. Too fresh to sleep, I am. Rarin' to go."

Minogue handed Kilmartin a bag of muffins.

"Kathleen says to ask the nurse if you're allowed to eat these yokes. I had them in the car with me."

"Gob and I'll try me best," Kilmartin affirmed. "And you'd no trouble getting in here?"

"No. The night duty boss is a girl from Feakle. I heard them playing twenty-five and knew the accent. 'Damn your sowl, why di'nt you lay the deuce and you with the knave in your fisht as well?'"

Kilmartin laughed lightly.

"Jases. The Clare mafia at it again."

Minogue wondered where Kilmartin's family was that they weren't visiting him. Sundays in Ireland

carried over to US as late as ~ 1950

involved visiting someone in hospital or else paying one's respects in a graveyard. Kilmartin scrutinised one of the muffins at close quarters, turning it around in his fingers and pressing into its side with his thumb.

"Full of nourishment, I'll wager. There'd be a ton of bran in them. Roughage, right?" Kilmartin looked up.

"That's it."

"Oh, suffering Jesus that died on the cross. 'Roughage.'"

Kilmartin's eyes followed his supplications heavenward.

"Me heart is broken with that word. I have books about fibre and roughage and the like that would give your arse heartburn reading them, so they would."

Kilmartin's brow lowered to gloom, then lightened. He pointed toward the chair.

"The main thing is that I'm on the mend and that's what counts, isn't it?" Kilmartin continued.

"Precisely."

Kilmartin settled himself against the pillow. He's actually happy to see me, Minogue realised.

"How's the family, Jim?"

"Topping. This is Maura's bridge night," Kilmartin said a little too earnestly.

"The young lad has a job selling ice cream in New Jersey, he wrote and said. He'll come back speaking like a Yank. . . . Isn't life wonderful?" Kilmartin added.

Minogue had an image of Maura Kilmartin with her overpowering perfume and her huge hands. She was from Leitrim and her flat drag-out-the-word-and-then-beat-it-over-the-head accent came through stronger after a sherry. Minogue had last met her at a retirement do for a Superintendent. He remembered her big, red farm-girl's face, the plump fiftyish body distending the sybaritic designs of her silky dress. She had whispered a dirty joke to Minogue. He was too distracted to get it straightaway, but she slapped her knees and almost dislodged her top set of teeth with laughter.

He remembered Kilmartin's sober face contorting in the kind of smile you'd see on a donkey chewing barbed wire. When Kilmartin said that he'd like Minogue to stand in for him and would it be all right to recommend him for a secondment for the six weeks, Minogue privately assigned a large percentage of at-fault — as regards Kilmartin's complaint — to Maura Kilmartin: Jimmy's shame, a farmyard wife too real for Dublin *politesse*.

"Ah, I feel sorry for the young people these days," Kilmartin drawled expansively from the bed. "So much pressure."

"You have hit the nail on the head," Minogue said.

Kilmartin warmed to the role of bedridden philosopher. He levelled a finger at the television set across the room.

"I blame that bloody idiot-box for a lot of it. You could watch that thing for a whole day, from early morning to late at night, and there wouldn't be ten minutes of it that'd be worth talking about. The rest of it you can throw your hat at."

"You're right, Jimmy, you're right."

Minogue wondered how much Kilmartin actually watched.

"Did you see the news?" Kilmartin asked.

"I heard it on the radio," Minogue replied.

"About that business up in . . . where is it?"

"Kilternan."

"That's the place. Do you know," Kilmartin leaned forward for emphasis, "but nobody tells me a damn thing here?"

"You're supposed to be resting yourself, Jimmy."

"Hoey and Keating doing the legwork?"

28

"They're very good. You have them trained to a tee, Jimmy."

"Well?" Kilmartin asked indignantly. "Aren't you going to tell me what's going on?"

Minogue thought that Kilmartin would not manage his retirement very well at all if this was what six weeks' sick-leave was doing to him.

"Sorry. Yes. A man by the name of Combs. His housekeeper said he's English. Mr Arthur Combs, seventy-three years of age."

"How was he killed?"

"Strangled, Jimmy. Hoey says he'd put money on it being a bit of nylon cord the way his neck was marked. There was no row or anything. The body was within arm's reach of the door he came in. It looks like he came home from the pub, in the door and . . . that was it."

"Stuff was robbed. Money, antiques," Kilmartin said tersely.

"The place was ransacked all right. I don't know what was taken yet," said Minogue.

"A crowd of young lads, I bet," Kilmartin tried again. "Looking for easy money. Give the oul lad a few digs so he'd get the money out of the mattress kind of effort. Was he beat up?"

Minogue shrugged.

"Doesn't look like it. No. We haven't placed him for the few days before the murder. Saturday night he was killed, it looks. The housekeeper only does the dinners for him on the weekdays, so . . . "

Minogue tried to let this part of the conversation die.

Kilmartin squirmed slightly under the sheets. He began to stroke his lower lip.

"I hope to God we have sheets on a few horrors who specialise in this class of crime. If you could call killing an old man and robbing his house by the title of 'crime' even."

"I hope so meself," added Minogue somberly and yawned.

"Um. Bastards. Cowards. Sounds like young lads to me still though," Kilmartin murmured. "Drink, drugs. They mightn't have records, these yahoos."

The conversation died on Kilmartin's contempt. Minogue resurrected a husk of what had been normality before Kilmartin's savage commentary.

"Wouldn't you like a bit of company in a semi-private room, Jim?"

Kilmartin glared at Minogue.

"I would not. Some fella coughing and spluttering next to me? Or someone with fifteen children from Ballyfermot and they all in visiting and blathering away? I'd as lief be here where it's quiet and I can read in comfort," Kilmartin declared.

He went back to stroking his lip. Minogue acknowledged the defeat of his diversion.

"Well maybe I can come by tomorrow. Will I give you a ring in the morning anyway, would that do?"

Kilmartin's eyes widened suddenly.

"Do that. Yes, would you? This place gives me the willies. It's full of sick people."

"Isn't that near one of your haunts, Matt?" Kathleen asked. Minogue watched his wife fork scrambled egg onto the plates. It was a quarter to eight. Minogue had woken up in the same position he last remembered before falling asleep. He was not sure if he was awake yet.

"Your home ground, like?" she persisted.

"Up near that ruin of a church?" their daughter Iseult added.

"Iseult, would you put down the book and be having your breakfast, love." Kathleen said.

"It says on the back that it can't be put down. 'Very gripping,' it says."

"There's a slim chance that your poor parents might want to hear from you," Minogue murmured. "To see how your life is running along."

"Isn't Daithi out of the bed yet? I thought I heard him stirring," said Kathleen.

"Who cares?" Iseult shot back. She yawned and laid the book face down by her cup.

"Yous should be glad that I'm able to read and amuse myself and still keep yous company," Iseult added moodily.

"In our old age, is it?" Kathleen paused with the fork.

Iseult yawned again. Minogue stole a glance at his daughter as she stretched. Why weren't girls called handsome? She rubbed her eyes.

"Well, is it up that way, Da?"

"It looks close on the map, I grant you. But there's topography to consider," he answered.

"Up near your favorite haunt, is it?" Iseult prodded.

A fleeting image of last night came to Minogue. Garish floodlighting around Combs' house, violence passing through the house like a whirlwind. Haunting; poltergeist.

"Could we try a different term than *haunt*, if it's not too much trouble?" Minogue asked.

"I think it's creepy up there, so I do, with all the trees and the bushes growing out over the road. The holy ground, I ask you . . ." Iseult said. She poured tea into her mother's cup and then into Minogue's.

"If there's any haunting going on up there, it's not the likes of me that'd be doing it," Minogue declared, with the sliver of rasher poised under his nose. "After all, I'm a lively type of character. Amn't I, Kathleen?"

"For your age," Kathleen said. Iseult laughed. Kathleen turned back to her husband.

31

"That's not up where those people used to worship the sun, is it, Matt?"

"No, actually. That's Katty Gallagher, the far side of the Smelting Chimney."

In a glade to the inland side of the abrupt stony lump that made up Carraigologan — or Katty Gallagher as the locals called it — Minogue had found a plaque. It had been placed there to commemorate a handful of Victorians who had for decades risen to worship the sun daily from the hill top. Minogue had sometimes imagined himself joining them each morning, with the Irish Sea unfolding before them. Inland, behind, a plateau of pastures was girdled by the ring of hills and mountains: the Great Sugar Loaf to the southeast, the foothills of the Wicklow Mountains to the west.

Often as he stood atop the hill, the wind teasing his jacket, Minogue thought that all the good land in west Clare would amount to less than the ordered land below him. Looking north from the summit, you could see the Mourne Mountains if the air over Dublin city wasn't bad. On a good day you could see Wales to the east. Minogue could almost feel the hilltop breezes tunnelling into his shirt still.

"Da. What do you do up in that place?"

"Tully? I visit the place is what I do." Minogue felt defensive yet.

"Yes, but do you do anything, though? Like, would you explore?" Iseult went on.

"Sometimes."

"And would you explore the graveyard, for instance?" Iseult harried him from behind a slice of bread she drew to her mouth.

"Honest to God, Iseult," Kathleen interrupted. "Do you think your father does be digging them that's buried there these hundreds and hundreds of years up out of their graves and talking to them?"

32

Iseult leaned back in her chair. She flicked her hair back over one shoulder, then another. She held her hand to her mouth and began coughing and laughing.

"It's nice to have the place to yourself at that time of day. And it doesn't cost me anything. So there."

"All right, Da. I believe you, but thousands wouldn't." Minogue tried to put some sense on the way the conversation was weaving.

"Anyway. I was a bit out of the way when that man was murdered. If you're looking for an alibi, I can only say that I'm very disappointed in you. All I can plead is that I was up at Tully, thinking," Minogue protested.

"That's your story and you're sticking to it, right?" Iseult added.

"Ask me if I can prove that I was thinking," Minogue retorted.

He lifted a quarter of a not-quite-ripe tomato off the end of the fork with his tongue. What he called thinking, his mother would have called romancin'. His father would have called it idling, and he would have been right for the wrong reasons, Minogue reflected.

"No way, Da. Not a bit of it." Iseult resumed earnestly. "Anyone can see that you do your thinking. Pat says that you have the look of a man that's always thinking."

"You may congratulate Pat for his prescience. But remind him that he'll have to find less obtrusive ways of ingratiating himself with his girlfriend's parents than by having such flattery reported indirectly. Suggest perhaps that he comment on your mother's cooking," Minogue said lightly.

Pat was Iseult's new boyfriend. He had appeared at the Minogue house riding an ungainly bicycle. In Minogue's youth such tall bicycles were called High Nellies. Policemen rode these heavy, gearless bikes imperiously on rural patrols, farmers rode them up and down bog roads with buckets dangling from the handlebars. Pat wore cropped hair in the manner of a foreign legionnaire or a jailbird. All his wardrobe appeared to be black.

Iseult left her dishes by the sink and headed for the kitchen door. Minogue and his wife sat without speaking for ten minutes. A bluebottle dithered noisily around the window, stopping and starting. He or she finally made it to the open window. The smell of cut grass came in from the neighbour's lawn. Minogue noticed Kathleen's hands as they fingered saucers, the sugar bowl. Back to the saucer. This is what life is, Minogue thought, it happens this way. He was waking up.

"Better be off. I'm Jimmy Kilmartin today. Work to be done."

"Matt. Before you go. I heard Daithi taking the Holy Name and effin' and blindin' out of him the other day when he thought I couldn't hear him. I take great offence at the use of The Holy Name, I needn't tell you."

Minogue almost agreed aloud that she needn't. Daithi had been saying such things for effect. They had found their mark.

"You'll have a word with him then, will you?" Kathleen said, "I'd only be giving out to him."

What word, Minogue wondered. Am I to keep the troops in line with orders from on high? Is she blind to the fact her husband is beyond this stuff?

"I'll have a word with him. Yes, I will, Kathleen."

"And if he's not willing to get up at a decent hour and do a day's studying . . . "

"I'll see to it," Minogue whispered. Kathleen picked up on his awkwardness. Daithi's repeat exams were coming up in two weeks. If he failed these ones, he'd have to repeat his final year. That was bad enough in itself. What Minogue and Kathleen most feared was that Daithi wouldn't have the interest to do the year again if he failed this time around. She looked at him. He did not want to leave her this morning with an acid remark hanging in the air behind him. She kissed him.

CHAPTER 3

James Kenyon walked out from Cadogan Gardens
onto a Monday morning Sloane Street. He walked
briskly, ignoring the noise of traffic. Kenyon crossed
with the lights at Pont Street and within ten minutes
he was passing the Chelsea Holiday Inn. Hyde Park
Barracks filled up the junction ahead, where Sloane
Street met with Brompton Road and Knightsbridge.

Kenyon glanced at his reflection as he strode by the
glass-and-chrome fashion shapes. Cecil Gee's wanted
four hundred quid for a two-piece suit that looked like
something a client would willingly leave behind in a
Neapolitan knocking shop? He took note of his own
preoccupied face sliding along the windows, a face
which usually said forties, not fifty-three this September. The mannequins in the windows repelled him.
They looked tough and cutting, determined survivors,
the grimly handsome of Maggie's shopkeeper Britain.

Kenyon had not met Alistair Murray in person, but
Murray's slight Scottish burr over the telephone had
irritated him. Maybe it was the air of unctuous assurance he heard in Murray's voice. He had noted some
faint condescension, as though Murray were using

his rank while he tried to soothe Kenyon. Kenyon didn't want soothing; he wanted facts. Murray had slipped up. Kenyon had to find out how much, and quickly.

Kenyon had been in the Security Service, MI5, long before the Soviets had rolled tanks into fraternal Czechoslovakia. Both MI6, what some politicians preferred to call the Secret Service, and MI5 had predicted the invasion as imminent four months previously, but the Foreign Office had pooh-poohed them. Since that intelligence fiasco the Government Communications HQ in Cheltenham had helped to improve on the divergences in different agencies' evaluations by bringing out and circulating daily summaries to agencies like the Foreign Office and MI6.

Aside even from the gargantuan cock-ups where MI5 was being run by a double agent, and the fact that the Americans simply didn't trust either service anymore, the gaffes and security problems had continued. There had even been a threatened strike at GCHQ, a place that the public was not supposed to know even existed, and the papers had had daily reports about the staff's efforts to join unions there. Comical, but with a sharp edge of lunacy. An East German defector had told Kenyon how his former boss had laughed until tears ran down his cheeks at the trade-union problem. His boss had said that the Worker's State would have taken out the malcontents and shot them.

Alistair Murray's title was that of Intelligence Analyst with the Foreign Office. He reviewed intelligence reports and memos which concerned matters in the Republic of Ireland. As well as skimming the daily release from the Government Communications Headquarters, Murray was also privy to intelligence emanating from covert sources in the Irish Republic and

Northern Ireland. After the phone call to Murray, Kenyon had decided that rank or not, he'd like very much indeed to cut Murray down to size. Especially if Murray ever tried to be coy and hint about the liaison he would necessarily have with the Secret Service to do his job well.

Kenyon had gone to Century House at nine-thirty last night and had pulled everything on Combs out of the Registry. Less than a half hour after he had corralled the files, Kenyon at least had some satisfaction in knowing that someone else's Sunday night had been scuttled, too. A Foreign Office request for the files on Combs had come in the person of someone called Thwaite — Murray's retainer, Kenyon found out later.

Kenyon had heard of an Arthur Combs, but that was three and more years ago. Combs was a relic, an artefact from a different age. Now that Combs was dead and it looked like murder, Murray and company had suddenly seen the light. They, too, wanted to re-evaluate the Combs' material in a hurry. To Kenyon it had all the signs of a potential cock-up.

By midnight last night Kenyon had still felt that feathery doubt in his stomach. Murray had done an evaluation on Combs before, but it had been at arm's length, relying mostly on what one source, a Second Secretary in the embassy in Dublin, had squeezed into half-page memos. Evaluate, Kenyon mused cynically. Garbage in, garbage out. Kenyon snorted.

The feature about Combs' material which stayed in his mind, above all else, was a quality that he had noticed in the man's more recent reports, the faintest signs of something which made his antenna quiver. He hadn't settled on a word for this quality: taciturnity, a tone of resentment, a faintly querulous tone which stopped barely short of telling more? Was Combs trying to explain something, was there that fatal germ of sympathy, an involvement of the heart to explain in what he said and wrote?

His stomach bilious from midnight coffee, Kenyon recalled a phrase from his university days. "More Irish than the Irish themselves." It referred to how Normans who had invaded Ireland assimilated to Irish ways. They proved to be the vanguard of Irish resistance to later Tudor ventures on the island. What was it about that damp island that insinuated itself through everything there? An atmosphere of disloyalty, some anarchic sentiment, another Italy? *Ortgeist*, was that the word . . . ?

There had been no sign of a failing mind coming through Combs' reports, and Murray should have known that. Combs' reports had sometimes been months apart. A half-dozen priority requests to him to be on the lookout for specific people had been replied to promptly. None had been of any use.

It took a detached scrutiny and several re-reads for Kenyon to finally decide that Murray's assessment had missed the mark. As a university student, Kenyon had read many diarists and his preference in books was still for memoirs. In the last year of Combs' reports, Kenyon felt a slipping away, a closing of some kind. It trickled out even through the typewriter of the officer who summarised Combs' stuff. There had been fewer and fewer particulars in the last year's material. Where before there had been an exact description number, there were now bland comments. "Party no longer resident in the area" or "X reported to have moved, whereabouts unknown." The phrases were almost ironic, as if they quietly parodied the monotonous language of reportese.

Kenyon waited for the pedestrian light opposite the Albert Gate into Hyde Park. While he stood by the swirl of traffic, he imagined Murray using the Combs' reports to feather his own nest in meetings. Murray could throw around phrases like "diminished activity there . . . Irish police and border patrols seem to have a better handle" and "support seems to be dwindling in that area." Was it something in Murray's nature and background that brought him to believe that superiors wanted only good news? Maybe it was inevitable that in the Foreign Office, or bureaucracies in general, sycophancy ruled and meetings were rituals for you to try and make impressions on your superiors. Everybody was bored to death with the Irish problem. A place where things went wrong anyway, without help from anyone. A bog into which things disappeared.

Kenyon had slept poorly last night, Murray's bromides circling elliptically around his head. He had been in the Security Service long enough to know that paradoxes were part of the day's work. His job was to ensure the security of ministers and senior civil servants, not to judge what they had done in the war. Kenyon's wife knew that he was a civil servant who worked for the Home Office. She didn't need to know, any more than any other Briton, that MI5 really answered only to the PM via the Permanent Undersecretary in the Home Office. That was only if the PM asked questions, too. Ministers could come and go, but the Defence of the Realm was sacred. Wendy, Kenyon's wife, used to quip about the phrase early in their marriage when her husband would come home after midnight. Kenyon now ran a desk in the Protective Security Branch of the Service. Very often it meant that he had to protect Cabinet Ministers from the deserving consequences of their own venal stupidity.

Kenyon had discovered very early in his career that when a colleague drawled out phrases like "Defense of the Realm from external and internal threat" in a caricature of the effete public school drawl, the colleague was deadly serious. The sardonic delivery was the sign of a mild heresy, sarcasm which only a true believer could utter so casually. The phrase was one of the few directives ever given to MI5 in written form by the Home Secretary. It dated from 1952, and it came from a one-page set of guidelines issued long before it was publicly admitted that Britain even had a Security Service.

While he had lain awake in the early hours, Kenyon had brooded about the damn island across the Irish Sea. Ire-land. Land of ire. Could it really ever be considered "external"? Should have sunk the place back in 1921. Murray would be hung out to dry if after all his assessments, it turned out that Combs hadn't been bluffing. . . . Still, it was Kenyon who was finally responsible for the damage when any trouble reached his turf. Sleep had come late to him. Kenyon had even woken up feeling harassed.

The lights changed and Kenyon strode purposively into the park. He crossed Carriage Drive. When he caught sight of the Dell restaurant, he was both relieved and immediately anxious to realise that he had made his decision. No matter what Murray would say here, Kenyon knew that he had to defend his suspicions about Combs. He'd have to brief Hugh Robertson, the Director of his section, before lunchtime. Better to squirm through that meeting, even if the Director General himself was there, rather than have this blow up in his own face. Kenyon also realised that he was hoping for a sign that would grant an instant logic and credibility to his suspicions. There was but the slimmest chance of winnowing anything like that from the man he had arranged to meet in the restaurant, one Alistair Murray.

*   *   *

Kilmartin's secretary, Eilis, greeted Minogue.

"I have it all waiting for you. And there's preliminary on Mr Combs, too."

"Aren't you great, Eilis?"

"It has been said, all right," Eilis answered in the exacting grammar of her native tongue, Irish. "Things are very efficient here now, don't you know? Now, Detective Keating phoned to say he's in Stepaside station with two detectives from the station. They want to interview three men at the station, and they're going to pick them up directly. Tip from an interview with a barman. Barman was on duty in Fox's pub Saturday night. Mr Combs was there, he says."

"Three men?"

"Three brothers by the name of Mulvaney, and they live in a place I never heard of before. Barnacullia. Up under Two Rock Mountain. These brothers are well known to police in Stepaside, being as they have criminal records. They say there may be difficulties getting the co-operation of these brothers."

She began unwrapping a packet of Gitanes. Minogue had known Eilis for some years. She was a single woman of thirty-eight or so, from the Dingle peninsula, who had tired of teaching Irish to fellow civil servants. The language had been a sacred cow in the public service, because it had held the bizarre status of co-equal with English as an official language of the state. Eilis had had enough of civil servants and teachers using Irish simply to get promotion, and one morning, stone cold sober, she unburdened herself of a life's rich gleaning of insults, all in her native tongue. While some of her baroque curses were narrowly local to her native County Kerry, she managed to touch most of the important taboos in her minute's fluency. It was one of her better students who deciphered some of her imprecations. Eilis was oddly satisfied to have taught him so well. After all, the one who reported her was a Dublin hooligan.

The civil service had a heart, however, and it listened to Eilis's uncle, a strong Party man who represented Kerry in the Dail, a man with formidable tribal connections. Civil servants who had gone mad, "had trouble with their nerves," "lost interest" or fell into any other nineteenth-century category which described people who were cracked, were often found work. One of these legion of disaffected public servants was well known to Minogue. He routinely saw the former Higher Executive Officer in the Revenue Commissioners — now a messenger — happily shouting his way around the streets, barking mad and refusing to take the pills which were supposed to render him subdued like other mortals.

Eilis was also a relative of Kilmartin's wife, Maura, but that alone was not enough for her to be taken on in so demanding a job as the police, not to speak of the Technical Bureau. A reluctant Kilmartin persuaded Eilis to take an intelligence and aptitude test, just as the Americans did, in the hopes of thereby demonstrating to his wife that he had tried his best to find something for Eilis but that, alas, she "couldn't function."

Eilis, who knew nothing of the shapes and questions which made up such tests, scored one hundred and seventy-four on an IQ test. She demonstrated a frightening ability in her deductive faculties, excellent creative thinking and indicated that she would have made a formidable jurist. Eilis now occupied a desk next to Kilmartin's office, chain-smoking and keeping track of anything that walked, crawled, ran or was telecommunicated to the section. Minogue had read in her the abandon of one who had found the world to be mildly entertaining. This was an attitude

43

which others construed as arrogance and contrariness, never stopping themselves to recognise a tragic sense because they could not know such things and be themselves again.

"I think that means," she paused to inhale more smoke, "that they're tricksters of some sort, I suppose. Do you follow?"

"I expect you're right. Have you the number of the station handy?"

Eilis drawled out the telephone number.

"Safe home, your honour," she added in Irish. He detected no humour.

Murray was groomed like a mannequin, right down to the cuff-links. Few things about a man's clothes show up the parvenu as easily as cuff-links, Kenyon believed.

"One Colombian coffee — nothing less, mind you," Murray said to the waiter. "And yourself, James?"

"Tea will do."

"You'll have read the Combs' material, James?" Murray began.

"Yes, I did."

"We can readily agree then, I'm sure, that we both know the background here. Even the ancient history," Murray said.

"Have you read up the material lately?" Kenyon asked.

"Really, James. You know quite well I did. But I sense that your evaluation may be different."

"There's the matter of his murder," Kenyon continued. "He was found Sunday evening, it seems."

"The police don't have a suspect, that I know."

"Who would want to kill Combs?"

Murray adjusted his shoulders inside his jacket.

"The Foreign Office would like to know, too. Even if Combs was small change. Very minor capacity. We'll find out from the police soon enough, I'm sure."

Kenyon made a conscious effort to keep the irritation out of his voice. Was it already time to tell Murray that he had not asked for a meeting to be showered with gratuitous *non sequiturs*? The waiter's return gave Kenyon time to figure out a new approach.

"Tell me, Alistair," Kenyon began, "what did you make of Combs' grumblings when he first started sending material over?"

Murray smiled wanly as he stirred his coffee.

"Oh those, yes. Well, that was over two years ago, of course. Combs obviously didn't like to be asked to live there, that was pretty clear, um?"

Kenyon nodded as he doctored his own tea.

"You see, our Second Secretary in the Dublin embassy at the time . . . well, he wasn't as experienced as we would have liked for this kind of work. All in all, a bit of a damp squib."

"You mean that Combs' threats were not taken seriously?"

Murray arched his eyebrows as he drew the cup down from his lips again.

"They were hardly threats, for heaven's sake. He grumbled about being there. I've been there on a few wet winter days myself and to be candid, I'd be grumbling, too. Dull enough work, too, I imagine."

"The embassy memo says the police suspect robbery."

"Um," Murray nodded and affected a consideration of Kenyon's interruption.

"What we had there with Mr Combs, James, what we had . . . we had an old man who was hitting the bottle rather hard for a long number of years. Prone to grudges, wilful misinterpretations. Quite paranoid, too.

45

Now match that with the Second Sec we had there at the time, his local link — a chappie fresh out of Oxbridge, who probably spent his weekends reading spy books. . . . "

Murray's faint smile trailed off into a look of indulgent regret. Kenyon said nothing. He waited for Murray to replace the dangling cup on its saucer. Murray's gaze swept over the view of the Serpentine before returning to Kenyon.

"What you get are melodramatic memos on the wire. Combs tried to put the wind up the boy and succeeded. Well, we didn't play Combs' game, as you can see from your hours in the Registry yesterday."

Kenyon did not return Murray's sardonic glance.

"We placed a new Second Sec there. He's one of our best, James. One of our best."

"Who was handling Combs, the new Sec?"

"Ball. Mervyn Ball. Fine fella, Mervyn. Soon put Combs to rights. Got him motivated, feeling positive."

Kenyon recalled dating the memos that had mentioned Combs' ramblings in those meetings which Combs had had with his novice handler from the embassy. Murray might well be right on that, he had to concede. There hadn't been a peep since Ball had taken up the station. But did that mean that Combs had simply swallowed his bitterness for two years? Had it really been just drunken complaining before?

"Was it your impression that Combs didn't mind the place so much after he had been there for a while?" Kenyon tried.

"Ireland? Well, now that you mention it, I had thought that he was a little more tolerant of the place, yes," Murray allowed.

Kenyon suppressed his rising anger. He remembered the feeling he had when he had read the place names, the mention of redundant information in

Combs' later reports. There was a quality of a surreptitious sneer about them.

"It strikes me that Combs may not have been the old fool you're implying. Much less the drunken old fool," said Kenyon in a restrained tone.

"Really, James?" said Murray, blinking with a new interest.

"You know his background. He was badly treated. He toughed it out during the war in very tight situations. More to the point, he was not a man to bluff. Judging by his record, I mean," Kenyon said slowly.

"Really, James? That's forty years ago. Personalities deteriorate. That's human nature. Aren't we talking about an old pouf-dah who had taken to the bottle? I don't wish to speak ill of the dead, but we have the living to contend with," Murray said, out in the open now.

"Look," he continued, "we kept tabs on him since he landed in Ireland. We think we know him rather well."

The barb registered with Kenyon, but he was grimly pleased to see Murray throw off the first of his gloves and turn to his prejudices.

"There's one flaw in what you're saying," Kenyon said coldly. "If he really was such an unreliable man, why did your office take him on in the first place?"

Murray blinked once.

"James, James. You know as well as I do that we inherited him. We looked around at what we had for assets in Ireland. It was a particularly bad time. We thought we could use Combs. Believe me, we wouldn't have chosen him if he weren't on the books. He was a relic."

"He was placed in Ireland on the condition that he live near Dublin?"

"Yes. He has been at us for years to be allowed back into Britain. It was decided that he'd be less of a risk if he were at arm's length. You know who he worked with during the war, I take it?" said Murray with a challenging edge.

"Yes. And I know what they did to him afterwards, too."

"Let's not get lachrymose, James. It's not for us to wonder why . . ., et cetera. Particularly after forty years, um? Combs was a security risk and that was that."

Murray made a church-and-steeple of his fingers.

"He'd only have agreed to go to Ireland for a period of time, I imagine," said Kenyon. "Under certain conditions, I mean. There's nothing in his file about the deal which brought him to Ireland."

Murray collapsed his chapel and smiled indulgently.

"Purely informal, I expect. Hardly a signed contract. Tricks men don't get the lawyers to sign deals."

"What conditions?" Kenyon persisted.

"Well," Murray began, "I believe that Combs was offered a deal whereby he'd be allowed to return here. A new passport, if he did a little work for us in Ireland for a short while."

"A short while?"

"Can't be precise. We couldn't expect more than a couple of years. Combs was getting on already."

Meaning that they knew Combs was drinking heavily and wasn't in the best of health to begin with, Kenyon reflected. Murray and company had had good odds that Combs would die before they'd have to live up to the deal about repatriating him. A relic, Murray had said: nuisance, expendable.

"What did you think of the stuff Combs sent? Overall?"

"My assessments are in the file, James. Remember, Combs was very low-level. Intentionally so, I don't need to add. We had nobody on the ground there at that time. The area in south County Dublin was a haven for IRA on the run. All we wanted from Combs were sightings, a name here, a car number there. Not too taxing. His material tapered off this last while, I must say. Could have been the booze, I daresay. Fact is, the IRA may have learned to stay out of that area. The Irish police did a few swoops off their own intelligence there, too. Several things combined to flush them out, I expect."

Murray took up his cup again.

"Combs reported to the Second Sec on a regular basis?"

"Yes. Ball tried to hold him to some reasonable schedule," Murray said vacantly. "Didn't really work, though. You've seen the calibre of stuff that came from Combs lately."

Kenyon nodded. The dull burn in his chest was not going away, he realised then. It was more than his distaste for what lay under the tailored facade which Murray had inherited from the other fops in the Foreign Office. Murray was playing down Combs' death. The Combs that Kenyon had read about in the Registry yesterday afternoon was a different entity from the man whom Murray was now discarding. As he watched Murray draining the cup, it dawned on him that Murray's assessment was wrong because Murray simply hadn't the experience, the depth — most of all, the damned imagination — to see into Arthur Combs. Just for the record, he'd ask Murray.

"So you feel confident that Combs would not have material which could be prejudicial to us?" he murmured.

" 'Us,' James?" asked Murray.

"What made this Arthur Combs enough of a security risk to bar him from Britain for nearly forty years? Was it what he was doing in Ireland these last two years?"

Murray paused and tugged at his cuff-links. Kenyon wanted to scream at the gesture. Murray seemed to be considering the question deeply.

"Oh balance, if it's a yes/no question . . . I'd have to say no. It's my sense that the matter is sealed."

"Excepting for the fact that he was murdered." Kenyon said, hearing the sarcasm plain in his own voice. "And we don't know why."

Murray sat up.

"Is there a need for melodrama like this, James? If our Mr Combs had damaging material to use he would have used it by now, I'm sure. He had no reason to betray his confidences. Really. We're talking about an antique queer who drank half the day. Do you think the Catholic Irish have some soft spot in their hearts for old bum-boys, old English bum-boys at that? Wait and see, you'll find something squalid about him — letting his inclinations get the better of him around some unfortunate youngster. You know what they're like over there. Touchy, temperamental. Peasants in many ways still."

Murray leaned forward over the table, a gesture of readiness to leave.

"Did I hear his place had been burgled, too? The very fact of him living there may have been enough to incense people. Terrible bloody country. A robbery attempt gone astray, I'd start with that if I were a copper. Combs must have looked an easy mark to a local hoodlum. Crime in the Republic is soaring, especially in Dublin. The peons want loot there, too, James. Their economy's on the skids. . . . "

"We can't leave the matter as it is," Kenyon said evenly. "You liaise with this Ball in the embassy, I understand."

"He is one of a number of personnel who reports to me regularly, yes. We have rather a lot on our plates with the border security conference coming up, you'll allow."

"I have to talk to him. It's better he comes here. Will I have difficulties?"

Murray regained his faint smile.

"Only too happy to assist our colleagues in the Security Service."

Which meant the exact opposite, Kenyon thought as he followed Murray out of the restaurant.

CHAPTER 4

Stepaside Garda Station was in the centre of the village. Keating met Minogue in the adjoining carpark. Keating was whistling, tongue behind his teeth. Curly head, mother's love, Minogue mused. He guessed that Keating might be the youngest in his family. Keating winked.

"You found the place all right, did you?"

"Course I did, Pat. I'm a detective. Now who are these Mulvaneys?" asked Minogue.

"They're a bit like hillbillies so far as I can tell from the lads in the station, sir. We have sheets on them for car theft, B & E, petty larceny. Three brothers and they live on their own up above Barnacullia. Up there," Keating nodded toward the rounded top of Two Rock Mountain over the hedges.

"Barman at Glencullen said that they had words with Mr Combs one night recently."

"Glencullen? You mean Johnny Fox's pub? But didn't Combs live in Kilternan? Why would he be going up there for his gargle?"

"Don't know, sir. Maybe he didn't like the one around the corner from him. The Golden Ball. Can't say I blame him either."

"Aha," Minogue murmured.

"And the barman says the Mulvaneys were in the pub with their usual carryings on. Mr Combs used to go in early in the evening for a brandy and a chaser. He'd be in about half seven and gone by nine o'clock, he says. Now one or another of the brothers Mulvaney had words with Combs. They were langers drunk. Drinking all day, by the cut of them," Keating said and paused to rub his eye.

"I think the barman is a bit leery of the likes of the Mulvaneys, sir," he added. "Now he has a chance to get a dig at them without having to face them. There's a lot of people up in these parts are not the full shilling, I believe."

"What was the row about anyway, did you hear?"

"Something about Combs' accent. 'Why is there an effin' Brit bein' served in this effin' pub with all the boys fightin' for freedom not a hundred miles up the effin' road?' and the rest of it," Keating replied.

"Barstool heroes. When they're not falling off them," Minogue muttered darkly. Three Gardai in shirtsleeves came out the back door of the police station. They carried batons.

"Come along up with us lads, the view is only tremendous," quipped a balding Garda. Minogue recognised him from somewhere. The Garda football club? A Cork accent, as thick as a ditch, and a clown's loaded smile. Another Cork exile here in Dublin.

Keating drove. The car made heavy work of the steep, winding road to Barnacullia.

"The official line is that we'll be requesting their assistance on several break-ins around the area. That way if they mention Combs at all, they'll be coming to him cold and we'll know what's what very quickly."

"Any assaults or threats on their records?" Minogue asked.

53

"Not yet, can I say, sir. Only resisting arrest, one of them. It's a bit thin, I know, but sure we can only try, can't we?"

Minogue nodded.

"They'll be dragging their arses out of bed around now. Says the sergeant below, anyway. Oh, the three brothers have names, too. Do you want to hear them?"

"Go on out of that. Are they special?" asked Minogue.

"The oldest one is called the Bronc. He wears a cowboy hat. The middle one is Seamus, but if you call him that, he'll pick a row with you. Everyone calls him Shag. Shag Mulvaney."

"Has a nice ring to it. And the third lad?"

"He's called Quick."

"Isn't that rich?"

"Quick has a bad leg now, so he's more law-abiding than the other two. He was the scourge of south County Dublin a few years ago. A real careful burglar, you know the worst kind, the ones who do it off a list, shopping for stuff they can fence straight away. We could never pin one on him. He could walk up a wall and do houses while people were fast asleep in the next room. He got a bit cocky, though, and started to take a few jars before a job. One night himself and another lad were half-way in the window of a house and didn't the man of the house hear them. 'Quick,' says Mulvaney and . . . "

"And what?"

"And that was all he said. Fell thirty feet into a bloody glasshouse, all over someone's rare tropical plants, and he didn't get up either. He has one leg longer than the other one since, and the long one is stuck together with a big bolt or something at the knee."

"A pin, you mean."

54

"A big fat pin. One of the lads at the station saw it."

Keating had turned onto a narrow road which meandered erratically under Two Rock Mountain. He guided the car cautiously through blind elbow bends. Minogue heard roadside grass lash along the door-panels. The glimpses of view between the bushes and banks to the right side revealed the city and south suburbs below. The sea-horizon was above Howth, they were that high. The Garda squad-car was waiting for them at the foot of a steep path, which led further up the side of the mountain.

"Jases," Keating said to himself, he thought. "We'll be needing mules next."

Rusting hulks of cars surrounded a cottage which crouched by the path. The path itself was no more than the dual tracks that cars had left in their wake. Other mysterious pieces of vehicles lay at the sides of it: bits of tractors, a piece of tread from a caterpillar, the frame of a lorry.

A district detective whom Minogue didn't recognise was leaning his elbows on the roof of the Garda car ahead. He came over and introduced himself as Eamonn Driscoll.

Then, like potatoes tumbling out of a sack which had fallen over, the three Gardai emerged from their car. There was much tucking in of shirts, fingering of batons and scratching of noses. They left their hats in the car.

"Do you want in on this, Sergeant?" *sotto voce* from the Corkman.

Playing it up a bit, Minogue considered. Maybe he thought it was all terribly funny to have to pick up the Mulvaneys for these detectives out from Dublin. Did he already know what Minogue had suspected, that the Mulvaneys weren't in a class to kill someone? Minogue said he'd come along.

"I hear these lads hunted with Finn McCool," Minogue said to the Corkman.

"Wisha Sergeant," he whispered. "Not to be disappointing you now, but these three Mulvaneys have been trading on their reputations a long time now. There's nothing to them. Petty thieves. Whoever tipped you off to these lads wasn't Charlie Chan. But we'll try anyhow."

Minogue followed the Gardai up the path. Driscoll fell back from the group and introduced himself to Minogue. At the top of the path, Minogue chose a deceased '57 or '58 Ford Prefect to lean his weight on. A dog began barking as the Gardai and Driscoll approached the house. Curious at first, the dog settled into a staccato, monotonous yelping. It didn't sound like a chained dog to Minogue. Then he caught sight of it, an old collie sitting surrealistically in a path of lettuce plants. If the collie was all they had to contend with, then the three brothers could take all their attention.

Driscoll's knock on the door went unanswered. No faces appeared at the windows. The cottage had small windows with sashes that hadn't been painted for a long time. Several panes had been repaired with tape and patches of what had been clear plastic. Minogue heard rustling by a sagging shed, which lay to the rear of the house. The old collie kept up its rhythmic barking. Minogue tried to listen again. Was it a small engine, a power tool of some sort? The shed door opened slightly as though a breeze had caught it. A large Alsatian shot out the gap in the door. The dog hesitated on its hind legs for an instant, caught sight of the group by the front door and began to race toward the policemen.

Its path brought it by Minogue. As the dog hared past him, Minogue stepped out from behind the car and landed a sharp kick on the fleeting dog's backside. It was enough to throw the animal off-course with a yelp. Two of the Gardai turned at the sound.

The dog had spun with the kick, righted itself and turned to face Minogue. Having nothing to hand, Minogue summoned up saliva and spat at the growling dog. The Alsatian's tail wavered. Minogue bared his teeth and crouched slightly, his arms out. He made to spit again, but the dog had already backed into the weeds.

"Hey, look it!" Minogue heard one of the Gardai shout.

A gnomic head peeped out of the shed door.

"Ya dirty animal," the head called out.

The Alsatian backed away further from Minogue then loped back to the shed. Driscoll ran up to Minogue, looked at him and then called out.

"Quick, come outa there where we can see you. Tie up that dog of yours or I'll do for it. Do you hear me talking to you?"

The dog wriggled through the door opening and disappeared. The old collie was still barking, as though having remembered how to do it, he was loath to surrender the skill to forgetfulness. A short, barrel-chested man came out of the shed door and closed it noisily behind him. He walked sideways to the policemen, dragging a stiff leg.

"Get those two brothers of yours up, Quick," Driscoll said.

"Dirty animal," Quick hissed.

Minogue watched the sideways gait of the balding man, a face on him that looked like it had been caught in a door.

"Jases, disgusting so it is. Spitting at an animal. I never seen such a disgrace as that," Quick said.

"I suppose he slipped the leash by accident all of a sudden," Driscoll said.

"Can I help it if the smell of yous rozzers drives the dog wild?" Quick retorted.

Minogue studied Quick's uneven face. Quick's beard served to emphasise his resentment at the world. He wondered if such spite could lead him to strangling an old man.

"Show us your search warrant," Quick sneered.

"Get up the yard with yourself, Quick," Driscoll broke in. "You're not watching the telly now. Let's have your driving licence and your insurance, too. Then you can start showing us all the jalopies you have around here and where you got them."

Quick's expression didn't change. He sidled crookedly by Minogue, looking him up and down at the sea off Dublin. Kilternan was hidden behind a rise of woods below and to the south of where he stood. He recalled the Cork Garda's remarks about the brothers. A household of three drunken bachelors, their forte would be squalid misdemeanours or, at the apogee of a binge, a brawl.

Minogue checked the time. He did not want to wait around long enough to be disappointed. He asked Hoey what time to hold the confab back at headquarters. Hoey said that four o'clock in the briefing room would be manageable from his point of view. Minogue could be in the city by one, his dinner eaten by half one ... ready for business by two ... and a break in Bewley's Cafe after three. To gather his thoughts, of course.

A breeze searched his jacket. Motive, he thought: why is this old man dead? Simple bloody question, no answer. He thought again of the drawings in Combs' house. Tully church, the pagan symbols on warm, smooth stones ...

Quick's limp had soured his face into that of a malignant dwarf. The Bronc was hatless, also wore a beard and smelled like a damp ashtray. He seemed mild, almost co-operative, as he stepped out in his socks onto the flagstones by the door. Evenings, and perhaps mornings too, had left him with an overhanging belly which his vest could not get under. There'd be no competition among the policemen as to who could sit beside The Bronc.

"Yous have nothing on me. Not a fuckin' sausage!" the Bronc hissed.

Minogue watched them trek down the path. Shag was the last of the brothers into the Garda cars. His eyes were darting about, but he remained silent.

"That was easy enough," Keating murmured.

"They were flattered by so much attention, I'm thinking," said Minogue. "Here, I'm off to town directly we get back to the station. Is someone going to go over the place for rope here?"

Keating concealed his surprise.

"Em . . . Driscoll and another fella will do it while these three divine persons are down in the station."

"Phone me in the unlikely event that . . . " Minogue didn't finish the sentence. "And can you be in by four along with the others? We'll go over what we have."

Alistair Murray wrote the cable message in longhand, authorised it himself and had it delivered by hand to the Communications Section. Ball would be waiting for official word that MI5 had inherited Combs. Information was to follow in due course, Murray had written in officialese, as to what dispositions and assistance Foreign Office staff could make for Mr Kenyon should the Security Service request same.

Murray omitted the second letter of his initials in the "reply to" box. The omission was a signal to Ball to telephone him at a public telephone booth in Knightsbridge at one o'clock this afternoon. He settled back in his chair and stifled a yawn. Maybe he should have let Combs off the hook sooner, he reflected. But getting him out of Dublin would not have been risk-free either. A cantankerous Combs would have nourished his resentment and had it flower sooner or later, at a time when he, Murray, would have less control. Kenyon and the Security Service would nose about until he had exhausted his irritation and assured himself and the Service that Combs could be boxed and buried permanently. Combs, whether he had liked it or not, had earned his keep. Under the circumstances ... Murray's thoughts slid away.

His memory drew him back yet again to the drizzly expanse of aerodrome tarmac, the blanket of grey clouds low over the small groups in uniform huddled under umbrellas. He remembered the savage ironies; here he was, standing in the rain at an RAF base where England's finest hours had been played out in the war, with fliers limping back to base in that spring of 1940. Heroes' return ... and so many never returning; England's best.

A clear enemy then, ranting dictators and masses of goose-stepping fanatics. England had never been more united. Who was the enemy now? he remembered wondering as he had looked out through the rain at the regimental honour guard, the drizzle beading and dripping from their brims while they waited for the coffins to emerge from the plane. No Members of Parliament to welcome back *these* soldiers, to stand vigil and honour their dead. No Ministers or their Secretaries. No Kenyons either. Just the faint hum from the motorway in the distance, the families standing in puddles, the uniforms. Small sprays of lilies standing out against the greys. No, no hero's return, no medals pinned, no wife's embrace. He had watched from the car as Ball had walked behind his brother's coffin, hatless and pale. Who was the enemy now?

Murray had waited for several weeks before contacting Ball. He had to wait for it to sink in with Mervyn Ball as it had sunk in with himself three years before. He waited for Ball to understand that his brother's funeral marked the end of it. There would be no public outrage, no questions in the Commons. Just another British officer's death sinking into history — not even history, mere numbers. And all for what? The sniper still crept over the rooftops of West Belfast, claiming more victims, the bombers still thumbed the buttons. A holding operation, governments too wary and timid to ask the army to do better than watch as parts of soldiers were shovelled into plastic bags amid the rubble.

Months later, Ball at a Foreign Office reception, glass in hand, weighing Murray up as the party went on around them: *Yes, Mervyn, we have something in common. Your brother was in the Royal Greenjackets, I think. . . .*

While Minogue negotiated his way into the centre of Dublin, Kenyon was walking back to his office in Cadogan Gardens. Kenyon was finding it difficult to order things in his mind. Several times during his walk he resolved to wait until he reached his office before trying to run over the facts again.

He was dimly aware of a threat lurking somewhere. It was contiguous with, but also hidden by his own anger and alarm. Back in his office, Kenyon listed plusses and minuses on a sheet of paper. Then he sat back in the chair and waited for the issues to announce themselves.

The first thing Hugh Robertson, the Director of his section, would ask him would be if he was being as objective as he could be. No, maybe he'd ask if Kenyon wasn't overly sensitive in the atmosphere of publicity around the Service's operations. As for the objectivity question, Kenyon had to point out that there was too big a gap between what Murray was saying and what he himself was beginning to conclude about Arthur Combs. The Combs that Kenyon had read was still a younger man, rebellious and steely. Evaluation, objective evaluation, Kenyon echoed as he sat back in his chair.

He unlocked his desk and removed a sheet from the top drawer. The sheet contained a list of names. Seven of the fifteen people whose names he had gleaned from Combs' file in the Registry were dead. Of the remaining eight only two were British. One of those two lived in Spain. None of these people was under seventy. As far as Kenyon knew, none on the list had any connections with security or intelligence organisations. Combs had been fluent in German, of course. Probably bits of Greek and Spanish, definitely French. So? Kenyon almost said aloud.

Another possibility was local to where he had lived, near Dublin. Unlikely, he whispered aloud. Combs had resisted going there in the first place. Garrulous people, "the world's best grudge-keepers" had been quoted directly from an interview with Combs. Funny, but macabre now.

Kenyon buzzed Bowers and sent him out for two cheese croissants. Then he stood by the window, not needing the paper or lists to command the issues now. Just before Bowers' return, Kenyon was brooding about the perennial injustice of other people's chickens coming home to roost with him. Injustice indeed: Combs would have known about that. Kenyon swore aloud at the impossible logistics he'd have to outline if he was going to go through with this operation.

All at once Kenyon realised that if he was already thinking details, it meant that he had made a decision. He had assented to a plan, but he hadn't quite admitted it to himself yet. He'd stick with that decision. This insight provided a moment of relief, but when Bowers knocked, Kenyon was again worrying about an important detail he might have missed. Christ, there had to be someone significant in Combs' life. His family was gone years ago; there had to be someone he'd trust.

"Sir."

Bowers pushed the door open. Kenyon turned and glanced at the doctorate in political science who was five months into working for the greater good of the United Kingdom. Bowers' glasses reminded Kenyon of Carl Jung. Sex, anyone? No thanks. Bowers/Jung might reply, I must go for a bracing walk in the Alps.

"Good. Still hot? Would you phone the Director's secretary, Gillian, and set up a meeting with him. ASAP. Tell her I can go meet him if he's out, all right?"

Murray taxied to Knightsbridge. The telephone booth next to Mappins was empty. He stepped in and checked for a dial tone. Hearing one, he looked at his watch. Two minutes to one. A woman struggling with shopping bags stopped outside the booth and opened her purse for change. Murray stuck his head out the door.

"The phone's broken, I'm afraid. I'm just trying to get my money back out of the stupid thing."

The shopper blinked at the well-groomed man leaning out of the door. She shrugged resignedly and took up her bags again. The phone rang a minute early.

"All right," Murray began. "Five has launched an investigation."

"I understand," said Ball slowly. Murray heard traffic from some Dublin street.

"Hold on a minute," Ball muttered. "I have to plug more money in already. . . . "

Murray listened impatiently as the coins rang into the telephone.

"I had a meeting with Five's man. He thinks our friend may have done something underhand. Wrote a bloody memoir. Left some documents, or told someone. They'll want you for a debriefing, too," said Murray. "And I expect they'll do a sweep of the house, too," he added.

"I'm ninety-nine percent sure the place is clean. There was nothing."

"They'll be thorough," Murray replied. "They're very tender about the border security conference here. Everybody's edgy."

Ball read the rebuke between Murray's words. *Couldn't have come at a worse time . . . was there no better way to fix it?* Ball said nothing.

"What exactly did he say to you when he called you on Thursday?" asked Murray.

"He phoned me at the embassy. I met him in a pub that afternoon. He'd been drinking — "

"But did he say how he'd do it?" Murray interrupted. "What did he say he could do? What would he use?"

Ball paused before answering. This was his third time trying to reassure Murray.

"He said he wanted out and that we had better listen to him this time around. I got him calmed down. He didn't say how but that he'd see to it somehow — "

"Somehow," Murray repeated. "Somehow."

"Exactly. He thought we had his mail opened and that we knew when he went to the toilet. He had no real plan, nothing. He went off at half-cock, without thinking it out. He said I should 'walk the plank' for it. You too."

"He didn't know me," Murray said quickly.

"I know. More bluff. He only met you once. He called you 'the ringleader.' How do you like that title?"

Murray did not care for Ball's grim humour one bit. There was a taunting edge to it: Ball, the action-man, chiding Murray, the desk-man. Murray thought back to the meeting in a seedy Dublin hotel. Combs had already been into his second — or was it third? — Scotch minutes after the hotel bar had opened, looking sullenly from Ball to Murray, hardly bothering to conceal his hostility.

"But he had no inkling after you met him Thursday? That we wouldn't buy, I mean?"

"Right." Ball said sharply. "I got him calmed down and I gave him what he wanted. I told him it would take a couple of days to get the passport through, so it'd be Monday at the earliest. But that we'd hurry things up. . . . "

"Yes," said Murray, distracted yet.

" . . . Stroked his hand, cooed his ear about the work he had done. I sent him home happy. At least more sober than when he arrived at the pub. I told him we had been about to wrap the whole thing up soon."

"You're certain he wasn't specific even then?"

"Absolutely. He didn't say what he would do, or would have done. That's because he didn't have anything prepared," Ball added slowly for emphasis.

Except his instincts, Murray almost added aloud. Kenyon's reading of the Combs' material. . . . Would Combs have suspected something from the way Ball had behaved at that meeting, that he'd never be let go knowing what he knew? Was Combs really the boozy, truculent character that Ball had been dealing with, or had Kenyon scented something more basic in his make-up?

"All right," Murray said finally, staying his own wandering. "Expect to be called in about Combs."

Murray hung up and hailed a taxi. He tried to ignore the garrulous Cockney cabbie. Ball was experienced, dependable. His motivation was at least as high as Murray's own. Mervyn Ball had dealt with Combs for two years, babysitting him, humouring him — his had to be the more accurate assessment. Most of all, Ball had not flinched, even when Murray himself had thought it precipitate to silence the old man.

The taxi joined a traffic jam near Oxford Circus. The cabbie's eyes sought out Murray in the mirror.

"Bloody bomb scare, I shouldn't wonder," said the Cockney. "Who's it this time, I wonder? The bloody Arabs or the Irish, eh?"

Murray ignored the question. Combs' "Somehow": it was very telling, all right. A loose threat, stillborn. He wondered if Ball had felt much pity for the old man. Hardly. Ball had been tough from the start. Perhaps not tough — more like firm, uncompromising — but still able to coax the old man. Did Combs wonder how Ball could cave in so readily to his demand last Thursday, though? Combs might have sobered up and then wondered why, after years of the cold shoulder, he was suddenly being granted what he had been asking for at least thirty years. . . .

Murray recalled the black-and-white framed snapshot which he kept in his desk. The confident, boyish face and the haircut they had laughed about. It was 1971, of course, and even Murray himself had grown sideburns. "Passing out at Sandhurst" had been the joke when Ian Murray had his arm around his younger brother's neck in a chokehold, laughing into the camera. Ian the doer, Ian the adventurer. A ham, a litany of broken arms and legs through youth, the ebullient extrovert. The same Ian Murray on a greasy footpath in Belfast three years later, dead before he hit the pavement, the dumdum spraying his brains and teeth twenty feet further down the path.

Did Mervyn Ball have a photo like that, too? One of his own brother, one he looked at before he went to Combs' house that night? Donald Ball had been a Royal Greenjacket, Ian Murray a Para. Ball told him that he had a letter from Donald describing the mountains outside Belfast — "once you're out of bloody Belfast, it's a marvellous country, believe it or not". Three days later, his brother was dismembered by a bomb in a roadside culvert. . . . believe it or not.

The taxi inched forward.

"It's the silly season, in'nit then?" said the cabbie.

Murray took out his wallet and looked at the meter. He handed three pounds to the driver and opened the door himself.

"Ta, mate. Bloody bombers are probably back safe in bloody Ireland by now, sitting in a pub laughing. The bastards."

Murray paused before slamming the door.

"Safe in Ireland?" Murray echoed with a sneer. "No such thing."

CHAPTER 5

Minogue had finished a jumble of cauliflower, potatoes and stringy mutton. The vegetables were barely
tolerable and he had little relish for the mutton. For
his pains, the waitress could only offer him the choice
of jelly or ice cream.

"I'll go jelly then," he said.

"Tea or coffee?"

"Neither thanks. I'm saving myself for Bewley's
later on. Don't tell anyone or I'll be in trouble."

When Minogue saw the cubes of jelly shivering on
the bowl under him, he knew that he didn't have the
heart for it. Still, he trapped a cube under the edge of
the spoon, cut it and tasted it. Wicked. Was jelly the
kind of thing that old people living on their own would
eat? Like in America with the TV dinners you bought
and could just sling into the oven and eat right out of
the package? Old people living alone. . . . Maybe Mrs
Hartigan had fed Combs right. Minogue felt his
thoughts slump. Damn and damn again. There had to
be something she'd know to get this moving.

When Minogue reached the Squad HQ in St John's
Road, the smell of Turkish tobacco stopped him in his

tracks. Yes, Paris, Minogue remembered, with his wife giggling at his French: the smell of Gauloises, piss and diesel in the early morning streets by Montmartre.

Eilis nodded at him. Her air of impatience served to keep groundlings at bay. She had had enough of humans, it seemed, but not enough that she did not entertain a Trinity College professor as her lover. So the rumour went anyway. The ones who raised their eyebrows the most were the policemen who were about the same age as Eilis, married men.

"It's yourself that's in it, is it?" she breathed. Wisps of her dark red hair had escaped the clasp gathering her hair over the collar of her blouse.

"And how's our Inspector?" she continued in Irish.

"Fine and well," Minogue replied in her vernacular. "He says hello to all and sundry here."

Eilis sat down. She almost smiled at Minogue's pun. On the surface, "fine and well" in her vernacular of Munster Irish meant that the party so described was happily drunk.

"I have reams of stuff to give you, you'll be thrilled to hear," Eilis muttered around her cigarette. The smoke was irritating her eyes, the more so as she leaned over to unlock a cabinet.

Minogue took the folder and decamped to his desk and chair. Combs' passport number along with a black-and-white snap — one taken in a Woolworth's box, by the cut of it — clipped onto a sheet was on top of the sheaf of papers. Combs had been looking back at the lens as if to challenge it, to make sure it reported a true picture of him. He looked older than seventy-three even then. Froggy, tired eyes on him, loose skin bundled under his chin. Sick-looking? Fleshy-looking anyway. How often did UK citizens have to renew their passport photos?

69

The photocopies of the visa pages from his passport showed a stamp from Malaga declaring that Combs had been a *turista* when he went there two years ago. Could have been over and back to Britain a million times, too; no passport needed. A poorly typed summary — a reluctant Hoey clattering on the keys on late Sunday night — listed names: Mrs Hartigan, James Molloy (barman), Joey Murphy (wit. in Fox's pub), Jackie Burke (do.), Larry O'Toole (do.), Mulvaneys (Barnacullia).

"Somebody phone the embassy of next-of-kin?"

"Master Keating did," replied Eilis.

Minogue returned to his papers. Copies of car insurance, an Irish driver's licence and, handwritten below, two account numbers for the Bank of Ireland, College Green. Minogue called the bank and asked for Bill Hogan, another Clare expatriate.

"You'll phone me then, Bill, will you? Here's my number. I'll follow up with the paperwork later on in the week. What's the story on any safety deposit boxes or use of a big bank safe, will you find out about that?"

Hogan would. Unasked, Hogan would also offer Minogue twenty quid at four to one against Offaly making it all the way to the hurling final. Minogue asked if Hogan could perhaps effect a loan on his behalf for that amount. Hogan barked a laugh and hung up. Minogue then phoned Keating at Stepaside Garda station.

"What about your three divine persons?" Minogue inquired.

Keating couldn't keep a touch of disappointment from his voice.

"You were right, sir. They're bad articles, but they're all blather."

Minogue heard the pages of Keating's notebook turning slowly.

70

" . . . Moved a few hot cars along and delivered the odd shotgun no questions asked. Shag was convicted three years ago for fencing stuff. He did six months . . . We questioned them separately but they came up clean so far. They're no strangers here. They want to know what we're holding them under."

"And is there anything ye can lean on them with? Anything around the house?"

"No, sir. A few dirty books and a new set of mechanic's tools that the likes of the Mulvaneys can't afford. And they have an independent alibi, all three of them, up 'til five o'clock in the morning. Sort of tears the arse out of things," Keating spoke slowly.

"Well, they weren't saying the rosary all night. They were playing cards and drinking at a house in the village."

"All of them?" Minogue interjected.

"All of them. One of them, let me see . . . Shag, yes, Shag. He was put out of the game because he was blackguarding with the cards. But he sat in the kitchen, drinking with another fella."

Keating filled in more details from the interviews. Minogue was half-listening. The other half of him was thinking of the drawings in Combs' house. The whorls in the granite had been rendered in all their stark softness in his drawings: stone gnawed over by centuries of wind and sun and rain. How many hands had caressed those stones? These extraordinarily ordinary images in a house that was empty of any trappings of family life, those other artefacts from which Minogue had fashioned bits of his own religion. Trappings, perhaps that was a word for it, all right. Maybe Combs never wanted to be entrapped by a family, and these drawings could only be produced by a man outside the rag-and-bone comforts of a family, those things which had brought Minogue back to life. Combs a transient? For two years? A man who couldn't conceal his feeling for such stones and signs was hardly a transient. It looked like he had found something.

Minogue gathered himself from his wool-collecting and took leave of Keating, but not before trying to buoy him up.

"Tell you what. Give it a rest. Shea can tidy up bits there, do you follow me? Get yourself a cup of something, polish up a summary of those three brothers. Get here for the four o'clock powwow here with me. Can you do that?"

"I think so, sir."

Bill Hogan phoned as Minogue was replacing the receiver. Hogan liked doing favours which showed his acumen and authority in the bank, Minogue remembered as he listened to Hogan's flamboyant greeting.

"Mr Combs had the two accounts, all right. One was for savings and the other was a current account. One of the girls remembers him. He used to wait for her so she'd do his business for him. There. Aren't we quick off the mark in this bank, Matt?"

"I'm blinded by your efficiency, so I am," Minogue said. "Listen, was Combs a big depositor?"

Minogue knew that his request was beyond the pale. Hogan could well ask for the official request in writing, in between apologising for the formalities of course.

"Let's say he was comfortable, Matt. More comfortable than you or I."

"Any large transactions in the last while?" Minogue tried gingerly.

"No. He never left more than three figures in the savings. The current account was just to receive remittances from banks in England. Credit memos. Now, don't you want to ask me where these remittances came from?"

"Well. I suppose I do . . . yes, I do," Minogue said, taken by surprise. Had he such currency with Hogan, a man who had grown up as a townie in Ennis while Minogue was mooching around in the sodden fields with clay under his nails?

"National Westminster Bank. NatWest. A branch in London. Every month, a credit memo at the beginning of the month and then another one at the end of the month."

"A pension, Bill?"

"Arra, I dunno. If either one was a pension, then it's in England the pair of us should be living and not here. One of the memos had the name of another bank as source. Sampson Coutts. Sounds very 'nobby, doesn't it?"

"Like they supply snuff to the Queen."

"Well. That's as much as we know here. Oh, he had nothing in the safe with us here."

"Aren't you great, though," Minogue declared. "There wouldn't be more later?"

"Nothing of any import."

Minogue had to sit through a crude joke where only Hogan laughed. Then he returned to the itemised list of Combs' effects.

There was no sign of a will. There was a box which seemed to have contained the receipts that had been scattered about the kitchen. Receipts for the electricity, receipts from a garage for a new clutch in the car, bills for water. Combs owned the house freehold. There was no safe or cubby-hole in the house. No money had been found. Combs' wallet, if he had had one, was missing. Minogue read through Hoey's report for mention of an address book, a diary, any notes for appointments. There was none. There was, however, a photocopy of a list of telephone numbers which had been taped to the wall beside the telephone. Hoey or somebody had tried the numbers, because red felt pen marks were next to all of the numbers. A doctor in Stepaside, the housekeeper's number, numbers for two bookies (ah, a racing man), the B&I ferry office, Aer Lingus, British Airways. One number had the name "Ball" next to it. "British Embassy" had been written in red on the photocopy.

Minogue leaned back in the chair. He almost toppled back onto the floor. Recovering his poise, he leaned his elbows on the desk. It was gone three o'clock. Eilis was burrowing in a filing cabinet. There was a smell of tea lurking somewhere, not yet suffocated by her Gitanes. It was a toss-up whether he should visit Bewley's in Georges Street (in which backwater you were liable to fall asleep) or go for the real Bewley's in Grafton Street or Westmoreland Street. Minogue took stock of what he needed. Meeting at four to put the nuts and bolts together. Combs didn't seem to have any solicitor in Ireland. Did the bank deal with this kind of thing, seeing as Combs had been a customer? Eilis to phone Bill Hogan back. Listen to his jokes, too?

But this was all a bit too routine, Minogue sensed, when he stood up from the offending chair. Beyond the sketches there was little enough personal in Combs' place. Did no one write him letters? No grandniece to send him a postcard about her holiday in Brighton? No shoebox of snapshots and cards? Mrs Hartigan's mention of Combs' corresponding with others . . . but no sign of him hoarding any letters he had received in reply. Minogue's house held mountains of knick-knacks, all sacraments sufficient to his own faith. He didn't know how a person could live comfortably without such a glut of signs. He looked at the copy of the passport pages again. Went on holidays to Spain on his own. . . .

Minogue was almost by Eilis when her phone rang. She beckoned to him before he could reach the door. The call was from the British Embassy. Minogue listened to an English accent announcing that she was Miss Simpson, that Mr Combs was unmarried and that Mr Combs did not have any family extant. Extant?

"Mr Combs' sister, Janet Combs, died in Bristol in 1979. We know of no relatives."

Just like that, Minogue thought. The way Miss Simpson had said it added a weight to the feeling he had held aside so far. Silly maybe: he had almost said "poor devil."

"Oh, I see. Now can you tell me where Mr Combs used to live in England? In Great Britain, I mean. Did he have a house there himself, like."

"Mr Combs last lived in London."

She gave Minogue an address which meant nothing to him. Some place called Wood Green. It sounded nice, but wasn't London very crowded? He scribbled while she spoke. A delphic Eilis sat behind a slim thread of smoke watching him. He tried not to be distracted by the way Miss Simpson was ending her words so precisely.

Mr Combs had retired from his job as a Customs Inspector at the Port of London. He had sold his house over two years ago and moved to Ireland. He had established contact with the embassy in Ireland as a matter of course. The address she gave him was the same house in Kilternan.

"I see, Miss Simpson." Minogue said.

"Would there be an Irish background here at all, his parents perhaps?"

Miss Simpson didn't know and she said so.

"Is there no one we can tell he's dead? Relatives, I mean, of course."

"I expect that his will may tell you something."

"Yes, indeed," said Minogue, adrift again. "But we have none. Will, that is. Solicitors I suppose. If there are any."

"Your Department of Foreign Affairs usually looks after the return of remains," she said lightly.

Minogue realised that she was trying to be helpful.

"Yes, Miss Simpson. Thanks very much now. And I hope we find someone for Mr Combs. His relatives I mean, as well as the perpetrator. However distant the relatives. Oh, before I forget, is there a Mr Ball working at the embassy?"

"There is. He's a Second Secretary. . . . Did you want to . . . ?"

"Not at the moment, no thanks. It's just that we found a telephone number in Mr Combs' house for your Mr Ball."

"One of Mr Ball's duties is to see to inquiries and communications with citizens of the UK resident in Ireland. As I mentioned, Mr Combs registered with us here."

"That's a lot of work, though, isn't it?" asked Minogue. "All those Britons who come here to live, even for a while, like."

"Not everybody would do so, Sergeant. Some like to do it, but Ireland, the Republic, is not a foreign destination for Britons really, is it?"

A sense of humour maybe?

"True for you. I hope to have better news for you if I'm in touch again, Miss Simpson."

Miss Simpson said that would be nice and rang off with a "cheerio," something Minogue had heard only in films. Eilis was lighting a cigarette from the butt of her last one when Minogue put down the phone.

"Poor Combs has no one to come and get him, it seems."

Eilis drew on her cosmopolitan, continental cigarette.

"London. That's a very big place now, The Big Smoke. You'll be wanting to speak with someone in the Met there, will you?"

"I suppose I'd better. Will you find me a name and a number, please? Is there a fella we've dealt with before maybe?"

"There are several, so there are," Eilis replied drily. "The Inspector had need to be communicating with the authorities beyond in The Big Smoke and he keeps in touch with several. 'It's good to have them when you need them,' says the Inspector. Especially when there's wigs on the green over a political thing, I suppose. *Extradition* and the like. The inspector does be very nervous when that word is mentioned."

"That's a word that'll bring the walls of Jericho down, all right," Minogue agreed.

"I'd suggest that the Inspector could pop a name at you that'd ease your way if you'd like me to phone the hospital for you." Eilis concluded her poor rendition of an imaginary Mata Hari.

"Or I could just pull a name off the card index . . ."

Kenyon's croissant had given him indigestion. He wanted to summon up a belch so that he might dislodge what felt like a piece of the croissant jammed in his sternum. He would have done so in his own office. Here, however, he could not be sure of concealing the belch under his palm should it erupt now.

Hugh Robertson, the Director of the Protective Security Branch, was reading Kenyon's summary. Although Robertson was Kenyon's immediate boss, Kenyon's liking for him supervened over rank and duties. Robertson had been a Colonel when Kenyon first met him. It was in Malaya, two years after Kenyon had joined the Service. As the Empire had contracted, so had the overseas doings of MI5 become more limited. Robertson was one of the leading brains behind the successful counter-insurgency campaign against the communists in Malaya. He had shunned jockeying a desk in favour of field operations.

Robertson had astonished Kenyon and many others with his bluntness. At a boozy farewell dinner in 1955 for a large contingent of MI5's field force — to hold the party itself was tantamount to mutiny — which was preparing to leave Malaya, Robertson had spoken his mind. He voiced his opinion about the shrinking Empire by saying good riddance to the damn colonies. He had looked around the room and said that now Britain would have to find something else for its second-rate sons and daughters to lord it over. It was only when the audience guffawed that Kenyon had realised Robertson had been speaking to the converted.

"Now, James. Who killed Cock Robin here?"

"I don't know."

"Did the IRA kill him?"

"Very, very doubtful," Kenyon replied. "They'd be sure to tell, loud and clear. That's their propaganda bread-and-butter."

"Burglary?" murmured Robertson.

"The police press release says they're pursuing it as robbery with violence."

Robertson gave Kenyon a stage frown.

"Did we kill him?"

"No."

"That's a relief, I suppose. But what do you want from me?"

"I need your approval. Then I'd be asking for staff to go surveillance on Combs' contacts. We have to get someone into Dublin, too, and pick up the bits. I want the Second Sec at our Dublin embassy for a few sessions. The chap who ran Combs. Name of Ball. That'd be a start."

"Contacts?" Robertson asked.

"These people on the list. The asterisk means that the party is dead. There are eight left. Combs may have sent something to any one of them. We have to find out, that's what I'm saying."

" 'Something,' James?"

"I'm taking Combs' threats seriously. He may have prepared some record of his grievances."

"Several years back, wasn't it? I thought that the new man Murray had put in knew his onions, claimed to have this Combs toeing the line. You're discounting the reports sourced through Murray and company."

"I am," Kenyon answered, with enough emphasis to cause Robertson to look up at him.

"Bit of a twerp, is he, James?"

"More than that. He's covering his arse. I don't like the way he's treating Combs' murder. He couldn't or wouldn't say what deals were struck to bring Combs to Ireland in the first place. It's a crucial matter if I'm to make sense of things."

"He doesn't have to, James," Robertson rounded on him politely. "You asked a lot of him, seems to me. We don't give out our more clandestine endeavours, you know."

"I'm not a reporter from the *Mirror*. We're supposed to be on the same side. I won't be happy until we've had a thorough search through Combs' stuff ourselves," Kenyon retorted.

"Threat, you said," Robertson diverted. "A threat to go to the IRA or someone and tell him that he was doing odd jobs for a British intelligence service?"

"Hardly, Hugh. He had no time for them, I'm sure."

"Or a threat to give out with his war stories, shall we call them? He could have sold that stuff for a tidy bundle here. He was a commie, was he not?"

"He passed some stuff to a Soviet ring in Berlin, yes. That's what we rapped his knuckles for. The real trouble started when he turned us down on staying in East Germany after the Liberation. Never trusted after that."

Robertson cleared his throat.

"Mr Combs didn't say at any time what exactly he had in mind, did he?"

"No," Kenyon conceded. "Murray puts it down to alcoholic raving. I still think that if Combs was threatening anybody with anything, it'd be what we did with him during the war and after. I don't see him betraying any of us to a bunch of thugs like the IRA."

"So . . . some documents on that, perhaps . . . notes he might have made?"

"Yes."

Robertson looked up from the papers.

"I see no mention of a joint op with the Secret Service in your brief. Or the Foreign Office itself. Don't trust our friends, do you, James?"

"Ask me after a few drinks at the next Christmas party," Kenyon joked morosely. "But first I need to confirm Murray and this Second Sec at the embassy."

"As to what they do?" Robertson half-smiled.

"For whom do they do what they do?"

"Why they work for our gallant Secret Service, James, our MI marvellous six."

"Just Foreign Office cover?"

Robertson nodded.

"So what is Six doing about this?" Kenyon asked.

"They're doing bugger-all at the moment, James. Naturally they'd like to know who killed Mr Combs and why. Howandever, the Home Secretary 'advised' that we carry it from here. Six will get around to their own investigation, but it won't be fast enough for the PMO. We have finally gotten the Irish to the table on border security. The PMO is more than keen not to have any, let's say, fans invade the pitch . . . so the game is called off."

"Speed, as well as jurisdiction?"

"How politic of you, James. Yes, yes," Robertson said quietly. He put the sheets back in order and laid the folder on the table between them. "You base your proposal on what you have assembled from Combs' file?"

"Yes. I talked to Murray this morning, too," Kenyon replied.

"You're saying that the risks are too high not to assume some dossier, some notes?"

"Right. Whether Combs was talking in the bottle or not, I'm assuming he made some note or notes. Even scattered notes, something to organise his thoughts. There's the two sides to the knife, though. One is how peeved we were — or SOE was — when we found out he was feeding some material to the Soviets back in '44 and '45. The people running the show back then include a former Minister and a D.G. of the Security Service. Anyway, Combs fouled his nest finally when he refused to go into the East and do low-level stuff. Turned us down point-blank. Wouldn't shop the Soviets, he said. Our allies in a common cause. . . . When we told Combs to get lost then, he knew we were serious, that we wouldn't tolerate any public disclosures. And I must say, the climate was tough enough then with the blockade on Berlin and Stalin throwing his weight about with a well-equipped army sitting half-way across Europe. Still, Combs knew some nasty trade secrets. He knew, for example, that we shopped a fella called Vogel to the Nazis because we found out

Vogel was reporting to the Soviets, too. Of course, Vogel was played to set up something better. Combs was particularly bitter about that."

"And he knew the same could be easily done with him?"

"Yes. But all that is wrapped under Official Secrets. It was renewed for another twenty-five years with the national security clause last year. At any rate, SOE made him an offer he couldn't refuse then. The feeling was that what he had done for us outbalanced what he had been passing to the Soviet networks . . . and he had done good work."

"So he sailed off into the sunset. The cattle ranch in Canada or the outback?"

"Neither, actually," Kenyon answered. "Left in a huff for Spain. Now, the other side of the coin is what he was up to in Dublin. I asked myself: What if he has prepared some account of what he was doing in Ireland?"

"Christ," Robertson sighed. "Every nonentity seems to want to write a bloody memoir these days. The Irish could skewer us at the conference with that."

"They could threaten to release it, or even leak it to any of their hardliners. Combs did very low-level eyes-and-ears stuff, but there'd be an uproar. Hardliners in Ireland carry enough votes to get any government to walk away from the table. They'd put us to the wall on it."

"I expect they would," Robertson agreed. "As we would them, I believe."

"And, for once, we need the Irish more than they need us on this. The South is still holiday-land for IRA on the run. It was tough enough for us to get them to the table at all. There's an election due within two years, and there are some marginal seats with

Sinn Fein slavering in the wings. It could add up to a lot of fall-out."

"Indeed. If the assumptions are strong." Robertson's brows knitted and then raised abruptly. "I'm very familiar with Combs' file too, James. Were you aware of that?"

Kenyon tried not to appeared startled.

"Yes. I read it when I got this job. I have a diarised memo to read the file twice a year. Tell me you're not surprised, James."

Kenyon managed a wan smile. So Robertson had not simply been passing on a routine inquiry about Combs.

"I'm less surprised because of the timing," replied Kenyon. "The Irish delegation feels it has conceded too much *de facto* on their constitutional claim to Northern Ireland by discussing the problem at all. The logic is that by negotiating border security, the government in the South implicitly accepts the fact of a border."

"Nicely packaged, James. Sure you wouldn't like to chuck what you're doing and go into the negotiating business?"

"And get an allowance to dress like Murray?"

Robertson fixed a look both bemused and distasteful on a point somewhere over Kenyon's shoulder.

"Let's not fret over whether Murray and his cohorts should be in the business of gathering any intelligence in Ireland at all, James. It's at our door now. I happen to know, because I don't ignore comments from the people I dine with, that the Foreign Office was rather red-faced some years ago as far as Ireland is concerned. There was flare-up in assassinations of police and troops in the cities in the North. We knew of IRA redoubts near Dublin. The Foreign Office suddenly discovered that, lo and behold, they had no one at ground level in Southern Ireland. The PM gave one of her grim-reaper looks during a meeting, and Murray and company fell over themselves trying to get anyone they could at short notice. Hence Combs. Fact is, and I'm sure you'll agree, Combs dead or alive could be messy."

Kenyon nodded. He could not banish the image of Murray from his mind. The sharp cut to the suit, the Rolex watch which he had fingered during their discussion.

"I asked you to look in on the business about Combs so that you'll support my conclusions. Can you live with that? Good."

Kenyon's breathing had quickened. He felt the beginnings of anger.

"You are quite right," Robertson continued, "to believe that there is a lot in the balance. I needn't lecture as to the arithmetic. It's our troops and police being shot at. I too tend to the conclusion that our Mr Combs was not a man to bluff. I'm old enough to remember what a war is. Mr Murray and his acolytes wouldn't know their arses from their elbows about men who have been through a war. Nuffink. Even if I did suspect it was a lot of hot air, I'd still want a complete re-evaluation on Combs now."

Kenyon could not resist any longer.

"So why are we treading water?" he asked. "Why are we still at arm's length?"

"Come on now, James, no righteousness please. Jurisdiction. I made representations about it when I saw that memo about Combs' death."

Robertson leaned back in his chair and smiled an unsmile at Kenyon. At least he's on the defensive for once, Kenyon thought.

"And you are quite right," Robertson added. "Let's face it. They were under pressure; they placed Combs in there quickly. Inertia takes over pretty quickly. Combs was left in place. Now they realise they may have cause to regret their haste. To hear you now, it seems I chose the right person to go for the neck."

Kenyon felt his own excitement edge his anger aside.

"Now let me ask you: what was it that tipped the scales for you with Combs?" Robertson asked. "Was it his record during the war?"

Kenyon paused. He'd have to stay out on a limb and tell the truth.

"No," he said finally.

Robertson sat up and placed his elbows on his desk.

"Ah, what a relief. Trumps, James, trumps. I thought you'd lecture me by telling me how abominably we treated him after the war."

It was Kenyon who felt defensive now.

"I shan't do that, today anyway. But selling out another operative, that Vogel chap. That stank to high heaven."

"The case-officer was a highly decorated and effective intelligence officer. Since deceased, James. Honourable service. We were fighting for our lives against Hitler, man."

Kenyon read Robertson's raised eyebrows as roadblocks to further rhetoric.

"What really persuaded me was reading the last reports he sent in," Kenyon went on warily. "I think I'd better explain that, and I'm not sure if I can give you a rational picture for what is a hunch. They started out precisely and in the last year I noticed a ... well, it's that vagueness. Like I said, it's that drop-off in real information, I mean, it's quite noticeable. Distinct even."

"You mention here his use of place names," Robertson said.

Kenyon winced. Robertson was pushing him while letting him stew in his own suppositions.

"An impression that he was getting used to the place there. Yes, but — "

"Stale, you mean?"

"No. The tone was as if he were guiding us around a spot he knew well. And we were rather like, well, ignorant tourists."

Robertson smiled.

"Redundant stuff, about some place being near an archaeological site."

Robertson's eyebrows still held onto a trace of amusement.

"Gone native, James? Kurtz in Ireland, something like that?"

That was enough to provoke Kenyon.

"Look, Hugh. It's difficult enough to defend it if one takes a stony empiricist approach, for Christ's sake. I never met the man. I admit that my impressions come from the windy side with these sources. But I look at what he sent out this last year and it's nothing really. And then Murray: 'What we have heeere is an aul poof-dah on the bottle, a dispirited and cynical man, James.' "

Robertson smiled.

"You do that rather well, James. Combs has been on the books for more than forty years. There are none of his contemporaries left in the Service. As for those memos about Combs' being less than satisfied about what he was expected to do in Ireland — "

"Murray kept on telling me how Ball's predecessor as Second Sec was a softie, someone Combs could push around," Kenyon interrupted.

" — they did dry up, those complaints. That's not to suggest that Combs' grudges simply disappeared, is it?"

"Tell that to Murray, Hugh. Let me just reiterate that Combs had two levers if he ever really wanted to strong-arm us for concessions. I don't know if he understood that he wouldn't get much mileage out of his wartime mess. If he realised that, he might have opted to tell anyone that he was doing jobs for us."

"But if he spilled the beans, James, he'd have no more arrows in his quiver."

Kenyon made no reply. It wasn't a question. This was the Hugh Robertson he knew best, a man who kept his own conclusions to himself until he had heard his staff out.

"The stakes are high here," Kenyon murmured. "I think we should be as thorough as we can on this."

"Thank you, James," said Robertson without sarcasm. "Let's just do our job, seal it as tight as we can."

Robertson's face brightened.

"Don't take my caution too seriously. I have to meet with C at four. Now I can confidently tell him that my most able officer has independently reached the same conclusions as I have. Your conclusions will become his conclusions, James, after I air them with him. I have just stolen your ideas. Feel flattered."

Kenyon managed a smile.

"Now. As to the field men. Where again?"

"Spain and Greece. Malaga and Athens. There's that friend of Combs in Britain. One to Ireland of course."

"Indeed. They aren't bound by an Official Secrets Act, our Irish neighbours," Robertson said wryly as he stood up.

"You'll be by about a quarter before four then?"

"For . . . ?" asked a puzzled Kenyon.

"A briefing with C? God!"

Kenyon nodded. Robertson enjoyed his surprise.

CHAPTER 6

Bustle greeted Minogue in Bewley's restaurant. To be indoors was a relief from having to negotiate the crowded footpaths outside. Masses of people flowed from Grafton Street around by College Green, spilling out into the street. The crowds thickened further as they massed in Westmoreland Street, unwilling to test the reactions of drivers speeding down the quays by O'Connell Bridge. Double-decker busses wheeled across five traffic lanes in front of the entrance to Bewley's and screeched to a halt at their stops along the street. Lunatics on bicycles hurtled through the traffic and diesel fumes.

Safe inside the door, Minogue wondered where all the people came from. A huge proportion of the population was between eighteen and thirty-five — a fact unprecedented in Irish history — Minogue remembered from an otherwise dull and farcical debate on the telly.

Bewley's always smelled of burned coffee beans. The cafe had been gutted by fire several years back due to an over-zealous employee roasting beans in a hurry. So used to the smell of burnt coffee beans were the patrons, passers-by and employees, that a delay in alerting the fire-brigade ensued. Much of the restaurant had been destroyed as a result of this habituation.

Minogue eyed the self-serve section before slotting himself into the queue which was waiting for coffee. He spent little time on non-essentials, choosing an almondy-looking bun of irregular shape so that the coffee wouldn't lack for company as it hit his belly. The room was full of cigarette smoke, talk, dishes clashing, young people. Minogue glanced from the table, half-expecting to see an Iseult or a Daithi there. If Kathleen were with him now, she'd probably mutter darkly that it's in pubs he should look for Daithi, not Bewley's Oriental Cafe. Minogue's turn at the coffee came.

"A large white, if you please," he said to the girl.

She was working behind a brace of bulbous boilers which served to heat water and to build up steam for scalding the milk — which in turn became a constituent of white coffee. The whole apparatus reminded Minogue of a submarine, but he didn't know why.

The afternoon sun cast broad beams of coloured light through the stained-glass windows, dividing the room into several realms. Along with the wreaths of smoke, the effect of the light entranced Minogue. Here a blond head of hair afire with light from behind, there a group softly adumbrated. The patrons seemed to take their cues from the light which their placements afforded them. Those outside the direct light looked subdued. They smiled ruefully, distracted perhaps by the sight of the blazing angels who laughed and gestured in the full light nearby. Newspapers were up like flags at many tables. There were race-horses to second-guess, letters-to-the-editor to compose, births, deaths and bankruptcies to savour.

The girl doling out the coffees had a compact, determined face. Her expression suggested detachment from the din about her. The steam scalding the milk for Minogue's coffee burbled and hissed in the cup. He stole another glance at her profile. Maybe her ancestors were the Vikings that helped settle this shambles of a city and she had one of their axes ready behind the counter for the likes of a bogman interloper like Minogue. Irish: kings and queens all, lost entitlement. Did Combs, with the dry sense of humour, cotton onto that trait? Queenly? The woman was tired, Minogue's common sense reprimanded. She probably had to wait a half hour for the bus home.

"If you went on at the steam yoke for a bit long, you'd have the makings of a *cappuccino*," Minogue observed.

"A what?"

"It's a style of coffee that they favour in Italy. Oh, but you'd want to have strong coffee to start with. Espresso. Black stuff. Like tar, for all the world. There's the stuff that'd keep you up all night, I'm telling you."

"Jases, mister, I wouldn't want that," the girl intoned slowly. Minogue recognised a Dublin accent all right, along with the carnal import. Sleep was a very underrated form of birth control, he thought.

"The French are very partial to espresso on its own, I don't mind telling you," Minogue went on. "Yes, indeed. Myself and the wife were over there for a holiday and you'd see fellas standing by a counter knocking back an espresso. Out of a cup a bit bigger than a good-sized inkwell. In an instant, bang, down it goes. Then they leap out the door, back to whatever they were doing. High as kites, I'm thinking."

"Go way," said the girl, turning off the valve.

"It's a fact. You get used to it, I suppose, like anything. Am I right?"

She threw a damp cloth on the counter to wipe up a spray of milk.

"You're right there," she said.

"Thing is," Minogue went on, heartened by her approval, "I'd say there are people that are so used to it that they might wake up in the middle of the night squealing and bawling like a goose caught under the gate looking for a hit of espresso. Caffeine's a very powerful drug. Do you know what I'm saying?"

Minogue had not noticed the queue gathering behind him. He was relieved that yet again he could count on someone from the real world to unwittingly help dispel the gloom which had unexpectedly settled on him as he had walked to Bewley's. Thinking about Combs again. Had Combs ever patronised Bewley's? She left him the trace of a smile as she looked to the next in the queue.

The coffee did indeed perk Minogue up. Still, it took him only a few seconds of thinking to dismiss those three topers, the Mulvaney brothers, as distractions. The drink led them to their choleric behaviour and brought out an innate need to be disputatious. The only people they'd be killing, singularly or collectively, would be one another. The weapons used would be drink and pique and time and bitter memory.

Minogue sipped at his coffee again. He congratulated himself for keeping out of the way of vexatious interviews with the troglodyte Mulvaneys. Mulholland and Murtagh had interviewed two men with lengthy records for burglary. One, Malone, had a record of assaults to match. Neither of the two was a suspect yet. They were unconcerned that their alibis were being checked.

His thoughts let go of the Mulvaneys abruptly and ran to Daithi and Iseult. Then he sat up with a start: he was to bring home a cake this evening and he had nearly forgotten. Iseult's fella was coming for tea. As for Daithi, Minogue was more anxious. If Daithi couldn't get his exams this time ... well, that wasn't the end of the world. But to persuade Kathleen of that ... ? *Have a word with him, Matt. Bring him back to the fold. Like the other sheep?*

Minogue had felt Kathleen's anxiety and anger keenly this last year. She wondered aloud if every parent saw their children grow into strangers. He wondered if life was the business that ensued when you were busy worrying about your irretrievably adult children going to pot. Kathleen probably remembered these two vaguely familiar adults as infants, those small snoring bodies that had kicked the bedclothes off and lay in battlefield poses in their beds. *Have a word.* Minogue almost smiled then: Kathleen asking the fox to mind the chickens.

Minogue did not feel despondent as he drained the cup. Daithi floundering, not sure of a future? Maybe the boy needed something tangible to kick against still. Minogue imagined a horse in a stall, the clear thud of a hoof on the planks, patient eyes: can't I get out and gallop in the field, master? So why couldn't Minogue be a parent like any other, a grit for his children to spin a pearl about? What practical use was a father who loved Daithi almost unbearably but who abjured too much of the dogma that their society had prepared a father to enact? Would Daithi and Kathleen be driven to wringing their hands, telling him that he was supposed to be doing something else, that he was supposed to be somebody else? Abstractions. Rubbish. It was Daithi's life. Minogue felt almost happy with his elbows on Bewley's marble table-top. Dublin: decay, scattered, alive.

He bought a cake with icing and a wafery thing on top. He was cautioned, as he took his change, to carry it upright. He took the Garda notice off the dash, returned the glares of two skinheads with a grin and drove down the quays toward Islandbridge.

Hoey was back from the wilds of Stepaside, waiting for him. He drew up a chair and sat by Minogue's desk.

"Keep your eyes offa the cake, Shea. It's spoken for," he murmured as he brought out the file from his drawer. "Now, aside from entertainment value, what of those three clowns, the Mulvaneys?" Minogue began.

"Pat Keating's on his way into town. He had an hour and a half with them. They have two people to vouch for them that night and nearly into Sunday morning, too. Playing cards and drinking. It's well for them that don't have to work for a living."

"Saturday night. They claim that Combs was provoking them with a remarks about the North and stuff like that. 'He called the lads cornerboys and scum,'" Hoey quoted from his notes.

"More luck to him for saying it," said Minogue without rancour. "Any of the three strike you as capable of doing something like a murder?"

Hoey shrugged.

"We interviewed them separately, sir. I suppose that Shag could be belligerent. But if the chips were down, though, they'd be mice, the whole pack of them. Shag was the one who went on about the homo bit. The other two didn't mention it."

"Homo?"

"Said it was common knowledge that Mr Combs was homosexual."

Minogue wondered if this devious Mulvaney was leading policemen down the garden path. Shag

Mulvaney wasn't one to care a whit about a man's reputation if it could be turned to advantage in making iijits out of the Gardai.

"They stayed in the pub after Combs left. All of them. Around nine, Combs left. The Mulvaneys were drinking goodo until closing time."

"Hmm. Say ten minutes for Mr Combs to get the car started and get back to his house. Nine fifteen," Minogue murmured. "Consistent with the pathology estimate. . . . "

Hoey nodded.

"And you checked out their bona fides that night?" Minogue asked.

"Yes, sir. They were in a house the Sandyford end of Barnacullia. House owned and occupied by one Eoin Reilly and family. Reilly goes by the name of Chop. He is well known in the area. He's not a criminal. Reilly gives Shag and The Bronc occasional work as labourers at quarrying or as mason's helpers."

Hoey went on to give Minogue the gist of his own interview with Shag. Minogue half-listened. He hoped that Keating had more than this. Each of the brothers had signed statements accounting for themselves on the Saturday evening.

"What about that mountain of junk around their house? The shed?"

"We had over three hours while they were at the station, sir. Nothing. The boys went through the place good and thorough," Hoey said, not bothering to conceal his weariness.

Curly, Byronic Keating shambled in by Eilis' desk. He saw Hoey and Minogue. He looked at his watch as if to stave off the four o'clock meeting. Minogue read the gesture to mean that Keating had nothing better than Hoey. Chasing after straws. As he passed the smoking Eilis, Keating confided what Minogue guessed was a remark with amorous overtones to her. With the expression of a tired croupier who was used to impoverished amateurs, Eilis batted her eyes but once at Keating before smiting him.

"Come back when you're grown up, Pat Keating."

Minogue held up his hand. Hoey stopped reciting.

"Lads. Get yourselves tea or something. There'll be a briefing in ten minutes," Minogue said sharply.

He watched the two detectives leave. Jimmy would have been proud of me, he thought, laying down the law. He had admitted to himself that the first stages of the investigation and the concomitant up-down of the detectives' hopes were played out now. Hoey, more experienced than Keating, had been more circumspect, knowing not to raise false hopes. It was now necessary to make a break with expectations of a quick and ready resolution and get down to slogging over details.

Minogue ruminated again on Shag's declaration that Combs was homosexual. Bad enough that Combs had called the IRA "heroes" in a tone that even the Mulvaneys could detect was sarcastic, but to be a nancy-boy. He looked up to find Eilis by his desk. Behind her were three of the Gardai Minogue had met that morning.

"Well lads, four o'clock is it? Will ye go with Eilis here and I'll be in, in a minute?"

By five o'clock Minogue understood that the murder of Mr Combs would stay an enigma for some time today and tonight and tomorrow. And probably the day after that, too. He wished Murtagh would stop talking. Murtagh had very bad breath indeed. Murphy's Law had Murtagh unconsciously edging closer to Minogue as Minogue drew back from the rancid smell. Minogue had to give up before being trapped against the wall. He was now breathing through his mouth.

"Malone says it has to be new boys," Murtagh was saying. Malone had an alibi. He had been in bed with his brother's wife in Inchicore. His brother was doing time for car theft.

"Malone's all right for Saturday and Sunday. He's of the opinion that only lunatics would do a house on a Saturday night. He says drugs."

"Very helpful of him," said Minogue wearily. "He means city thugs, I suppose."

"That's the gist of it, I think — "

"Local though," Minogue interrupted. "Someone local had to hear about or know about Combs. Knew he lived alone, might have a few shillings around the house. Has to be local."

"There's the Mulvaneys, sir. Their stories might leak yet," Murtagh tried to inject some enthusiasm. "And some fellas in or around Sandyford used to do houses. Stepaside are doing them now. I have the names here . . . "

Minogue copied four names.

"Wait a minute, sir. Sorry. Driscoll says the last one, that Molloy, he's in England since Christmas. Nix him. . . . "

"And was it yourself that got the statements off the neighbours?"

"Yes, sir. Me and Driscoll. Driscoll and I, yes."

"There's the matter of Mr Combs' sexual orientation we can't be ignoring," said Minogue.

He saw weary curiosity in all the faces save Keating's. Keating was chewing the end of his pencil. The lead didn't seem to be affecting his brain yet. He stretched one arm out in search of additional comfort to prolong his slouch. Minogue addressed Murtagh.

"Sean. We need photos of Mr Combs; get personnel to go to various pubs with them. I mean pubs where gay people go."

Murtagh rubbed at his nose.

"Do you know which ones I'm talking about?"

Keating couldn't contain his smile any longer.

"Like the back of your hand, Seanie, am I right?" he said. One of the district detectives laughed aloud.

"Fuck you and all belonging to you, Pat Keating," said a blushing Murtagh. "I'll put money that it's your name and number I'll find on the wall of the jacks in that class of pub. And the price listed, too."

More laughter.

"We may be looking for a young lad who turned turk on Mr Combs after a pick-up, don't you know," said Minogue. Murtagh nodded solemnly. Minogue saw Hoey look at his watch again. Taking the hint, he delegated to Hoey the task of going to Stepaside station the next morning to co-ordinate the second interviews both in Kilternan and in Glencullen.

"I'll hear from ye during the day," Minogue said.

Minogue nodded toward the district detectives from Stepaside. He visualised them returning home later and enlarging upon their meeting with members of the Murder Squad. Excitement. Drama. Tall tales.

"I'm obliged to ye for coming in, all of ye. It's no small matter to be running around and taking statements like ye did today. Ye've laid great foundations, I'm sure," Minogue said above the screech of scraping chair-legs on the linoleum.

He remained seated, watching the policemen leave the room. He had been more embarrassed by his little morale speech than by the plain fact that they still knew next to nothing about Combs' life. It was almost two full days since the man had been murdered. He looked at the card which Eilis had left on his desk.

Along with a long telephone number, the card also had Inspector Newman's address — down to his room number — with the London Metropolitan Police. The card mutely informed Minogue that Newman was the head of a section called C11 in C Department, the office which travelled under the agreeable name of International Liaison. Would this crowd be working after five o'clock, though?

It took Minogue but a half minute to hear a man's voice announce himself as Inspector Newman. The accent made a funny "r" at the end of his rank, not an accent that Minogue expected. Not like Alec Guinness in *The Bridge on the River Kwai*, for example.

"Detective Sergeant Minogue calling from Dublin, Inspector. I'm in the Investigation Section of the Gardai here. The Murder Squad, that is. I'm calling on behalf of Inspector Kilmartin. He's indisposed at the moment. . . . " Minogue paused to allow Newman to digest his intro. Should he tell him that Jimmy had his arse in a sling?

"Yes, I know Inspector Kilmartin. And you're . . . ?"

Minogue repeated his name.

"We're looking to a murder here, Inspector. A citizen of the United Kingdom. He last lived in London. A place called Wood Green. Am I making sense?"

Newman said that he was.

"Mr Combs. Mr Arthur Combs. Will I spell it?"

"Honey — C—O—M—B?"

"The very thing. Do you want a date of birth and the like?"

Newman said "righto" each time he recorded details. Recounting those details, Minogue wondered at what meagre things these accoutrements of a life were. A middle name, a height, a weight, a job. All pegs to keep you rooted while life buffeted you, its

98

gusts and lulls alternately testing the pegs. Finally to have a lid closed over you, cold in the earth.

Minogue told him that the Gardai had not assigned a motive for the murder. He did not tell him that the other two of the policeman's morbid trinity — opportunity and resources — were as wide as a barn door with the wind whistling through. Mr Combs had been strangled rather expertly by a person or persons who had been waiting for him as he entered the kitchen door of his house. The Gardai would be glad of Newman's help in furnishing information about Mr Combs before he came to live in Ireland, and after too, if that was to be had. Newman said that he would do what he could. Minogue liked the sound of that. Inland Revenue, army service, would that be a start? Minogue said that would be a great start. Would the Inspector be needing written requests to get it going? He would not. Then he surprised Minogue.

"What kind of weather have you in Dublin?"

Newman pronounced the name of the capital city as if there were a hyphen in the middle, much as a respectful traveller might try to say "Zambesi" without offending the sensibilities of tribesmen leaning on their spears nearby.

"Oh, it's very nice, you'd love it," Minogue said. He had guessed right from the accent. Newman was no sooty Londoner but one of God's chosen, a countryman like himself.

Newman paused.

"Well, that's very nice," he said finally.

"It certainly is. We get buckets of rain here by times, summer or winter. The bit of dry weather does wonders for the morale," Minogue enthused.

"Ay, ay. I'll have an officer start a file on it, and you can call on that when you need it, too," Newman said.

"That'd be great. Yes."

Minogue replaced the receiver and clapped his hands. They weren't bad lads over there at all. Maybe Kilmartin had him over here on a golfing holiday or something, that Newman was so helpful. He glanced at his watch. Holy God: twenty after five. Hoey and Keating could hold the fort and show off all they'd learned off Jimmy Kilmartin. Damn: forgot to phone the same Jimmy . . .

C had completed the requisite number of patrols, mixed in with the odd full circuit of the room, to whatever end he alone knew, Kenyon guessed. Now he was seated with his legs crossed at the knee. He had taken but a few drags at a second cigarette before leaving it to smoulder. The smell of the burning filter was distasteful to Kenyon. He stole another glance at the balding, basilisk C. Some of the senior staff called him F. Hand-in-hand with his eccentricities, the current Director had the reputation of being a vengeful bully.

"So: find if this Combs committed any gripes to writing," C declared as a question.

"Writing or perhaps tape," replied Kenyon.

"Tape, file, dossier," C murmured. "Would this Combs have secreted material with someone else?"

"There's a possibility, sir," Kenyon answered quickly. "But it just doesn't make sense that Combs' grievances dried up when Ball became his handler. I strongly believe that Combs was at the end of his tether. He may have felt that he had nothing to lose."

"But Combs didn't issue any threats this last while," C stated.

"True, sir. But at the very least, Combs may have made some record. Named names."

"Low-level intelligence work," C murmured. "You don't say. Do we call it that because it was done in Ireland?"

Kenyon mustered a polite smile.

"Bloody burkes," added C. Neither Kenyon nor Robertson needed to wonder if it was the Foreign Office his remark addressed.

"And we have to pick up the bits after these brainwaves. . . . Yes. Tape, file dossier," C murmured again. "It's altogether too like a bloody sordid little treasure hunt or something."

He turned to Kenyon.

"You know now that Hugh and I have had this pot heating before we looked to you for a fresh appraisal?"

Kenyon nodded.

"The most problematic part will be that bloody miserable island of nutters next door to us. Murphy's Law, home of. How do you plan to do business in Dublin with this? You're willing to act on the theory that Combs put something by locally, right?"

"Yes, sir. He may have believed that we had his post screened, too. . . . "

"Was this Combs' thing picked as a complete fiction then? How much cardboard is behind this character? Will it hold up?"

"I think it will," Kenyon took up the question. "As long as there's no leak from our level. We held the death certificate when Arthur Combs died, so the Irish police will get the goods from the Met here and it'll be bona fide. I have an alert with them if anyone inquires after Combs. Nothing from the Irish police yet. Combs was sixty-seven when he died, six years ago. Not married, no family either. Retired Customs Inspector. One of Six's better fits, I have to admit," Kenyon said.

"No one there in Ireland he'd pour out his heart to?" C persisted. He seemed to Kenyon to be talking to himself.

"Seems not, sir. He had a more general or, shall I say, abstract attachment."

"Meaning?"

"The business about local history there. Old artefacts, ruins, things like that."

"Bit of an old ruin himself, come to think of it," a mirthlessly sarcastic C murmured.

"You're relying on D notices and the Secrets Acts to tame our journalistic friends should they receive anonymous parcels of notes from Ireland?" C challenged.

"Yes, sir. They'd cough up, I'm sure," Kenyon tried to sound confident. Robertson cleared his throat, a cue for Kenyon to get to the main course.

"I believe that we can best get out of the Irish, er, bog, sir, if we insert a man who can legitimately go over Combs' place, his effects. A good sweeper."

Kenyon returned Robertson's glance before dropping the log.

"And with our man there straight away, the need for a joint op with anybody, even Six and the Foreign Office, would obviously be close to nil."

"Obviously," C intoned, again close to sarcasm. "We're not discussing something like the Immaculate Conception here, are we now, chaps? The Micks are hardly going to fall for a long-lost-relative-showing-up routine."

Kenyon sidestepped the leaden mirth.

"Combs' estate is a problem, sir. To be disposed of, the estate needs an agent. Has to be probated."

C snorted faintly.

"Somebody say agent, eh, Hugh?" He looked to Robertson and graced him with a rare grin. Kenyon continued.

"A lawyer. Combs has no will, I believe. Foreign Office worked up a pension for him years ago, and the bank source it as a pension from Customs and Excise.

He also had an annuity. That part of his income comes through a small merchant bank here in the city. They list it as income from stocks. We can surely work up a lawyer to represent either bank involved," Kenyon flourished with a rhetorical lilt.

C was nodding his head lightly.

"Rather elegant solution, James. You'd want to cull some legal type from our own fold here, I take it."

"Ideally, sir. Should have had some field training."

"Find someone, then. Cite my authorisation to hive off this person from what he's doing at the moment. I'll give it priority. Put the fear of a Presbyterian God in the fellow to keep his cards close to his chest. Someone who can get around the police there, maybe listen in on their investigation?"

"That would be quite a coup, sir," Kenyon said.

Kenyon made a mental note of the inquiry which had come through to Newman in the Metropolitan Police. The Garda's name was Minogue, a sergeant. He thought the name looked familiar, but the more he tried to recall where he had seen or head it before, the less he was sure of ever having known it.

Returning to his office after the meeting, Kenyon had felt his elation being swallowed in the maw of anxiety. He had graduated to despondency within the last few minutes. As Kenyon was stepping out of Robertson's car, the door still ajar, Robertson had looked out under the roof at him. Kenyon crouched by the open door. Why did he still feel that Robertson was leaving him out on a limb?

"Keep me posted, James?"

Bowers was propped in front of the terminal.

"Find me somebody, would you? Two people, actually. I need a man in the Service, someone with a legal background and some field training. Let me think, was there somebody a few years back that . . . "

Kenyon realised that it was six o'clock and that was why he wasn't firing on all cylinders. He'd phone home before going out for supper.

" . . . Knows something about Ireland, if you can. Get me a list of eligibles. I need this fast. I'm staying on duty for the evening. Can you?"

Bowers detected the tension in Kenyon. He said he could.

"The second chap, sir?"

"Oh, that's a different matter. It's by the way. I seem to remember his name a few years ago, too. An Irish copper, Minogue. Forget it until we've found our own man."

Bowers' face took on a puzzled expression. Kenyon noticed his bewilderment as he was elbowing off the door-frame.

"Some incident a few years back. More than three, let's say, if my memory is sound. We'll be working near him, so I'd like to size him up."

Iseult's wooer, Pat Muldoon, was over six feet tall. His clothes were black again today, save for a dark grey shirt which was not ironed and not meant to be ironed. A long face on him and a bony nose, missing two days' shaving but with lively eyes atop. The eyes were blessed-virgin blue, with a touch of mockery not far behind them. During the tea, Minogue felt he was sitting next to a priest. Pat never laughed outright but smiled enough and gave considered nods of his head. Minogue was a little nervous. Iseult was very animated. She was on guard against lulls in the talk, filling in details which Pat sometimes forgot. What Pat really means, what Pat is getting at . . .

"He got first in his class last year, so he did. Didn't you, Pat?" Iseult enthused. Kathleen's eyes widened in approval. Pat looked up under his eyebrows as he worked the rind off a rasher, as though to remonstrate with her. Iseult beamed. Kathleen made herself busy with her knife and fork. Was her subconscious leading her to toy with the cutlery, the better to drive away a suitor to her overloved daughter? Minogue wondered.

"Da worships the sun, don't you, Da?" Iseult said guilelessly.

"And the moon and the stars," he said, feeling his cheeks redden. "A bit of everything."

"More luck to you," said Pat. "Nice sermons, I'd say."

Everyone laughed. Pat was studying psychology. When Kathleen had asked before, he allowed that it was very interesting. Was there anything in particular? He liked experimental psychology. Minogue thought about rats with wires attached to their heads.

Kathleen stabbed the Bewley's cake and apportioned slices to the plates stacked by her side. The sun was peeping around the back of the house now. It was Minogue's time of day. He could almost feel his planet turning. Daithi plugged the kettle in and remained leaning on the edge of the sink. No one spoke. The chairs had been pushed back from the table. Birds called out to one another from the garden. Minogue stole a look at the faces around the table. Kathleen was smoothing an imaginary fold in the tablecloth. As his gaze swept by Iseult, she winked at him. Her face seemed bigger. It was entirely possible that his faculties were declining with age, he thought. Damn it, he thought then, her face was glowing. She must have fallen for this lad. The kettle whispered. Minogue looked over to Daithi. He was fidgeting, restless. No doubt he'd want to go out tonight and have a few jars with his cronies. Kathleen had now joined her hands under her chin, elbows on the table.

"Here, Da. Tell us a bit about Paris," Iseult said. She turned to Pat.

"The pair of them are like love-birds so they are, Pat. They up and went to Paris a few years ago."

"To see the sights," Kathleen insisted.

"Some sights you'd see there, too, I'm sure," Iseult taunted. "And they wouldn't take their only daughter to give her a bit of culture. The meanness of it."

"Do you know, Pat," Kathleen countered by turning to the one who might well steal her daughter, "maybe you know something from your studies, but why is it that children turn contrary and get to being punishments for their parents?"

"I don't know, Mrs Minogue," from a diplomatic Pat.

"Here now," Minogue rose from the table, "if ye are really interested in talking about Paris, there's only one proper way to do that."

"And how's that, may I ask?" Kathleen inquired.

"With a bottle of anise and a few tumblers. You bring up the tea if you want, and we'll lay waste the rest of that cake, too," Minogue said, rubbing his hands. "We'll away up to the end of the garden and catch the last of the sun. Now, where's the tape-recorder? We'll bring up your man Offenbach and a bit of Chopin. Who in their right minds wants to be indoors on a summer's evening?"

A Dublin-born Daithi rolled his eyes at the vagaries of a bogman father.

"To hell with poverty, we'll kill a hen!" said Minogue.

The batteries on the tape-recorder died after twenty minutes.

"I thought that Offenbach sounded a bit off-colour," Minogue remarked indolently as he watched Kathleen walking up the garden toward them. She stopped by the rhubarb, toed something delicately in the clay, and continued her slow walk. My wife, I'm her husband, he thought. He had watched her at mass on Sundays for years, her head bowed after communion, eyes closed in prayer. A fine-looking woman.

The sun leaned into the garden now, lighting up the shrubs and branches from the side. Iseult was fidgeting.

Minogue poured more Marie Brizard. He could think of nothing to say. Kathleen was helloing a neighbour across the wall. Then she stood by the garden chair where Minogue was dishing out the anisette. Pat, formerly quiescent with the food and drink, led with a high card.

"You're County Clare, aren't you, Mr Minogue?"

"Absolutely," Minogue affirmed. He raised his glass. Iseult sniggered. Pat raised his glass the length of his arm. Had Iseult primed Pat?

"A hundred and one percent," Minogue added with feeling.

"I heard recently what a Clareman's idea of heaven was, you know," he continued.

"Tell us so," said Minogue.

"Cork beat, the hay saved and a girl in Lisdoonvarna."

Even Daithi laughed. Kathleen and Iseult poked each other, laughing both.

"You should be on the stage," Kathleen said to Pat. She was standing behind Iseult now, absent-mindedly patting the dark hair that fell on Iseult's shoulders. Iseult didn't notice. In Minogue's uncodified religion, Kathleen's gestures had the force of a transfiguration. For several seconds the garden and the orange wash of the sun, the smiles, the smell of clay, the birdsong fell away from him. It will be very hard on Kathleen if this Pat fella does win her, Minogue thought.

"The next stage leaves town at eight," Iseult said.

Minogue was thinking that the unconscious was too strong a force in life entirely when he heard Daithi calling from the kitchen window. He walked down the lawn and entered the kitchen. Daithi was doing the dishes and that gave Minogue pause to wonder. Perhaps the boy was washing his hands in advance of some divilment later on tonight. Neurotic. A girl?

"Phone, Da. It's from work," Daithi murmured.

It was Hoey.

"Sorry to disturb you at home, sir. Stepaside station phoned. Driscoll. They have a fella that maybe we'd be wanting to talk to. A fella that was snooping around Mr Combs' place, like."

"Yes, go on."

Minogue believed his anisette breath would surely stick to the phone like spray paint.

"It was by chance that someone saw him going up the lane. He went into a field and then came back up to the house and started looking in the windows. He tried to get in the door, too."

"Did he try to make off with anything? Use any force trying to get into the house?"

"No, sir."

"Who is he?"

"He's a tinker, sir. He calls himself Michael Joseph Joyce. He's living in a caravan down the back of Loughlinstown somewhere. He has a lot of drink on him and he's not inclined to be very direct with answers."

"Did he resist being brought to the station or that class of thing?"

108

"No, sir. He was spotted fiddling with a horse in a field belonging to Combs."

"Right, of course. That's it," Minogue said.

"That's what?"

"The horse. I knew there was something I was trying to remember. When I saw the horse, I was wondering who'd be feeding it now that Combs was gone. The horse was tethered up to the gate."

"That's what Joyce said he was about. The arresting Guard wasn't impressed with that one, I'm afraid."

"Hold on there a minute. You said 'arrest.'"

"The Guards here told him that he was under arrest for trespassing. Just to keep him in and question him, sir. They'll keep him overnight so we can see him in the morning. No harm will come of him staying over. You can go straight to Stepaside in the morning, sir. When Joyce is sober, you see."

Minogue noticed the tentative tone in Hoey's voice now.

"Look it, Shea. We can't be locking people up overnight, especially a traveller. It's a fright to God to travelling people to be confined. I don't want us to be giving testimony at an inquest as to why some poor divil woke up in the middle of the night and hung himself. To quote Jimmy Kilmartin, we're not a banana republic. Yet, anyway."

"I know what you're saying," Hoey answered slowly.

"Here. I'll call Stepaside and I'll tell them myself."

"Ah no. It's all right, I'll phone them back myself," Hoey said.

Minogue delayed by the telephone, distracted by the sweet burn of the anisette at the back of his throat. A traveller, tinker. Combs and drinking. A homosexual? Couldn't ignore it. But so squalid an end? Daithi opened the kitchen door.

"I'll be in early," he said.

Daithi seemed relieved. Perhaps it was because he didn't have to face Kathleen who would have pressed questions on him.

"Oh," Minogue shook himself out of his thoughts. Daithi turned quickly as though expecting a rebuke.

"Did I leave a tenner for you under the toothbrushes? Go up and take a look, would you? Maybe I left it under the clock in the kitchen, though. That's old age for you, the first signs. Try upstairs like a good man, would you?"

Daithi's face lifted. He sprang at the first few steps. Too proud to ask for a few bob. As stubborn as an ass. Must have got that from his mother's side. Minogue found a ten-pound note in his pocket and left it under the clock. He stepped down into the garden then, finding that the planet's tilt had raised the sunlight to the tree-tops. The edges of the sky were already primrose. A breeze stirred the poplars next door. Their leaves' soft clacking sounded like the sea. He heard Iseult laugh. He'd have to tell Kathleen about the extra pocket money, he knew, and why he had given it to Daithi if he thought there was a chance he'd be buying pints with it. We're only human, he'd tell her. Would she believe him?

He went outside again. He listened for a while to Pat explaining conditioning in the higher animals. Primates. Weren't cardinals called primates? Even Iseult kept a respectful silence. Then he walked arm-in-arm with Kathleen through the darkening garden. She stopped by the kitchen door. He yanked on her arm.

"If they wanted to smooch and carry on, they can do it anytime," he said. "It's not like we never did it."

"You were all right in that department," Kathleen murmured, not willing yet to release the smile. Minogue, a pagan, kissed his Christian wife.

"And I didn't have to get you all excited talking about monkeys and electrodes, did I?" he said, grasping her tighter.

CHAPTER 7

By eight o'clock, Kenyon had settled on an officer
from the Sci and Support Services branch. The man's
name was Moore, an Irish name. He phoned Moore's
acting section head, cited his authorisation and asked
him to hunt down his quarry. The night-duty man
was back in ten minutes. Moore had been in his flat.
He'd be in Century House within a half hour.

Bowers had given him seven names. Moore was
the only one who had articled at law. At first Kenyon
could not understand why a barrister would drop a
practice and join MI5 unless he had been groomed as
an undergraduate.

He noted that Edward Martin Moore had been
recruited by the Service six years ago and had climbed
four grades since entering. Although he was given
field training during his probation period, Moore had
been posted to Sci and Support section. He had used
his legal training only occasionally since joining. Moore
came from landed money, a farm in the home counties. Evidently he didn't need a barrister's income. He
may not have wanted to do law in the first place. His
forte at the moment was protective security measures

in British university laboratories where Defence work had been farmed out.

Moore was unmarried. Both his parents were alive. Moore had toured Australia and the Far East before joining the Service. No Army or Territorial service. Probably not a boy scout either, Kenyon mused. An able administrator, lots of liaison with intelligence services in Europe, some with the Yanks. No tricky stuff with arms or poisoned pens. Moore spoke French and "had a conversational facility" in German.

An administrator? So what? All Kenyon wanted was an astute, observant man to get close to the investigation in Ireland while he settled Combs' affairs. Then, if and when the police found a written record of Combs' rambling, Moore could be on the spot. With good timing, he could well get his hands on it before the police did. If the police found anything first, Moore could push hard with a legal approach and lay claim to papers as effects of the estate. If the Irish police balked at that, what then?

Kenyon's stomach, rising slightly in reaction to the question, signalled something which didn't need to be otherwise articulated. Throw more legal pepper around, bafflegab? Make a diplomatic kerfuffle about getting the papers back intact, unread? Fat chance. . . . There'd be leaks from any Irish copper who'd read that stuff. But at least there'd be nothing in their possession to substantiate rumours. QED?

Kenyon shifted in his seat at the thought of going blind into that dark room which constituted "Anglo-Irish co-operation." It was a phrase as unlikely as anything he had come across. The blunt facts had to admitted: Combs' solecisms could easily become a stick to beat the Brits with, if indeed the Irish read them and took them as fact. All it would take was a nationalist-minded copper there to turn them over to a journalist. The timing couldn't be much worse with negotiations in the balance. Had Combs known that . . . ?

It dawned on Kenyon that this possible outcome was why he had had such ready access to C. It was a good bet that C had realised how much could hinge on this if his, Kenyon's, evaluation was true. No wonder Robertson had worn that stoical face at the meeting, probably hiding an anxiety which he didn't want to rub off on Kenyon.

Bowers distracted him from his gloom.

"Found reference to your chap in Dublin, sir. That copper. Minogue, as in rogue, I believe. I found him in an Army Intelligence Report from four years back. There's more to him than that, actually. Seems he was on the spot when our Ambassador was killed. Minogue was part of the police guard in a convoy, following the Ambassador back to his residence. Do you remember?"

Kenyon did.

"Minogue was almost killed in the bombing. The Irish police took him back after a spell in hospital, and he showed up again when he was seconded to their Murder Squad. I don't know why. Minogue almost got himself peppered rather severely by our army unit at the border. Apparently he tried to intervene in a tip-off situation, a set-up with a car suspected of carrying IRA weapons. The Irish police gave us a hands-off, and they trailed the car from their side until it got to the border. A young woman, a student, was killed in the car when the driver tried to run the Army check-point."

Bowers stood by Kenyon's desk, one hand pocketed, the other holding a notepad which he referred to occasionally. His brow wrinkled as though he were reporting something regrettable. Kenyon sighed as he launched himself up from his chair. All he could

conclude was that the policeman investigating Combs'
death was not an off-the-shelf copper. He looked out
the window. It was one of the rarest of summer evenings. The sky had been cloudless all day and now
only the tops of the taller buildings remained in the
sunlight. Bowers was still standing by the desk when
Kenyon turned from the window.

"Come with me when we go to see Moore. Keep
notes and type them up before you leave this evening.
I'll be briefing him later in the meeting, but you needn't
stay for that part. He'll be coming here tomorrow
morning after we run up a background for him. A
good, staunch firm of barristers and solicitors will be
dispatching our Moore to Dublin within twenty-four
hours . . . to recover our dirty linen."

A half hour into the meeting, Kenyon, Bowers and
Moore were served weak tea and ham and cheese
sandwiches. Kenyon had found himself looking into
Moore's eyes whenever Moore was talking. He was
trying to figure the man out. Save for under his eyes,
Moore had a pallid complexion. There were dark saucers there, signs, Kenyon guessed, of a heavy reader
whose habits taxed his capillaries. Moore looked any-
where between thirty-five and forty-five. Kenyon remembered seeing him somewhere before, probably
in a pub crowd around Christmas or a retirement do.
He read Moore for an academic despite the worldly
and even raffish hints which Moore's file had suggested to him. Moore didn't smile much. He carried
signs of the self-contained, which many would inter-
pret as arrogance or being wilfully remote to affect
some superiority. It was as though there were a slight
draft off Moore, cool and with the prospect of a chill if
circumstances drew him to disapproval. Moore fitted,
all right. Kenyon was searching for a sign that would

tell him that Moore was wily as well, behind the facade of being distant.

"Absolutely," Moore said without enthusiasm. "It's quite routine, here in Britain anyway. For all intents and purposes, Mr Combs has died intestate. If he has left a will with someone and it shows up later, while I'm there, even, I'm still intact. I'm acting for the estate, appointed by the bank."

"Right. That was how I saw it," said Kenyon.

"But the business about looking over police shoulders in Dublin?" Moore probed.

"You'll have to be versatile," Kenyon said. "Get your feet moving under you when you land in Dublin. Play it by ear. Get close to the chief investigating copper."

"I'll have to tell the police there that I'll be approaching people who are involved."

Kenyon nodded. They fell silent for a moment.

"Remember," Kenyon said as he reached for the teapot, "we're looking for something he concealed. Papers, a tape cassette even. Concentrate on finding a person that Combs trusted. Will this person come forward now because Combs so instructed him? We don't know. There may be a time lag where Combs posted something, to himself even. It's very unlikely he posted it abroad."

"No friend, no one he trusted?"

"No. That's part of the problem. His link was a Second Secretary, Ball, in the embassy. Ball would be the last person on the planet that he'd leave anything with."

"I expect I'll have to effect entry to the premises," Moore said, dryly mimicking his former profession. "Legally, I mean. The embassy. Do they — will they — know me there? Do I need a contact there?"

Kenyon sat up slightly in his chair.

"Yes. I'd prefer otherwise. We'll give you a link to a staffer in the embassy. He's not your control, remember. He's last-choice support if you need it."

Kenyon glanced from Moore to Bowers and back to Moore.

"Before you go, I want you to be aware of what our situation is," Kenyon continued. "What your overall guidance should be, who you're working for and why. We in this section are finally responsible for keeping our civil servants, our senior civil servants, out of the way of whatever may compromise them while they pursue their duties. If it smells really badly, then they have to go, but at the right time, with minimum fuss, with the best timing. There'll be time enough for drinks in the pub with our, er, friends in the F.O. After we settle the matter. Let's soothe any ruffles then, but for the moment this is our show. The Home Secretary knows what we're trying to do. We know for certain that some staff in our Dublin embassy are under surveillance from Irish police intelligence. That doesn't matter. If nothing else, it'll help prevent the IRA taking potshots at our staff. Just be aware of the context if you have to go to the embassy for some reason. Remember: our show."

Moore nodded and looked off into the middle distance as if considering the aftertaste of the tea. Kenyon looked at his watch.

"Travel under your own name. You'll have no problems. You'll be working for the bank's law firm. You'll have your cards, stationery and credentials. If the Irish police check on you here, all inquiries will be handled by the firm. I expect you know from your own work that several of the principals were in the Service and that they have done work for us before. The firm helped to set up Combs as an entity, so he and his affairs will not be unfamiliar to them. Have no

117

concerns about that, you'll be well covered from this end."

Moore shrugged. His hand strayed lightly over the sandy hair. For a moment, doubts wormed deep in Kenyon. He searched the face opposite him. Moore, parachuted into an operational role, this time as a lawyer; whatever field instincts he may have had rusted by now. But the assignment didn't require James Bond; just someone who was observant, methodical. Was that enough? Moore interrupted his drift.

"I'll need a letter of authorisation, an introduction, as well as proof of accreditation here."

"You'll have them by the morning. Draw what you need to get settled into a hotel there. We'll book you on a Dublin flight tomorrow, mid-day. You'll have your letters and background paperwork waiting for you here. Briefing at seven-thirty. Any difficulties with this schedule?"

Kenyon thought he saw a smile start on Moore's features, but he couldn't be sure. Moore shook his head once.

"We'll get you to Heathrow. Run yourself up a three-piece pin-stripe or something. Don't bring a bowler hat to Dublin, though. Only the Orangemen wear them there."

At least Bowers smiled. Kenyon gestured for him to leave. Moore sat gazing at the tea-tray. He didn't acknowledge Bowers' leaving.

"Now, I know it's short notice and all that," Kenyon began in a conciliatory tone. Moore looked at him as though to agree, but with a heavily ironic emphasis.

"I expect you want to know more about Arthur Combs and why we're falling over our arses trying to get at him now that he's dead."

Minogue's mouth was chalky, cloyed from the anisette. Iseult and Pat were in the kitchen now, as was

Kathleen. They were drinking mugs of tea and attacking the leftovers of the Bewley's cake.

Minogue poured himself more tea. It turned out to be the bottom of the pot. He filled the kettle from the tap. While he waited for the kettle to fill, he tried to look through the blued reflections of the kitchen which came back to him from the window. He could make out the bushes and the grass where the kitchen light reached. His own blurry shadow, fattened, lay in the distorted rectangle of yellow light. The shrubs beyond the light were faint but dense masses, as if the night had clumped them there, giving them a protective bulk. Was there no moon? He didn't see one, but he did notice a slight fan of blue behind the tree at the end of the garden. Would that be the beginnings of the moon he wanted? Combs, coming home in the darkness to a lonely house. A bit unsteady on the legs after a few drinks? Didn't notice anything amiss. Was there someone with him, a boyfriend? The anise had stilled Minogue, making his movements laborious. He knew it was a fake sleepiness. He wondered what the night-time was like at Tully, the whorls on the stones now faded into the shadow, the ruins no longer standing out against the sky.

The kettle filled, he placed the lid on and plugged it in. How does one draw or paint night anyway? Anytime there was a bright moon Minogue could not resist turning out the lights in the room to admit the moonlight. Moon, *luna*. Lunatic.

"Don't be falling asleep there, Da," Iseult said.

Kathleen resumed her interrogation of Pat. She asked about his brothers and sisters. Pat likely knew that this wasn't the first time he'd have to account for himself and his background to his girlfriend's mother, Minogue thought. Mrs Hartigan, the housekeeper. How could she not notice if Combs was homosexual?

He unplugged the burbling kettle and poured a little of the water into the teapot to scald it. Minogue would only drink tea that had been drawn in a fresh pot which had been scalded first. As he poured the tea, he tried again to shake himself of the passport photo: Combs' flabby, tired face, those candid eyes staring into the camera.

Minogue allowed himself an hour and a half of Tuesday morning for the State Pathologist's report, additional pages from Garda Forensic and the State Lab, and typed-up reports based on interviews done by Gardai in Stepaside. Arthur Combs had consumed approximately four small whiskies and one, perhaps two, half-pints of beer in the two hours before his death. Fond of it? Minogue wondered. Murtagh's trips to the gay bars had produced nothing. Only one pub had phoned back when the new shift had had a chance to see the photo of Arthur Combs. A barman in Lydon's pub thought that an older man, like the one in the photo, had come in some Friday nights over a year ago. If his memory was good — and Minogue couldn't silence the cynical gargoyle within — the man had read a sporting paper, probably horse-racing, and had left the pub after a couple of drinks. Alone. What next? the gargoyle whispered. Go to all the bookies in Dublin? Another motive for doing in a man who owed money to a bookie? But no, Minogue realised: Combs wasn't short of money. Horses, a little betting. Tinkers?

He rang Stepaside station and asked for Driscoll.

"One Michael Joseph Joyce, sober," said Minogue. "Reliable, usable testimony. It may be twelve and me getting there but . . . "

"No bother. He can cool his heels here."

Minogue turned to the forensic report. No pressure prints or UV traces of prints on victim's skin. No cord, twine or string of any description found on premises. Shoe-prints in the laneway matched brogues found in Combs' kitchen. Thirty-seven recoverable prints lifted from kitchen. Twenty-two from Combs, twelve definites from Mrs Hartigan, awaiting more intensive comparison checks on three marginals. More from the car and other rooms in Combs' house. All matches to Combs, none pending even. Tire treads that matched the radials on Combs' Renault. Didn't trust himself to drive up the narrow laneway after a few drinks? Didn't mean that no other car had parked in the laneway, Minogue brooded. Clues like asymptotes: nowhere he could see. Ahhh . . .

He phoned the Garda Forensic Lab and listened for almost twenty minutes while he was told much the same as he had read. Still no prints outside of Mrs Hartigan's and Combs'. Only eight pending for matches now. Any amount of ones smudged, unrecoverable. No, no one had done the end of the laneway. Why not? It was examined and found to be virtually all stones coming up through the soil. No tire marks visible. Clothes, any struggle at all, nails? No. Had to be something in all these pages, some clue.

Michael Joseph Joyce, itinerant, age thirty-eight, currently residing in Heronsford, Ballcorus, Co. Dublin. Married, wife Josie (Josephine), seven children. Minogue pushed away from his desk using his knee. He didn't get far. One of the rollers under his chair was seized.

"Tea, your honour," from Eilis, by his side. He hadn't heard her walk over to him. Smoke followed her and began to settle on him, a smell from the Levant. A souk, coffee-like tar in thimbles? Maybe a stone-flagged square with gristled and moustachioed men at dusk. Anatolia, Minogue wished. Wouldn't mind being there.

121

"Thanks, Eilis."

Eilis slouched back toward her desk. It was a quarter after eleven. It had been lashing rain since Minogue awoke at six.

Joyce: no relation to the one writing the dirty books beyond in Paris, of course. Joyce is a Galway name. Galway is the City of the Tribes. Travellers, itinerants, often converged on Galway city, the gateway to the west. Michael Joseph Joyce had been found malingering around the outside of Mr Combs' house by a member of the Gardai. Garda Eoin Freely was answering a telephone call from a concerned citizen, one Brian Mahon, who happened to be driving by with his brother. Happened to be driving by? Mahon lived in Stepaside. He had come by to see "the murder house." More lurid sightseeing, Minogue snorted.

Joyce had drink taken. Not completely legless but intoxicated enough not to be sensible to the waking, official world. Michael Joseph Joyce told Garda Eoin Freely that he was on Mr Combs' property to see to it that "the horse was fed and watered." Garda Freely did not report that he laughed at this explanation. He did report that he promptly took Joyce to Stepaside Garda Station for further questioning. No questioning had been done of course. They had rung Hoey by then and Minogue had issued his edict. Heronsford, where Joyce was camped, was three miles and more from Combs' house. What really brought Joyce that far from home at that hour of the night?

Minogue sipped more tea. It tasted slightly of washing-up liquid. Garda Freely would hardly have called Joyce a Mister any more than he would have listened to the man's protestations last night. Joyce was, after all, a tinker. Tinkers were shifty, dishonest, cunning. They drank themselves into a stupor, they stole things. Tinkers left mounds of rubbish

122

behind them when they moved their caravans to a new site.

Tinkers had to be taken in hand, evidently. Garda Freely was no different from any of his colleagues: no song-and-dance stuff, pick him up and make no bones about it. Let the social workers and the do-gooders blather on about "itinerants" or "travellers," the Gardai held the fort against tinkers.

Minogue paused at the phrase "currently residing." He imagined a leaky caravan or a canvas tent surrounded by bits of scrap iron and clothes, a gaggle of half-dressed children, treacherous mongrels growling under the caravan. They lived over a ditch and moved to a new ditch when they were thrown out of an area. Travellers, that's how they described themselves; and they usually kept horses or donkeys, if not by their camps, then with another member of their family. At thirty-eight, Joyce had lived the same portion of his expected life as Minogue, at fifty-four, had of his own. The settled Irish conferred very little romance on these <u>descendants of dispossessed peasants</u>. They were the starving losers in a run-in with Oliver Cromwell and his mounted metal men who hacked at the Irish by way of bringing in the Modern Age.

NOT GYPSIES

Tinkers like Joyce sent their women and children out to beg. O'Connell Bridge in Dublin usually drew a dozen of these shawled outlaws with ruddy faces cajoling and pressing for money or else sitting in the rain by a piece of a cardboard box with pennies in it. The men would go door-to-door, too, but looking for scrap iron. Wary householders generally held that tinkers a-begging at their door were really sizing up the houses for burglarising later.

Because of his gormless explanation, Michael Joseph Joyce nearly didn't get to go home to his Josie and his seven children. Had he actually entered the

123

house? Unless he knew the Gardai had seen him, Joyce would hardly admit to that. Minogue put his mug of tea aside. Hoey was standing by Eilis' desk now.

"There's a reply from the London police on the telex. Do you want it?" said Eilis.

The afternoon stretched out ahead of him as he read the half-page telex message. If it was raining here in the city, then Kilternan and Glencullen would be awash. Combs had retired as a Customs Inspector, sold his house in a suburb of London and moved to Ireland. What would Joyce and his family, the seven children who were probably the survivors of a family which could have been twice that number, what would they do in rain like this? Her Majesty's Government sent Mr Combs a pension and the bank with the funny name sent him an annuity, which Combs had bought with some of the money from the house he had sold. Tinkers are like untouchables among us, he thought, a Christian country full of churches and priests and nuns and roadside statues . . . and people living under canvas in the ditches. The Sampson Coutts crowd said they'd be sending someone to look after Mr Combs' estate in Ireland and —

"Very quick off the mark," he murmured aloud.

"Who is?" Hoey yawned.

Minogue read the last sentence aloud and added in "Reply for attn. Inspector Newman. Rgds."

"What's 'rgds'?"

"He means 'regards' I suppose," Hoey replied.

"Oh. So this policeman says that a bank is sending over a lawman to settle Mr Combs' affairs here . . . " Minogue's voice trailed off.

"That's banks for you," Hoey said vacantly. "Rob the eye out of your head and come back for the eyelash, telling you you look better without it."

"Today or tomorrow, it says," Minogue said. Keating appeared at the door. Minogue promptly appropriated him and the radio car.

"Stepaside, Pat. And don't dally about," he said.

Moore was not detained in passport control at Dublin Airport. A middle-aged man with a skeptical cast to his face and glasses down on his reddened nose asked him if he was importing any plants. Had he been to a farmyard in the immediate past? Moore had been allowed to keep his clothes as cabin baggage along with his briefcase. He found himself precipitously outside Customs, looking down the hall at windows running with the downpour.

The airport could have been in Britain, he thought, when the plane had skimmed under the low clouds into a grey, green world. He noted signs in Gaelic on the sides of vans and on advertisements in the terminal. He saw no armed policemen or army. He noticed the two plainclothes police near passport control, though. They wore their indifference rather affectedly. Neither gave him more than a momentary glance.

Moore had never been to Ireland before. His only connection to the place was his surname. His great-grandfather, a bricklayer, had emigrated to Britain in 1892, had married an English woman and had spent the rest of his life happily becoming as English as he could. Moore's grandfather had bought some real estate and in two generations had brought the Moore family from provincial town builder to the appearances of landed money.

Moore rounded a partition and found himself facing a throng of people who appeared to be waiting to greet passengers off his plane. He looked at several faces. He felt he was on show. He gathered his wits and headed for the greater spaces of the terminal. As he followed the signs for the taxi rank, he shelved his efforts to put a finger on what exactly was so different about the faces here. He asked a woman who was leaning listlessly on an information counter how much taxi fare to the City Centre was.

"Why would you want to take a taxi?" was the reply.

"I have to make good time actually," he answered.

"To the Burlington Hotel? You wouldn't see much change out of a ten-pound note."

"That's near the City Centre, I understand," Moore said.

"And a bit more too, now. It's over the south side. Tell the driver to take you over the new bridge. Otherwise those fellas would drive you all over the country."

"Ah, I see," Moore said.

"Why don't you take the bus and save yourself a bundle of money?"

Moore telephoned the hotel to confirm his booking. Although it was almost one o'clock, he wasn't hungry. He stood by the window watching people running in from the rain, surrendering bags to the security check by the doors. A double-decker bus drew up at the stop outside and that decided him. He entered the bus, paid and opened out a map of the city. Combs' house was beyond the suburbs even, on the map for County Dublin.

Moore followed the bus route on his map as it made for the city centre. The driver was whistling in a dispirited way, losing track of the air and changing his whistle to one made between tongue and teeth. He stopped his whistling only to mutter to himself or to wipe condensation off the side window. As Moore was leaving the bus, the driver spoke to anyone who would listen to him.

"Ah, you'd be tired of all that sunny weather, wouldn't you?"

Moore got into a taxi at O'Connell Bridge. The Dublin he had seen while he was coming in on the Airport Road was a dishevelled, grey sprawl. There were kids all over the place, on bikes, running, walking in wet groups. From his street map he knew that the trip to the Burlington Hotel was a short one.

The hotel was a clone of every and any nondescript hotel that had been designed in anonymous American Vulgar. It was like an office block, quite without features local to where the developer had slapped it up. Moore thought that the taxi-man had gone less directly to the hotel than he could have, despite his protestations of roads being "up" and one-way streets. Moore declined an offer of help from a doorman with a florid drinker's face, a stage Irishman who probably even enjoyed donning the silly livery he wore. The gear reminded him of Emperor Bokassa.

Moore followed a young woman from the Reception. She flicked his room-key against her thigh as she walked. Her badge said Maura.

"That rain is down for the day," she said without turning to him. "As soon as I woke up and looked out the window this morning, I knew we'd be swimming in it all day."

"Yes," he said.

"That's Dublin for you," she added and showed a distracted smile while she watched the floors light up in the ascending lift. Moore was wondering how best to explain his business here in case the police asked. Would they know enough to wonder why Combs' bank had not simply called on a law firm here in Dublin to do the work? He could say, as Kenyon had suggested in his briefing this morning, that his firm prided itself on being on the spot promptly and that it had the necessary expertise to negotiate affairs in the new Europe. The European Economic Community and all that. He could deflect any curiosity by talking about how much new law membership in the EEC had brought with it. Even if they knew he was lying, they'd probably believe that he was boasting more than anything else, or greedily chasing commissions even outside Great Britain.

Maura stopped and unlocked the door into the room. Moore couldn't understand why she had led him. Why not give him his key and let him find his own way? He had already refused help from a doorman and a porter at Reception. Couldn't they take a hint?

She entered the room and stood to the side of the bed. It was clean, luxurious even. There was no smell of stale ashtrays from the last boozy travelling sales-man either. Moore didn't hide his approval.

"It's nice, isn't it?" she said.

Moore snorted lightly at the incongruity of it all. What kind of a place was this where a porter or portress would stand in his hotel room and comment on the place? More amused than baffled, Moore agreed. She left without hanging around for a tip. He sat on the bed.

Yet again, Moore mentally rehearsed a scene where anyone might query his haste in coming to Dublin to settle an estate. At least it was easier than having to explain why he was there in the first place: inventory effects as soon as possible and thereby secure them for disposal later. Had to be tactful, though, about insinuating that an Irish thief might be a shade quicker off the mark or more heartless about breaking into a dead man's house and lifting stuff. Moore had heard of instances in Britain where thieves had kept an eye on death notices in the papers and plundered houses even as the funerals were taking place. He could mention that, and emphasise that it happened in Brit-ain, of course. Of course. . . . Plus the idea that Combs may have had valuables around the house.

Moore found the telephone book in a drawer. He didn't know what "Cuid a hAon" might mean, but the numbers were for Dublin. It took him two calls before he heard a woman with a thick singsong accent, but who sounded bored too, tell him that he had reached the Investigation Section. Moore glanced at the name in his notebook again as if one more look might finally tell him how to pronounce it now that he had to try and utter it.

"Sergeant Min-ogg, please."

"Sergeant Minogue?"

"Yes. May I speak with him please?"

Moore's gaffe with the pronunciation abruptly reminded him that his own accent was beginning to sound different to him. A foreign country, just off the coast of Britain?

"He's not here at the moment. You might leave a message."

"It's in connection with a Mr Combs. I have just arrived from London to try and settle Mr Combs' estate."

"Give me your name and where you can be gotten in touch with," Eilis said instead.

Moore wondered if her offhand manner was typical of what he could expect from anyone else on the island.

"The Burlington, is it?" she asked.

"Yes. I'll be starting just as soon as I can, you see, and I need to okay it by the police rather than surprise them at Mr Combs' house."

Moore, like many other well-meaning Britons, assumed that a little humor oiled the wheels when dealing with the Irish on their home turf.

"You had better not stir as regards the matter until you meet up with Sergeant Minogue," Eilis said stonily. "I'll see to it that he telephones you within the hour. Is that good enough for you?"

CHAPTER 8

It took Minogue forty minutes to get to Stepaside. To be exact, it took Keating forty minutes to drive himself and Minogue to Stepaside. Minogue dozed on the trip. He stretched before opening the car door. Two Gardai ran by them to the door of the station, one with a newspaper held over his head.

Michael Joseph Joyce was sitting alone in a room on the upper floor of the station. The door to the room had been locked. The Garda who led them upstairs called himself Tobin.

"How's it going on this thing anyway?" he asked as he clumped slowly up the stairs ahead of them.

Tobin cast a glance back at Minogue. The look on Keating's face drew his attention then. Tobin read what he suspected from Keating's wide eyes. He tucked his head into his shoulders, averted his eyes and made speedier progress up the last of the stairs. He rattled the lock as he was unlocking the door. An unconscious gesture of authority to the nervous man within, Minogue thought. A heavy, noisy man in a uniform. Not Minogue's cup of tea, this Tobin who had been devoured by his uniform. The place smelled mothbally, damp. Minogue stayed Tobin's arm before he had turned the key fully.

"Joyce has been here since this morning, am I right?" asked Minogue.

"Yes, sir," Tobin answered. "We put the heavy word on him when we brought him home last night. Begob if he wasn't sober and dressed up in his finery waiting on the squad car this morning. Shaking like a leaf he was. The DTs, I'll bet."

Minogue fixed a languid smile on Tobin.

"A spot of tea for him too then, Garda. Lots of sugar, if you please. Any chance of buns in the village here? My colleague Detective Keating and I frightened one another on the way here with the way our bellies were growling. We've had no dinner, you see."

Tobin headed back down the stairs. Minogue knew by Keating's face that Tobin had given him the look of incredulity which he didn't dare show Minogue. Minogue rested his hand on the doorknob. The room smelled of woodsmoke and unwashed clothes. Joyce was standing by the window. He was indeed nervous, his hands in and out of his pockets, reaching for buttons on his shirt, touching his belt, rubbing his nose.

Joyce had the puffy, tired face of a heavy drinker. Watery eyes darted from Minogue to Keating to the door. Minogue noticed a faint smell of shaving soap. Joyce had several nicks on his neck. Although he was wearing the jacket of a suit over what had been a white shirt, Joyce was shivering slightly. He ran his hand quickly over a full head of red hair, which might have owed its styling inspiration to a 1955 Elvis Presley. Joyce looked out under his eyebrows at the two detectives.

"Mornin', sirs," he said hoarsely. He licked his upper lip with rapid side-to-side stabs of his tongue.

"A poor one, I'm thinking. I'm Sergeant Minogue. This is Detective Keating."

Joyce looked plaintively to the closing door.

"I have to go to the toilet, sirs. I'm here all the morning," Joyce said.

Minogue nodded to Keating. A fidgety Joyce followed Keating out the door. Minogue saw only two chairs, one with a bockety leg, to go with the formica-topped table. He waited by the window for the pair to return, his own mind adrift as he gazed at the teeming rain on the glass. Tobin arrived with a tray before Joyce appeared at the door. He eyed the shifty Joyce as Minogue directed him to a chair. Joyce sat on the edge of the chair, blinking.

"But now, sirs, how is it ye'd be wanting to see the likes of me?"

Minogue had insisted on Keating taking the other chair. He slung a leg over the corner of the table and held out a cup of tea to Joyce. Joyce's jaw dropped.

"Deal out your own sugar," Minogue said.

Joyce spooned four heaped teaspoonfuls of sugar into his cup, spilling half of the last spoonful in transit.

"We want to know what you were doing at that house the other night," said Minogue.

"On my oath, I was up looking to the horse, sir, and nothing else, and I went up the lane a bit and I had my eye out for the horse. I needn't have looked far, but I had a bit of drink on me and I don't deny that. Sure wasn't the creature tethered up to the gate and he was after eating all around him, but if you — "

"Hold on there. Hold your horses," Minogue raised his hand.

"And here I am locked up in the barracks all morning — "

"Look it," Minogue said sharply. "Stop running away with yourself here." Joyce's nostrils went in and out

132

like bellows. He could not stop from spilling more tea. Minogue reached out, grasped his forearm and guided the tea to the table.

"Didn't I tell the peelers last night to get the man of the house and he'd know me?" Joyce blurted.

"Who?"

"Mr Combs. I told them to knock on the door and t'would be all fixed up as right as rain and they'd see what I was at and that there was no harm to it."

Minogue knew from Keating's stillness that he was startled, too. Minogue spoke very slowly now.

"Well now. Would you care to telephone Mr Combs now and we can clear it all up?"

"Sure wouldn't I be after doing that if I could have?" Joyce replied, a little less agitated now.

"Well, why didn't you then?"

"I don't have the reading and the writing, sirs, no more than I have a telly-phone. If ye'll find his phone number in the book, I'll phone him this instant and he'll tell ye what ye want to know."

"What did the Garda say to you last night when you said you wanted to knock on the door so as Mr Combs could vouch for you?"

"Didn't he laugh at me and tell his pal that I was arse-over-tip drunk!"

"You remember everything that was said and done last night?"

"Well, I do get a bit shaky every now and then, but I know what I know. Mr Combs will tell you, so he will. If he wasn't at home the other night, then he'll be home today and he's the man'll set things to rights. A shocking nice man is Mr Combs. He's after forgetting to untie the horse, but sure that's no big thing. Oh, yes, that's my horse above in his field, with one of his legs gone to the bad and him getting it tangled in barbed wire. I do go up and have a look at the horse

133

every now and then, and sure enough the animal is in the best of fettle now with a field full of grass inside of him and oats and the divil knows what else that Mr Combs does feed him. And he paid for the vet, too."

This overtaxed Keating. He looked up from his notebook and pointed his pencil at Joyce. Joyce gulped some tea.

"Mr Combs fed your horse and let it graze in one of his fields?" Keating asked in a tone of open disbelief.

"Bits of barley and molasses he did, something I never did in my life. True as God, the animal must have thought he'd gone on to paradise. I would have et the stuff myself," Joyce said with new assurance.

"So this horse of yours went to the vet, was fed and watered by Mr Combs, not to say pampered entirely," Minogue said, "and he let the horse roam around that field and graze where it pleased?"

"He did, sirs."

Tethered, Minogue wondered. Had the horse tried to escape before? Bad-tempered perhaps?

"He had a soft spot for horses, so he did," Joyce added. "He told me once that he had a pony and him growing up, years and years ago in England. And that that pony was the best pal he'd ever had and could hope to have. Did you ever hear the like of that?"

Joyce showed brown teeth in a nervous smile.

"Tell you the truth, I think Mr Combs tied up the horse near the gate so as he could pet it and what have you. Don't tell him I said that. Sure an old man couldn't be chasing a horse around the field, could he? Sure that same horse was fit and able to come home with me last week. But I think the poor man likes the bit of company. I wanted to sell the horse last week, and that's what I went to tell Mr Combs. I hadn't the heart to tell him until yesterday. The drink, you see. Didn't he buy a gorgeous bit and bridle for the animal, to dress it up, like? Presents, like."

"Presents for the horse, your horse," Keating said in a monotone.

"That's the way of the world, isn't it, sirs. Everybody's different in their own way. And there's no explaining it in the end. There's people that love animals and there's people that don't . . . "

Keating rubbed his eyes. He laid his pencil on the table to get a better knuckle into his eye. Minogue watched him massage his writing hand then, stretching out the fingers, flexing them. The sound of the rain was a constant dull percussion on the roof.

"Jesus and Mary and all the saints and archangels will tell ye that Michael Joseph Joyce had no mischief on his mind and, please God, never will have again. A man can have enough trouble and run-ins with the law in his life, and he can get sick of the badness. Sure aren't we all the same, sirs, all trying to keep the arse in our trousers and have a roof over our heads? Aren't we all the same? Under our skins, don't you see . . . ?"

Pleased with his logic, Joyce sat back in his chair.

"And can't I tell them, when I go home, that it was all a confusion like, and ye perhaps thinking I was a blackguard and up to divilment?" he added. "Oh, there's nothing like visit to the police barracks with hard-working gentlemen like yourself to waken a man up and put him to rights. Even if it is the wrong man ye have," Joyce added earnestly.

Barracks, Minogue was thinking. Gentlemen. Sirs. Language and suspicions that belonged in another age when more than the tinkers of Ireland were outcasts in the ditch by the roadside. The servility was a foil to conceal the contempt it was bred from. He felt Keating looking at him now, wanting him to pull the cork on Joyce.

"We'll be back in a moment, Michael Joseph," Minogue murmured. "Wait here like a good man. We'll not be long."

Keating followed Minogue into the hallway.

"Well?" Minogue looked at Keating.

Keating shrugged. He was a bored policeman with a sore hand.

"God, he has a desperate mouth on him for talk. When he wasn't putting me to sleep, he was driving me up the walls with the blather out of him. But not a hint of any homo thing."

"But he never once makes a slip," said Minogue. "Never once lets on that he knows Combs is dead. I think if he had his way, he'd march up up to Combs' place now so that we could talk to Combs and that'd be that," said Minogue with an edge of irony.

"You know," Keating began wearily, "the way he talks about Combs and himself having a drink in Combs' kitchen every now and then, it doesn't sound like he's telling a pack of lies."

"I can see that, too," Minogue agreed. "Well, after tea when Mrs H wouldn't be around to know . . . and be scandalised. I'm not saying that I buy Joyce's yarn though."

"He did say that Combs let him into the house once or twice and even gave him a bottle of whisky an odd time. Passed him a tenner for his family several times," Keating said, squinting at his notebook.

"I wonder how much of the tenner she saw," added Keating. "The bottle of whisky was no kindness to them."

"But well-meant," said Minogue. He was surprised to find himself leaning out to catch a fragment of Combs' personality, his open-handedness, lest it plummet to the ground after Keating's rebuke.

"But don't you think he's twigged that we're not here in Stepaside ~~him~~ about the weather? He must know about Combs," Keating said.

"Travellers don't be rushing out to buy the papers or listen to the news, now," Minogue cautioned. "We can't assume he knows."

Neither man said a word for several seconds. Joyce's grandiloquence was not a ploy to delude Keating and himself in particular, Minogue believed. Rather, his talk was the reflex of a man who moved warily around such prickly institutions of the settled Irish as policemen and publicans. The elaborate flattery and invoking of saints and angels was the language of a different century, a different mind. Joyce had adopted the wheedling way of the powerless peasant without a thought that he, no more than his forbears, could ever be any other person dealing with peelers. His whorls of self-pity and whining were the Trojan horses which carried an ancient and enduring hostility within. But that did not mean Joyce was lying.

Another burrowing notion elbowed its way into Minogue's attention: this odd acquaintance between a retired Briton and a traveller somehow fitted Minogue's picture of Combs. This surprised Minogue when he allowed the truth of it to settle on him. For the life of him, he could not backtrack through that fog, back to a clear and detailed "Mr Combs," which had to be somewhere in his head for Minogue to be able to think this way at all in the first place. Maybe it was those drawing in Combs' house, the signs of a local interest. A passion?

"I'll tell you this much," Keating said quietly, "he hasn't told us everything. It's a bit like a good yarn, you know, how decent Combs was to help him out and the rest of it. But he didn't go beyond that sort of thing."

Minogue gave Keating an inquiring glance.

"I mean some substance to the man he says he knew. Combs," Keating said hesitantly, as though the school toughs might jeer him after showing an interest during poetry class. "Maybe he's telling us what he thinks we want to hear. I'm not saying that he's fibbing or anything. It may be that, like you say, he doesn't know it's Combs we're on about."

"I think you're very shrewd entirely, Detective Keating," Minogue said absently. "But what way do you think we should go now?"

"I think we should tell him, sir," Keating replied without hesitation.

"And watch very closely how he reacts?"

Keating nodded ponderously.

"And watch very closely how he reacts, sir."

They had re-entered the room to find Joyce looking around with darting, bird-like glances. Now, he was perched on the edge of his chair . . . as though hunkering by a fire, Minogue thought. He seemed to be keeping himself taut by clasping his knees with his hands. Minogue knew Joyce didn't believe that Combs was dead.

"Ah, no. No," Joyce whispered finally. "He couldn't be. Sure didn't I call to see him last night?"

Minogue said nothing. Joyce seemed to be on the brink of a denial or on the very edge of blurting something out, but he was stopping himself at the last instant. At each surge, his body leaned forward slightly as if to breast a wave and out with his disbelief.

"Ye are trick-acting with me," Joyce said accusingly. He would not look up from the floor now.

"We're not, Michael Joseph," murmured Minogue. "Mr Combs was murdered."

"Ye're trying to get me into trouble."

Joyce's voice had a rising tone of apprehension to it.

"Not a bit of it," Minogue continued. "We're going to find out who did it. And put him in jail for it. That's our job, do you see?"

"Someone is trying to do me a bad turn and bring me down," Joyce mumbled. He looked up suddenly at Minogue.

"Trying to put a traveller away in jail, so it is. The whole world is up against the traveller," he said slowly. His watery eyes had settled on Minogue's. Their new intensity showed that he had cast off the protective air of servility.

"You're telling me someone has gone and done away with a man that had the time of day and the decency to bid good-day to the likes of Michael Joseph Joyce, when there's thousands of people born and bred in Ireland would cross the road sooner than say good morning or good evening to me, or so much as walk on the same footpath as myself . . . ?"

Joyce was almost keening now. It had an eerie solemnity to it. Minogue sensed that Joyce was beginning to believe them. Keating was visibly impatient.

"Listen now, Michael Joseph," Minogue interrupted. "Did Mr Combs ever suggest anything to you about his friends?"

"Friends? No, never did. He never mentioned a thing about them. I couldn't help but think to myself that he didn't have any."

"Men friends?" said Minogue. Joyce frowned.

"What are you saying?"

"Any idea in your mind that Mr Combs was a homosexual?"

Joyce sat back abruptly and stared at Minogue.

"That sort of thing? Men pretending they're women sort of thing? You must be joking. Mr Combs was a perfect gentleman, God rest him."

"And he never so much as hinted anything to you in that line?" Keating asked quickly. "Him giving you money and drink. What for? Didn't he want a little something for his troubles?"

"That's a dirty thing to say. And ye policemen?"

Tobin appeared in the doorway and pointed to Minogue. As good a time as any to leave Keating to do his work, Minogue shrugged. With a bit of theatre not totally alien to him in his domestic life, Minogue stood and addressed Keating.

"Detective Keating, would you carry on in my absence with Mr Joyce here? And Mr Joyce will furnish exact details and information about what he knows concerning Mr Combs. Are you with me on that, Michael Joseph?"

Joyce nodded. He rubbed his palm down his face and slouched back in the chair. He was sweating slightly. His face was even more lumpy and tired-looking.

"Every detail now," Minogue added. "Nothing left out."

Joyce looked with a bleak apprehension as Keating rearranged his chair opposite him. He looked up under his lick of hair at Minogue, aware now that his performances might not derail these peelers after all. He nodded again at Minogue.

Tobin closed the door behind Minogue. He had a cigarette going, cupped in his hand behind his back. His tie was loosened and the top button of his blue Garda's shirt was undone. He had meaty forearms.

"Divils for talk, hah, Sergeant?" he said, producing a packet of Majors from his pocket.

"No thanks," Minogue said.

"Once you leave them sitting on their own for a while here they get to being jittery."

140

"You say there's someone on the telephone for me?"

"Oh, yes sir." Tobin made for the stairs. "You can take it in the interview room below."

"Thanks very much, Garda Tobin. Now what can three hungry men here visiting the village of Stepaside do about a bit of grub? Nothing too substantial on account of it being half-way to the tea-time. A plate of chips maybe?"

He watched Tobin lumber heavily down the hall before picking up the phone. He listened to Eilis and then wrote the telephone number she called out.

"Moore? M-O-O-R-E?"

"Yes, your honour."

While he waited for the hotel to switch him through to Moore's room, Minogue let a phrase circle slowly in his afternoon mind. *Indecent haste.* Could hardly say it to this fella though; he was just doing his job. As the bishop said to the actress? Someone had to do it, sooner or later.

Minogue tried to remember his own odd grief at his father's funeral, the macabre sorting out and handling that was part of the ceremonials. Patrick Minogue, age fifty-seven. Minogue's mother holding out jumpers and socks and shirts and shoes and jackets belonging to her husband. Would they fit you, Matt? Or maybe you could get them taken in or altered? Great wear still left in these boots, hardly used at all, two pound ten in Limerick at the sales last year. Would they be your size? Jumpers that she had knitted for all the family, elbows patched, the tobacco-sweat-home smell of his father bonded to each fibre. The man who had chastised and loved him, worked alongside him in the fields, the man he had listened to in the pub, watched at the table, heard snore at night, fought against and cursed, implacable and infrequently gentle, but most often with a horse or a dog. . . . Minogue

141

had been invited to slip into these clothes and make them his own.

"Mr Moore? Sergeant Minogue, Mr Moore. Concerning Mr Combs?"

"Yes, yes. Hello, Sergeant. Thank you for calling back so promptly. I must say I didn't expect your call this soon."

Eilis, Minogue fancied. Left him hanging because of his English accent?

"Nothing to it. You're here to fix Mr Combs' estate, now?"

"I'm here from Mr Combs' bank, actually. I'm supposed to settle his affairs. For the moment anyway, until we can do a thorough search for relatives and locate a will."

"Where there's a will, there's a relative," Minogue observed.

"Quite so, Sergeant. I must remember that one. That's a good one."

They must be hard up for jokes across the water, Minogue surmised.

"No family, I hear, Mr Moore. Not like here. A man can't throw a stone over a wall without hitting a relative of his."

"Indeed, Sergeant. No family here at any rate. Odd but by no means unusual, I'm afraid. Some people actually resist making wills. As though a will might hasten death, I suppose," Moore said.

"Like a body with a pain in his chest wouldn't go to the doctor, for fear he'd find out there was something amiss?"

"How true, Sergeant, how true. You have that phenomenon here in Ireland, too, do you?"

No, Mr Moore, we eat raw meat. And pray to statues by the roadside. After we've mangled a few of our fellow countrymen with Armalite rifles and gossip.

"In any event, not a happy occasion really," said Moore.

Which is exactly when the law profession steps in and makes pots of money, hand over fist, Minogue reflected. He listened while Moore described what he planned to do. It wasn't that anyone feared that Mr Combs' effects would be interfered with, Moore stressed, but his firm prided itself on handling such matters promptly ... to ensure the integrity of the deceased's worldly estate.

Moore had a nice armchair BBC accent, Minogue thought. So far he hadn't laughed. A bit too tactful, though. Maybe he had been reading a How to Deal with People in Ireland, UK version, on his way over from London. Nice of him to be polite, especially on the telephone: absolutely no hindrance to the investigation ... could be of any assistance to the investigation, more than glad to ... a few days at most, an inventory, see to any possible claims on the estate from Irish sources ... arrange for the remains to be returned ... take advice, of course, from authorities here. Moore said that it was likely that Combs had a life insurance policy, but he didn't know where it might be.

"Of course," Minogue replied. "By the way, you speak the Irish very well."

"I beg your pardon?" from a tentative Moore.

"Gardai. You knew the word for the police here."

Moore gave a rather breathless laugh. Out of practice, Minogue wondered.

"We prepare ourselves. It wouldn't do for the legal profession to be putting their feet in their mouths."

The man was a comedian entirely.

"No more than it would the Gardai, Mr Moore. Look. I must tell you that I don't know the procedures on this class of thing. I don't doubt but there are affidavits and applications and letters of authority and God knows what else to be dealt with. I think that if it were Jesus himself being taken down from the cross, there'd be a line-up of civil servants with reams of forms waiting."

"Don't trouble yourself, Sergeant," Moore interjected. "This is merely a courtesy call to let you know I'm here. I have to settle my presence with some of your civil service departments, I believe. Your Foreign Affairs for a start. A Land Registry for ownership of the house and lands, I think. . . . Doubtless some officials who deal with death duties and taxes."

"Department of Finance, Mr Moore. Death Duty Section."

"But mainly to seal the house and see what the estate consists of. Frankly, I'd be relieved if I can find a will. Of course, for selfish motives, I mean; I would then be directed by a sound legal instrument. But just to do right by Mr Combs, there's that, too. Perhaps to benefit those he would have liked to benefit. A charity, some relative. To bring something out of this tragedy. Might I call on you or your staff, so that I can get into Mr Combs' house?"

"You can, of course. Can you find your way to our offices here in St John's Road? The middle of the day, say?"

Minogue allowed himself several seconds' pause after putting down the receiver. He heard men's voices, not their words, resonating in the building. Laughter then, a jibe: still no words. Was it still raining? He walked to the barred window. A margin of sodden fields rose sharply up from the village. He located a puddle and saw that it was not disturbed. Maybe step outside for a breath of air and not be drowned now. Minogue retraced his steps through the hallway. He stepped out the back door of the station into a yard which served as a carpark. The air was clear as though it had been scrubbed. What day was it today, Tuesday? Three days gone by. Minogue leaned his hip against a squad-car and drew in the mountain air.

It did not worry him that he might have been remiss about placing an appeal in the papers and on the telly before today. It was politic to wait and pull all the loose threads which he found locally. Minogue looked to his anniversary-present, fancy quartz watch and saw half three looking implacably back at him. Quartz watches didn't fib, that was the trouble. Keating could hold the fort here and finish off with Joyce. Could Joyce kill a man? Rejecting sexual advances from Combs?

Minogue met Tobin in the hallway. The Garda was balancing three plates of chips and dangling a bottle of ketchup as well. Minogue followed him upstairs. Tobin put the plates on the table and then stood inside the door, his hands in his pockets. Minogue saw that Keating didn't know how to get rid of the sulking Tobin.

"If I might lean on your generosity again, Garda Tobin. A pot of tea would be just the thing. If I could trouble you," Minogue added.

Tobin did not tell him that it was no trouble at all. He glared at Keating, who had wisely turned his attention to a plate of chips. Minogue sat on the edge of the table and picked a chip.

"Ye had better dig in, the pair of yous. Being polite will leave you hungry when I'm around a plate of chips."

While Joyce began working on one plate, Keating drew Minogue back into the hall. The two policemen stood plucking chips at the head of the stairs.

"While you were gone, sir. Joyce maintains he visited Combs several times," said Keating. "He called around

145

once in a while in the evenings when he knew the housekeeper wouldn't give him the bum's rush at the door."

"Combs would pour him a drink, and how could he refuse, says our tink — our traveller. They'd chat, if you can believe it."

"About what?"

"About everything and anything, he says. Combs seems to have been interested in finding out about Joyce's family and background."

"Any indication of the sexual thing?" Minogue asked.

Keating deftly caught a chip, which he had upset on the edge of the plate.

"I haven't put it directly to him, sir. I'm waiting for a hint. Then I'll press."

" 'Talk,' 'chat'? Yarns, like?"

"Maybe Joyce romanced about the gypsy-rover life. That'd have been good for a few evenings by the fire, I'm sure," Keating added with irony. He plucked another chip from the plate.

"Is he lying to us, Pat? Obstructing at all?"

"I don't get that sense. Yet, anyway. When I asked him about anything he might have learned about Combs' affairs, he got on his high horse a bit. 'A man has to mind his own business in another man's house' says he."

Minogue shook his head.

"And that was it?"

"Well, you were only gone the twenty minutes, sir. I took your cue and let him blather away for fear he might clam up and forget something. I had to go over dates with him. The man has no idea what a calendar is, I'm thinking. I think he believes us about Combs' being dead now, but he doesn't want to believe it. He'd probably believe it if anyone other than a police-man — a peeler — told him."

"Never bumped into the housekeeper, Mrs Hartigan?"

"He said he was turned away from the door by her once. After that, nothing."

Keating fell upon the remaining chips.

"So they'd have a few jars and yap. Did Joyce stay late?" asked Minogue.

"No. He made a remark about that. That Combs didn't want him getting jarred and into trouble, so he used to ration him with the drink and send him home. After their chat, like. He says that Combs used to like to hear about what went on around the place; you know, people in the area, the weather, the local goings-on. He was interested in where Joyce had travelled, all over the country. That class of talk."

"I see," Minogue murmured.

"And what it was like living by the side of the road; had, em, travellers anyone to stand up for them as regards housing or trouble with the law?" Keating was saying.

"Joyce didn't think that the man was a bit nosey to be asking him things like that? Prying, maybe?"

"You know how it is with this bloody country, sir. Even with the tink — travellers. Sure don't we pour our hearts out to Yankee anthropologists who'd be asking us about sex or the like, before we'd say a word beyond the weather to the man next door."

Minogue half-smiled at Keating's truth, a sizeable mental benchmark for living in this country. Keating had finished the chips.

"Do you know, but it's true for you," Minogue concluded.

He remained outside the door while Keating went to the toilet downstairs. He heard Joyce cough once behind the door. Minogue realised that he was tired now, irritable even. He watched Keating plod back up the stairs. Then Minogue opened the door to find Joyce standing by the table.

"Come on, we'll go home now," he said to Joyce. "I'll drop you off."

Joyce's suspicion gave way to a cautious relief.

"Are we done, sirs?"

Minogue gave his Fiat a tall order on his way home. He had left Joyce by the side of the road at Heronsford Lane. Joyce looked like a man who hadn't slept all night. He stood in the ditch, gathering his jacket around him, his shoulders hunched. Home was a cream-coloured caravan, still on its wheels but thrust into the brambles. A face appeared at the window, Joyce's wife. A child with a mop of red hair ran out onto the road from behind the caravan, a dog following. More faces appeared in the window. The dog sniffed one of Minogue's tires and lifted a leg. Joyce shouted at the dog and startled it away. He picked up the child. Boy or girl, Minogue couldn't tell. The child's belly-button peeped out as its jumper rose. A face streaked with dirt, a runny nose, an expression curious and defiant. Minogue saw the dog in his mirror this time as it made to piss on his car again. He drove off. A last glimpse of Joyce hoisting another one of his children, the two figures one now, becalmed in the wet squalor, surrounded by discarded clothes and bits of metal. Joyce half-waved.

Minogue knew what few others knew: there was a short-cut up this lane over a rocky track and down a worse piece of road back to the tarred lane which led by Tully. The closed gates might dissuade faint-hearted people if the potholes did not. Minogue knew what right-of-way was, so he unlatched the wide farm gate, drove through, parked and returned to secure the gate again. He stopped, his hand on the bolt, and looked down the fields. Three horses were grazing by a clump of trees in the middle distance. Minogue saw no harnesses or nose-gear on any of the animals. Free, to the edges of these fields anyway.

His mind swung gently from raiding chieftains on horseback to Joyce, a disinherited Irishman, but regal with a horse; perhaps Combs had savoured that irony, sympathised. Tinkers, we call them, men and women who sleep by the roadside but cling to their horses and let them graze by the sides of the road, while the motorised Irish look down their passing noses at these horsemen. Landless but horse-mad. His hand on the wet gate, another hand pushing home the bolt so hard that it shook raindrops off the bars, Minogue was surprised by the rush of anger. If he were Joyce, he'd steal Jags and Mercedes and money and anything, all day and all night until someone stopped him.

The Fiat wallowed and bottomed on its struts four times before Minogue reached the tarred part of the road. Keating was probably back in the city now, getting up a press release to appeal for scraps of information they hadn't trawled yet.

Minogue and Kathleen had but themselves for company at tea-time.

"And did I tell you that his bank already has a legal eagle here to close up the house and run up a list of pots and pans and knives and forks?"

"Go on," Kathleen said. "That's banks for you. Scavengers."

"I suppose. No relatives, so what do you expect? That's how they make their money and do their business."

"Maybe he came over to make friends. Someone may have told him how friendly we are over here," Kathleen offered.

"Nosey, you mean."

"But you say he kept to himself. So he didn't come here for the company, did he? Unless it was just to be with people without being too personal."

Minogue had no reply for that. He decided to leave the matter. They sat through a second pot of tea and listened to the half-past-six news on the radio. He rose from the chair and began to clear the table in advance of washing the dishes.

Iseult breezed in the back door. She switched off the tape-machine which was draped across her shoulder. She yanked off the headphones but caught a strand of hair to one side.

"Ow!" She drew her hair gently through to free the apparatus.

"Why are you shouting?" asked Kathleen.

"I had the volume up. I must be deaf. Ow."

"Can you still breathe with that thing unplugged?" Minogue asked.

"Nice welcome. Am I interrupting a comedians' convention?"

"I'll bet your head is like a washing machine inside after listening to one of those things. And you probably walking into walls and hopping along the street with your head full of that stuff," Kathleen observed.

"It's great stuff. It helps me think."

Iseult plonked down a bag with hairy tassels.

"I have presents for you. The both of you," Iseult said. She rummaged in the bag and drew out two postcards. She handed one to Kathleen, the other to Minogue. Kathleen turned hers over. It was a Modigliani, head and shoulders, a woman. Minogue snorted when he saw his.

"Isn't that the limit?" he smiled. "I've seen that one in the books but I never thought I'd ever get a postcard of it."

"Do you dig the title, though?" Iseult asked.

Minogue laughed again. Magritte had called his painting of a glass of water balancing on an open umbrella, *Hegel's Holiday*.

"Is it the right way up? Maybe it's upside down. What's the idea of the glass of water?" Kathleen asked.

Recovered a little, Minogue said that it was a cavil.

"How do you mean?"

"I think that Monsieur M. was taking a poke at Hegel and Idealists in general."

"I thought it was contrary enough for you, all right, Da."

"I think it has to do with standing things on their head," she added.

"Or on their ear, drunk," Kathleen said.

"Karl Marx stood Hegel on his head, you see," Iseult replied airily.

"He did what?" Minogue asked.

"Turned him inside out. Got down to brass tacks with the real world. Hegel was airy-fairy basically. Everything was ideas for him at the end of the day."

"Is this part of your training to be a teacher?" Kathleen asked.

"No. Pat told me. He's interested in that stuff, too. As well as the psychology."

Electrodes. Conditioning. Primates. Hegel, Minogue reflected. This Pat might yet be troublesome.

"Aren't you very lucky to have met a philosopher and psychologist in one?" Minogue murmured.

CHAPTER 9

Kenyon had his first contact from Moore just after three o'clock that afternoon. It had arrived from the bank, typed up, marked "transcribed and complete." The envelope, which was addressed to Mr Glover, had been hand-delivered to Bowers. On the face of it, Moore was reporting his progress to his liaison in Sampson Coutts Bank. He had telephoned and, as arranged, asked that his news be passed on the Mr Glover. His message was that he was landed and installed in a hotel. He had spoken with the investigating officer, Sergeant Minogue. He was to meet him on Wednesday at mid-day. Moore would phone later "re accreditation." That telegraphic term meant that Moore had sought what clearances he needed to get into Combs' house.

Moore's second message came at seven-thirty. The secretary who took the call merely announced herself and taped a monologue. It took her forty minutes to transcribe what Moore had said. She photocopied the three pages and telephoned Mr Glover. A messenger had the envelope on Kenyon's desk within twenty minutes.

Moore had moved quickly, he read. The leisurely, remote phone manner must have been for public consumption, Kenyon mused. Moore had been in Dublin only since lunchtime, but he had already contacted Minogue and a senior civil servant in the Department of Justice. He had also been in touch with a Mr Hynes, who went by the deceptive title of Assistant Secretary in a department called Foreign Affairs. It was Hynes who had prompted him to call the Department of Justice, where his call would now be expected, seeing as Hynes had referred to them the matter of what Moore might want. Moore, that bookish and slightly arrogant don, calculated that he'd have the necessary authorisation, in writing, by mid-day tomorrow.

Kenyon sniggered and shook his head. He felt his stomach loosen, a late reminder of the tension which he didn't want to admit. The phrase which offered him the relief and mirth had come at the end of the lawyer's call. Had Moore purposely uttered the phrase: subject to verification from my principals at the firm? Kenyon wondered if spy paperbacks which called MI5 "The Firm" were known at all in Ireland.

Minogue laid Mme Bovary and her waning fortunes aside. Iseult was baking something in the kitchen. This disturbed him. She didn't cook as a habit. Perhaps she was preparing for the domestic role with yours truly, Pat the Brain. Marx stood Hegel on his head. Ireland stood Minogue on his head. Pat the Brain has stood my daughter on her head. Was this a good thing?

He listened to Kathleen's fountain pen. The living room scene could have been a study for the Dutch school. Twilight, wan evening glow on the side of Kathleen's face. What on earth was she writing? Letters, still? Maybe she was writing poems. Had he not noticed? Maybe that's what one of her poems was about, too: "On the blind narcissism of men: my husband, for example." God help him if she slashed like Sylvia Plath.

"What are you at?" he tried.

"I'm writing letters. It's not often I do it, so I'm going to plug away at it until I get sick of it," she murmured.

"What's your daughter up to with the cooking? Nest-building?"

"Don't be interrupting me. She's making muffins."

Sorry for asking. Where was Daithi? Better not ask the boy's mother.

Minogue fingered the Magritte postcard. He looked at it again in the yellowing light. He was afraid to turn on the light for fear of disturbing Kathleen. She was pacing herself to the daylight. Like talk, it didn't matter that the daylight had almost gone. Soon she'd look up from her papers astounded: do you know, she'd say, I didn't know it was dark; no wonder I can't see what I'm writing.

Things inverted, things turned upside down. Very clever boyo, that Magritte. Look at it. The promise of water, all ready to drink in a tumbler, the umbrella skin-tight against its ribs waiting for the water that wouldn't come. Sort of impossible but possible too, maybe? It was an odd feeling, one that made him smile, a feeling of reordering after that vagueness of recognition. He thought of Magritte's *Key of Dreams*, pictures of objects with wrong names. Ha ha, very clever entirely.

The phone rang. Minogue knew it was Kilmartin before Iseult picked up the phone. She called out of him. There was flour on the handle of the phone.

"Hello, is this Matt?"

It was a woman's voice, not unfamiliar. She sounded breathless.

"Yes, it is. Speaking."

"This is Maura, Matt. I'm calling from the hospital. Jim had a bit of a turn."

Her voice wavered a little.

"Today around four. He called the nurse on the buzzer because he was feeling a bit queer," she continued. "But he was able to say a few words to me and he asked me to call you. Maybe it was something important ye were dealing with together, I don't know. Work."

"What is it, Maura?"

"They think it's a lightning infection," she replied. "They told us there was a big risk of infection on account of the part of the system, the body, don't you know. And he was taken very quickly with the symptoms."

Minogue heard rustling. Maura sniffed.

"How serious is this, Maura?"

"Wisha, you know how they fib to you. I think they don't know. Jim's no spring chicken anymore. They do be talking about an inflammation. Then it's something-itis. Then it's 'shock.'"

Minogue heard more rustling, the phone being pushed into clothes, held.

"You know how he consults you, Matt," she resumed nasally now. "This isn't the time to be beating around the bush. And I'm not phoning you to come in or anything. It's just that he mentioned you."

"I'll be in directly. Would you like me to bring you in a bit of grub? Have you tea and a few fags for yourself?"

"No, no, no. He's fast asleep, so he is. They have a tube in him and they want him conked out for a while. They have machines and yokes plugged into

155

him so he's in no danger. Ah no, there's no point in you coming in, thanks very much."

"Any little thing now, Maura?"

"No, no thanks. Tomorrow maybe."

Minogue remembered their son in the States.

"Have you anyone with you?"

"My sister and her husband are up staying. The will of God they came up to Dublin yesterday. Margaret'll stay as long as she's needed."

She sounded strong, too, Minogue surmised as he hung up. He went slowly toward the kitchen to make the tea which customarily saw Kathleen and himself in front of the telly watching the news. Kathleen came out from the living room, squinting.

"I'm half-blind, I am. Who was that on the phone?" she said.

"Maura Kilmartin. Jimmy took a turn in the hospital. Nothing we can do for her tonight, I'm afraid. He's looked after as best as can be done. It's an infection, some blood thing. He was very chipper the other day, I will say. Maybe that was a sign," Minogue reflected.

" 'You know not the day nor the hour,' " Kathleen whispered in awe.

Although the muffins were warm and piquant from the lemon, Minogue received little succour from them. Later, when the news began splashing images of Beirut on the screen, he levered himself up from the chair. As he stood up, the Magritte postcard fell out of his book. He picked it up and replaced it inside the front cover. Turned on its head; inside out. Inverted, the surprise: a fresh approach. Minogue took a swallow of tea and turned a page. The print was meaningless, but he tried harder to read.

Minogue abed could not sleep. He brooded instead. Better than four out of five murders were done by family or acquaintances of the victim. More concern for Combs now that he was dead. Living like that, awaiting disposal in the morgue. Who to send this man Combs back to? He heard Kathleen lock the kitchen door and test it. There was some odd, scattery music coming from Iseult's room. New Music, they called it, music with lots of beats in it. It reminded Minogue of Charlie Chaplin caught up in a conveyor belt.

The house settled on itself with ticks and creaks. The weather forecast had said that clear skies would be coming their way overnight, all the way from Norway, if you please. Jimmy Kilmartin might finally and involuntarily have secured a wife's attendance at his bed with the turn he took. Minogue wondered if it wasn't a bloodclot and the hospital had fibbed to Maura. He imagined a clot finding its way up arteries, around bends, unknown to Jimmy until it struck. More sounds from the end of the day: taps being turned on, brushing from the bathroom. The toilet flushed. Water spiralled quietly, gurgling down a pipe somewhere. All the things you miss when you don't pay attention to them, he thought. What would Jimmy do now? He might lose a faculty if it was a stroke.

Minogue was still pretending to be asleep when he heard Daithi come in the hall door. His movements had the excessive carefulness of the guilty drunk. He dropped his keys on the mat in the hall. Minogue heard him swear in what his son would have thought was a whisper. At least Kathleen hadn't stirred.

Minogue stole out of the bed. He managed not to step on his slippers as he eased his dressing-gown from the hook on the door. He glanced at Kathleen's face in the pallid light from the landing. Asleep still. He remembered the creaking step near the top of the stairs and avoided it entirely. It was quiet downstairs now. Had Daithi gone out again? The hall light was still on. Minogue stopped and listened. He heard the steady, brittle tick as the pendulum swung on Kathleen's antique clock in the living room. A scratch then, surely someone lighting a match. Minogue opened the door to the living room. The lamp over the television was on now. Daithi was slouched in the armchair with a cigarette handy in the ashtray. His eyes were closed. Minogue smelled the beer-breath from the doorway. His eyes still closed, Daithi reached out for the cigarette again.

"Smoking in your sleep, is it?" Minogue murmured.

Daithi started from the chair, his eyes bulging. The ashtray clattered to the floor. Daithi scrambled after it. He lifted the cigarette before it had burned into the floor.

"Jases, Da, don't do that. You nearly gave me a heart attack."

"I thought you were asleep. I didn't want you burning the house down."

He saw in Daithi's eyes the glaze of tiredness and detachment which drink brought.

"Just having a smoke before I hit the sack," said Daithi. He began stubbing the cigarette. "But sure it's past my bedtime."

"Hold your horses there like a good man. Now that we're here," Minogue began, "it's not often we get the chance, that our paths cross, I mean . . . "

Daithi's chin went down as he gave his father a baleful look. Minogue recognised the exaggerated gesture, even more ham coming from someone who had drink on them.

"You're not going to give me a lecture, are you?"

"I was half-thinking of it," Minogue answered. "But I don't want to waken the house. Can you keep your voice down?"

Daithi's face matched the conspiratorial whisper.

"Can't you do it tomorrow, the lecture?"

"It's not really a lecture at all. I just wanted to know ... how you are and so on," Minogue whispered.

He sat on the edge of the coffee table. He wondered if his anger was lurking about close by, somewhere he couldn't detect it. Daithi took the butt from the packet and relit it.

"Like, life? The meaning of life and all that?"

"Something like that, yes."

"Well," Daithi said as his eyes fixed on the thin rope of rising smoke, "I'm studying for me exams so I don't make an iijit of myself and fail them again. Then a job, I suppose. Am I getting warm?"

"You're not an iijit at all."

"I'm an iijit to the expen — to the extent, I mean, that I should have had me exam the first time around. It's a waste to be studying again."

"Don't you learn better this time around?"

Daithi drew on the cigarette.

"I dunno. It's not exactly the most thrilling stuff."

"Are you anxious for a change, maybe?"

Daithi blew out a think stream of smoke.

"Aren't we all, Da?"

Minogue almost stopped then. He felt the anger like a bull behind the gate, pawing the ground.

"Restless, though?" Minogue tried.

"You get fed up slogging away at the same stuff," Daithi murmured, watching the ribbon of smoke. "Especially if you let people down by not doing something right the first time around."

"Who's sitting in judgement here? You didn't let me down at all. Nor your mother. You're too tough on yourself. A harsh judge. Did you ever read any of that Scott Fitzgerald fella?"

Daithi shook his head.

"*The Great Gatsby*. Lovely stuff. Nick says this: 'Reserving judgement is a matter of infinite hope.' Nice one, hah?"

"Maybe I should have done the artsy-fartsy stuff like Iseult does, or Pat."

"The psychology, is it?"

"Yes. All you have to do is write a load of bullshit and they won't fail you. It's easy for them. There's no right or wrong answers."

Minogue thought about that for a moment. His son blew a well-formed smoke ring across the room.

"Did you get to thinking that maybe you'd have liked to try some of that stuff instead of what you're at now?"

Daithi's snort quivered a smoke ring hanging in the air between them.

"Does it really count in the end?"

"In the end of what?"

"Jobs, the future. The real world. I mean, does anyone really care about that stuff anymore? Everyone's still shooting and starving one another when you turn on the news."

Minogue's thoughts back-pedalled.

"It's true for you, I'm sure," he allowed. "Anybody'd get tired of stuff and they studying for so long. It's natural to want a break, isn't it?"

"You're telling me," said Daithi slowly. Minogue took his chance then.

"But hardly in a pub every evening."

Daithi stubbed out the cigarette with care and returned his father's gaze.

"It's not every evening. And who says I'm in a pub anytime I'm not here around the house?"

"I have no small experience with drink myself, Daithi. Before you were born, I'm glad to say."

"So you can't preach, then," Daithi said quickly.

It had slipped out, Minogue realised instantly. Daithi knew it, too.

"If you're looking for hypocrisy in people, you'll find any amount there, easy enough. But you won't find much else if that's your approach."

"I didn't use that word."

"You would have liked to. You'd have been entitled to."

Daithi shook his head in exasperation. Minogue's thoughts raced.

"Ah, Jases, let's forget I ever mentioned it." Daithi placed his hands on his knees, anxious to go.

"I wish you'd stop saying 'Jases.' It distresses your mother no end. It's a coarse expression."

"And she told you to lay down the law about it. Even though you're . . . "

"I'm what?"

"Ah, come on. Ma's the only Catholic left in the house. Didn't anyone tell you?"

"All I'm asking is that you don't give her offence with it."

Daithi stifled a belch and yawned.

"You know what I'd like to know? How come you never got up and emigrated to the States like you used to talk about?"

Minogue scrambled for an answer but found none.

"You see?" Daithi pressed home with his finger jabbing the air. "You're all right. You have your trips to Paris and your books and your ideas to play with, but what does it all add up to?"

Words ricocheted around Minogue's mind, but they would not settle. Daithi stood up.

"It adds up to a compromise, I suppose," Minogue said at last.

"Who's being hard on himself now, but?" a rearguard Daithi asked, swallowing another yawn. It seemed like a grimace of pain to Minogue. He wanted to tell Daithi that he loved him, but the atmosphere seemed to curtail emotion. The anger had receded. Minogue felt the first creeping touch of sadness, familiar and inchoate. Failure? Couldn't put it in words for Daithi. *My own son, I can't talk to.*

Daithi stumbled on the leg of the sofa as he headed for the hallway. Reflexively, Minogue grabbed his son's arm. Daithi turned, surprised. The embarrassment swept the slackness from his face. Both knew what had happened and that neither would say anything about it. Minogue's hand still remembered grasping Daithi's arm.

"There is life after school, you know," Minogue offered.

"So I hear," Daithi murmured. "The house, the kids and the mortgage. Mow the cat and feed the lawn and all that."

"You're not even asleep and you're having nightmares."

"Goodnight, Da."

"I'm going to work on a good speech, you know. I'll have all the answers next time," Minogue whispered after him.

Had Minogue caved in and taken a nip of whisky from the cupboard then, he might have been tempted to turn on the radio very low to see what classical music the BBC was putting out at this hour for insomniac aesthetes. At any rate, the BBC didn't carry the news until the following morning.

Radio Telefis Eireann called it "an ambush" in their late headlines, which came on just before the television service signed off at a quarter to twelve. The motorbike had followed Mervyn Ball along Ailesbury Road from Donnybrook — no great distance — but the tag car had been parked just beyond the Y turnoff to Shrewsbury Road. Ball had looked into his mirror to see the motorbike's beam still bobbing, following him onto Shrewsbury Road. He had a few seconds to decide that this might be something to worry about.

Ball down-shifted his Saab from the third gear into second. He kicked the accelerator onto the floor and held it there. The Saab shot ahead and he pushed it back into third. The motorbike kept pace, however. There were no other cars moving on the road. Ball thought there were two figures on the motorbike. He was less than two minutes from the British Embassy and residence on Merrion Road. Unlike the Ambassador's armour-plated Daimler, Ball did not rate a carphone. He glanced in the mirror again. The light seemed to be falling back a little. He was into the top end of third gear now, at seventy-five miles an hour, with a finger's width left on the tachometer before the needle would enter the red. Could it just be two twits fresh out of the pub, farting about, looking for a lark?

Ball almost went for his brakes when he saw the car pulling slowly out from the row of parked cars ahead. He held his hand on the horn and shouted instead. The car did not stop. It turned out almost broadside onto the road. Ball's foot itched and wavered over the brake pedal. The engine's torque slowed the Saab quicker than he had expected. He remembered that he was still in third gear. The car ahead stopped abruptly in the middle of the road. Ball shouted again, knowing that he had been caught. He remembered, or rather, his reflexes acted to head for the rear of the car which straddled the broken line ahead. Ball felt the surprise start at his diaphragm and run up his face like a current where it was now shock. Like an electric jolt, it raced to his scalp and seemed to leap off, taking the top of his head with it. He wanted to deny, to make something stop. Everything was so completely unfair. There had to be a chance to explain. He heard himself shout again and a part of him, oddly disengaged and slowed and crazily patient, told him he was panicking.

It had been drilled into Ball in training that a driver, no matter how experienced, almost never had a blocking car ready in reverse gear if the quarry tried to squeeze through the trap behind. The back of a car was lighter when struck and in any forward gear the car would have at least some give so that it could be shunted. If the quarry was going fast enough and the impact was near to ninety degrees, that is.

Ball's twelve thousand quid's worth of seven-month-old Saab screeched through the gap behind the car. It glanced off the back bumper, shuddering, and bounced to the side as it hit. Ball saw the other car hop, a hand come up against a face in the window. All the glass in the passenger side of the Saab came out as he careened off the parked cars. The Saab slowed as it ran along their sides. Ball saw the bonnet pop up in front of him, but the safety latch held. Sparks showered in through the broken windows along with the deafening shriek of metal on metal. The steering seemed to have given out. He wrenched the wheel and the Saab slewed into a course which wavered over toward the right-hand side of the road. The horrible rending of metal and glass stopped. Ball jerked at the wheel and felt the car's suspension hit bottom as he brought it back to the middle of the road. He was down to twenty miles an hour. There were car headlights in the distance.

Ball felt an exhilaration surging up through his chest. Everything was clear and sharp. There was a hissing in his ears. He looked in the mirror and saw a figure standing by the open door of the car which was now facing back up Shrewsbury Road. No sign of the motorbike. He pressed the horn and held it. The yellow quartz streetlights flooded, emptied and flooded a garish light into the car as it picked up speed again. He noticed that his hands had been cut. His face felt warm. Even with the air rushing in the windows, he could smell his own beery breath and the comforting stench of his own sweat. His head was pulsing.

He saw the motorcycle at the last minute. It was a big Japanese bike. Its petrol tank dully reflected the Saab's tail-lights as it drew alongside. The two helmeted riders looked like giant ants, Martians, something out of science fiction. Ball stopped thinking. For that endless second before the passenger pulled the trigger, Ball knew. The hand clasped over the clip to steady the pistol, the extended stock jammed into his hip, the passenger crouched for the recoil. Ball tried in vain to find eyes behind the tinted glass on the full-face helmets.

The first shots caught Ball in the neck and chest. His foot was jerked off the accelerator and he was beaten into the passenger seat by their impact. He was dead before the Saab wavered slowly over to the far side of the road and dug into a parked van. The car spun as it bounced and rolled over, scattering glass and chrome trim along the pavement. Engine off now, it lay on its side in the middle of the road.

The Kawasaki dipped suddenly on its front forks and skidded to a stop. The driver held his legs out to steady the bike as he turned it and cruised slowly by the wreck. The passenger stood on the footrests and fired into the car's interior until the clip was empty. The driver revved the engine, crunched first gear as he found it, and leaned over the handlebars as he opened the throttle.

"Who did you say again?" Minogue spoke through scrambled eggs. He was still tired after a night of dreams, most of which he had forgotten. He had tottered down the stairs still thinking of the dream about horses. Horses galloping, horses tearing away from tethers, horses rearing.

"Urr whurr the urr gurr murr durr?" Iseult said.

"Who was it?"

"Senility all right," Iseult said brightly. "Regression to cave-man talk."

Minogue had inhaled a piece of egg. He began coughing uncontrollably. He stood up and edged over to the sink, coughing and spluttering.

"Ah, go on, do you really think I'm that funny?" Iseult said.

"The fella in the embassy," Minogue wheezed out before another spasm of coughing erupted.

"Ugh. You talk like one of those dirty old men in raincoats," said Iesult.

Kathleen slapped her husband sharply between the shoulder blades.

"Are you trying to finish me off entirely, for the love of God?" he wheezed. "That's a very agricultural belt you landed on me."

"Whisht, would you and you'd hear the news."

Kathleen rested her arms on Minogue's shoulders while he leaned over the sink, listening.

"Very touching," Iseult commented. "At your age. Give her a squeeze, Da."

"I know him," Minogue croaked, wiping his eyes.

"You know who, lovey?" asked Kathleen.

"That man, Ball. He's a Second Secretary at the British Embassy."

He felt Kathleen withdraw a little. Any mention of "British" or "embassy" brought her back recollections of her nights in the chair by her husband's hospital bed.

"And what's more, I was due to talk to him, I think."

They listened to the announcer's bland, mid-Atlantic tones.

"A telephone call to the *Irish Times* claimed responsibility on behalf of the Irish National Liberation Army. The statement said that the INLA had received information that Mr Ball was in charge of intelligence gathering on its members in the South and that he was responsible for the murder of Mr Tommy Costello, a well-know republican and member of the INLA, abducted in County Monaghan two years ago. . . . Mr Costello is thought to have been the victim of a power struggle within the ranks of the INLA as to the movement's campaign of violence in Northern Ireland . . . "

"Madmen, the whole lot of them," Kathleen whispered.

" . . . The INLA statement also pronounced what it termed a sentence of death on Mr Ball and any other person co-operating with him. A spokesman for the British Embassy refused comment on the incident or on the allegations."

Minogue sat back at the table. Kathleen remained by the sink, her arms folded in front of her.

"What does this have to do with you, Matt? You said that you weren't involved in this racket any more. And I recall telling Jimmy Kilmartin that I didn't want my hus — "

"Now look it, Kathleen," Minogue began.

"Now look it, yourself."

"Don't be arguing in front of the children, you two," Iseult broke in. "I'm very impressionable and sensitive. You don't know the harm you could be doing."

Kathleen turned to her daughter. Iseult fled the kitchen.

"I don't want you getting involved with this stuff, do you hear me. You know what I'm talking about. Gun-play and those thugs. You've paid your dues and done more than anyone else in that line. How far are you from retirement now? There's your family to think of."

"And me long-suffering wife. If there's any chance of — "

"There'd better not be."

Keating was sitting on Eilis' desk and offering her gentle taunts when Minogue arrived. Minogue phoned the Special Branch and asked for Pat Corrigan. While he waited for someone to answer, he watched Eilis blow smoke up into Keating's face. It did not budge him off her desk.

"Don't be getting your knickers in a knot now, Detective Keating," she murmured.

Corrigan was not in his office, but he could be reached by cellular. Minogue redialled. Corrigan answered with a cough.

"Matt Minogue? The man himself. Where are you?"

"I'm in a space rocket and I'm hovering over your nice new shiny car with your shiny telephone, Pat."

"You nearly had me looking out the window for you. What's with you?"

"Think of me as Jim Kilmartin but without the rank. I'm working on a very odd case here in the Squad. I might need something solid to break open the damn investigation."

"You're always in the thick of things, Matt. Much in demand, hah?"

"Not as busy as yourself this morning, I'll wager," Minogue probed.

"Aha. You heard," Corrigan replied grimly. "Very bad work done on this poor fella. We warn them about socialising on their own, you know. It's not in my basket this morning, though, thanks be to God. There's a dozen security-types in from London already,

168

hush-hush. We're supposed to treat them like royalty and give them free rein. Did it come to your Squad yet?"

"A letter from Justice on Jimmy's desk this morning to tell us to wait until we're wanted. The English lads want it all to themselves on account of it being an embassy thing."

"You're as well off to be told to wait by the door with this. They'll use the Technical Bureau for evidence gathering, I hear . . . ?"

"That's all they want from us, yes. But Pat, I need to talk about this poor Ball fella."

Corrigan didn't reply.

"I'm working on a case where an Englishman was murdered. Ball's telephone number was on a little list he had in his house. They tell me that Ball's job was to look after UK nationals living here. Tell them when their pensions go up and remind them about free coal allowances, that class of thing. All very polite and above-board, thanks very much."

"But?"

"Well, I'd have had to be talking to poor Ball sooner or later in connection with this case, you see. It seems more important now, if you follow my meaning."

Corrigan caught the emphasis. His voice took on the ancestral tone of his peasant forefathers bargaining over the price which no one wanted to mention aloud.

"Oh yes. Oh yes. But this is a very delicate matter. There's going to be skin and hair flying over this effort. . . . This person was English, you say?"

"An elderly man. We're making rather heavy weather of it so far, do you see."

"Aha."

Minogue sensed Corrigan's interest. He felt his own impatience growing.

"Well," Minogue said finally. "If we can't be talking too much over this yoke, we had better meet."

"All right so," Corrigan said slowly. Minogue had the impression that Corrigan was distracted, writing something while he talked.

"Off the premises, if it's all the same to you, Pat. Bewley's Cafe in Westmoreland Street, the self-serve nearest Fleet Street. Is a quarter after ten good?"

Corrigan grunted.

"Same as ever, Matt. Fair enough."

CHAPTER 10

"Do sit down, James. Please."

Kenyon caught the sarcasm, but he didn't care now.

"Really, I insist. I'm not at all prepared for a fit from you."

"What the hell is Murray doing, running this operation?"

"Murray is not running the operation, James. He's part of a group gone to Dublin to sort this mess out. The offer of a chair still holds," Robertson added ominously.

"For Christ's sake, Hugh. His embassy man is shot to bits last night and Murray is already half-way across the Irish Sea by now — "

Robertson looked at his watch.

"Landed by now, I'd say, James."

"Landed in bloody Dublin after leaving us here tied up in knots. While *he* decides what has to be done and when. I can't believe it. And I'm being told that Murray isn't running the show?"

"James. Sit down, would you? I can't talk to a moving target. Let me go through it again. Murray is not running anything. We've just been asked to hold our investigation under advice from Murray. The immediate stuff has to be done first. The coppers in Dublin are being very damned co-operative. Murray has to be there if anything of Ball's work leaks out. That's all. Murray went through the Deputy Under Sec in the Foreign Office. He chairs the liaison meetings between the Foreign Office and MI6. Murray got territorial, that's all. 'Ball was ours, Combs was ours, let's fix this ourselves.' He convinced Chapman and they got to the Foreign Secretary. The Foreign Sec knows damn well that Murray is MI6. He took it up with the PMO and her ladyship issued her edict on it. She doesn't want a ripple. We're to freeze what we're doing and keep out of the way while Murray and company seal the business as best they can."

"Seal? Band-aid solutions. It's becoming unstuck every minute, that's pretty plain to me."

Kenyon sat down, still shaking his head.

"But can't you see we may have some edge out of this? The Irish are very embarrassed about security now that an attaché has been murdered. They'll be more tractable in the conference because of it, James."

"Stinks," Kenyon retorted.

"Tell me," Robertson tried to divert, "what should we make of this Costello business?"

Kenyon slumped further into the chair. He paused before answering his Director. Robertson waited, balancing his pen delicately in the palm of his left hand.

When Kenyon spoke, his voice had softened.

"It doesn't make sense to me. I just did a brief check on this. Costello's down as a part of a feud in the INLA. There was a run of killings then, all part of the same squabble. Some wanted to go more political and others wanted more military targets. Costello's death sparked off other revenge killings. He was shot to bits and had his throat slit. A real horror show, right down to the message daubed on the car window in Costello's blood. Something in Gaelic about him being a traitor."

"Good riddance, hmm?"

"No tears shed here."

Kenyon yawned. He remembered reading that a yawn was a sign of repressed anger. He had been up since three.

"So they used Costello's name as an excuse?" Robertson probed. "A martyr, sort of?"

"The INLA? You can't take anything they say at face value. They might have suspected Ball was an intelligence officer. I'm sure the Irish Special Branch had Ball as a probable operative, just by powers of deduction from our staff numbers. There could have been a leak from their police. You just can't believe anything the INLA put out. They could have said that Ball was the oppressor of the Irish people for the last eight centuries."

"Their myth-making is that, shall I say, hyperbolic?"

Kenyon shrugged.

"You should read some of the interrogation transcripts I got from Defence intelligence when they picked up some of them in Belfast last year. They have a looney logic to them. Costello would be alive today if the British had never come to Ireland eight hundred years ago. Ball is British. We think he's an intelligence officer. Therefore, Ball led to Costello's murder. Something like that. Anything goes with them."

"Refresh me a tad on the INLA, would you?" Robertson asked.

"They're mostly ex-IRA and a few with overlapping memberships and loyalties," Kenyon began wearily. "Some INLA operations have had the direct support of the Provos. The Provos used to use them, supplied them and sheltered them but denied any link. They're what the Ulster Freedom Fighters or the Red Hand is to the Loyalist mob, the UDA. They're also nutters. Grown up under the gun."

"Something like the PLO-Black September exercises?"

"Yes. But they have their family squabbles, too. The INLA are very bad news indeed. That Costello killing had all the marks of an INLA job. They like to 'make examples.' They think the Provo leadership is too soft and they won't listen to them. We've put over twenty of them through the Diplock courts in Northern Ireland. All except three or four were for murder. They had a campaign going against prison warders and police. They're worried about the INLA in Dublin, too, I expect, and not just because of this thing last night alone. Three of their police were killed by the INLA, if I remember. Scores of bank jobs and a few punishment killings in the South, too. Then there was that feud started off by the Costello thing. . . . "

"So the mention of Costello is misleading?"

"Ask Murray. He handles the breakdown for the Foreign Sec and the Home Office, too."

"Um. Let's not keep coming back to Murray, James."

"I was just stating facts," Kenyon muttered. "Murray was the analyst. He'd know more than I would."

"All right, I see that. Don't forget, though, Murray has his way for the time being. The edict is that whatever we're doing in Dublin has to come through Murray for the moment. Murray has taken direct control of all intelligence work out of the embassy right now. We simply have to be sensitive to the negotiations."

"It's a security alert,'" said Kenyon.

"It's a security alert," Robertson continued, ignoring the sarcasm. "We're to keep out of his way and anything we are running there is his business, as of this morning. That's the directive. He can tell us to shut down and get out if he thinks the work is at risk, James. Tiptoe, softly softly."

"Murray hasn't actually told us to get Moore out of there, has he?"

"Not yet he hasn't," Robertson replied with an effort. "We can continue until such time as he thinks we're a potential balls-up. I outlined the operation because the PMO asked me to. That's how Murray knows about Moore snooping around for us in Dublin. I may not like it — you evidently don't like it — but if we can sign a border security deal or get better extradition for IRA men and that saves the life of one of our lads there . . . ?"

Kenyon breathed out heavily.

"Hugh, you make me feel like a shit. But don't ask me to approve of Murray. Look at the mess he's gotten us into already."

"He may be a double-dehydrated shit, James, but we have to swallow our puke for the moment."

The image repelled Kenyon. He shivered.

"Any yield from Moore, and he has to at least show it to Murray in Dublin; that's the net effect right now. Murray may have to evaluate it on the spot and do whatever he needs to do security-wise then and there. I want you to tell Moore to stand by for an order to get to hell out of Dublin if that's what Murray thinks is necessary. And if he does find anything, he has to set up an RDV with Murray and show him any material he has."

Kenyon let out a long breath.

"Will do, Hugh," he said softly.

"Now, what's the risk to Moore at the moment?" Robertson asked.

"I don't see how they could connect Moore to Combs. All Moore has to do is to do his job and keep his eyes open."

175

Robertson nodded.

"He'll know what is happening," Kenyon added. "If he thinks there's a mark on him, we'll pull him out immediately. He can walk in the door of the embassy as a last resort. We have no reason to worry about him right now. Moore is actually doing quite well. . . . "

The atmosphere in Robertson's office felt less strained now. The silence between the two men floated on a vague hum of traffic outside.

"Can I quote you on that, James?" Robertson tried to bring some relief to his subordinate. Kenyon picked up on a less agreeable interpretation. He left Robertson's office with the question trailing him, driven home by Robertson's parting remark, one which was far less ambiguous.

"Be sure to call me on any contact with Moore, James. Just so as we stay in touch on this."

Corrigan was a robust Garda Inspector in his mid-forties. What could have been a belly on him was on his chest instead. Minogue noticed that Corrigan had had his hair styled. When Minogue last worked with him, Corrigan had been a sergeant in the Special Branch. In the five intervening years, he seemed to have gotten younger. Perhaps it was the confidence which rank brought him. He had all his own teeth or else very good dentures, Minogue observed. Probably the latter, Minogue guessed as he walked away from the cashier, seeing as Corrigan had a broken nose from his favourite sport, hurling. As he drew closer to Corrigan's table, Minogue noticed the eyes again. For a tough nut — and he was Wyatt Earp when he had been stationed at the border — Corrigan had clear, soft grey woman's eyes. Minogue would have liked to tag the word *vulpine* on those eyes, but he could detect no signs of concupiscence in him. As though to compensate for the gentle eyes, Corrigan's eyebrows were bushy prominences.

Corrigan tested the seams on a classy-looking light sports jacket when he reached out to shake Minogue's hand. Minogue, no willow himself, saw his cup of coffee shake in his other hand while Corrigan pumped vigorously.

"How's the man?" Corrigan smiled. The lines out from his eyes drew the eyebrows down more.

"Pulling the divil by the tail, Pat. And how's yourself and all belonging to you?"

"Great."

Minogue dug a lump of dried brown sugar out of the bowl and plopped it into his cup.

"And how do you like your new premises, the Puzzle Palace?" Minogue inquired, referring to the Special Branch's move from Dublin Castle to Harcourt Square.

"It's like Phoenix, Arizona, or someplace."

Minogue laughed aloud and let the pleasantries settle while he stirred his coffee.

"Well, thanks for coming over, Pat. I hope you're not discomfitted. Do you know about this Combs man?"

"Murdered? Over the weekend?" Corrigan asked.

"That's the one. The well is dry on this so far, you see. But the name Ball — your business — his telephone number was on a little list that Combs had by his phone at home."

Corrigan nodded noncommittally. Both men made use of their cups and spoons now, each pretending to be absorbed in his coffee.

"The thought crossed my mind, Pat, that — "

"That your business might be connected with mine?"

"You're very quick off the mark. What do you think?"

Corrigan paused and breathed out heavily before he sat up, elbowing onto the table.

"Let's be practical now. I checked your Mr Combs after you phoned me. There's nothing in our files. He's not connected with the British Embassy so far as I know."

"Well, Pat, I asked myself if it was enough for Mr Combs to be English for the IRA or their likes to kill him. Only a passing thought, really. They wouldn't kill him the way it was done anyway, though. Maybe I shouldn't be asking you."

"Go ahead, you can if you like. The crowd that killed Ball last night, they meant business. There was at least three of them. More, I'll bet. Someone tagged him at that eating house or pub he was at and they let him drive his moth home. Very chivalrous. The fella on the motorbike used a sub-machine gun on Ball. Typical of the action men in the INLA out for the kill."

"Have you got anyone picked up for it yet?"

"We picked up two INLA fellas in Castleknock, see if we can shake anything out of them up in the Bridewell," Corrigan went on. "But they were gangsters from the North, we're almost certain. There were four or five jobs like this one done in the North since last September. We think they have a unit that specialises in this stuff only. We had one strong name from the Brits, but he's at home in bed in Derry this morning."

"What about them telling the papers that Ball was some class of intelligence man?" Minogue asked.

Corrigan scratched the back of his ear.

"Ah, they'd have to say something like that. You know yourself, Matt. Make it sound like they had a reason."

Minogue spoke to Corrigan without looking at him.

"Is it all classified, Pat?"

Corrigan made an effort to smile.

178

"Sure isn't everything classified these days?"

Corrigan hadn't been quite able to carry it off.

"Did the INLA work something out about Ball and intelligence work here?"

Minogue watched Corrigan work harder at appearing relaxed.

"Sure isn't that what I'm telling you? They'd make up any kind of a yarn or excuse for a bit of gun-play. You know, make hay out of it for their outfit."

Corrigan leaned further over the table to confide.

"Now you know and I know that there's still an unspoken agreement for there to be no stunts like this here in the South. I can say this in confidence to a fellow member of the Gardai. Now you know more about the INLA anyway, more than would others, so what I'm saying will be no big news to yourself. What has me and my higher-ups jittery about this is that the rules aren't sticking. . . . "

Minogue nodded.

"Yes, Pat. But the INLA are out of their minds at the best of times," Minogue said gently. "Since when did they care a damn what the public thinks? Didn't they break away from the Provos because they thought the Provos cared too much for what the man in the street thought?"

Minogue looked into Corrigan's eyes as he spoke. The friendliness was quite gone now, as though a window had been closed behind them.

"True for you. But like I was saying, that's what we're wondering about. If this is a whole new way of operating on their part. A new campaign. New rules."

Corrigan sat back in his chair, disengaging himself. He drained his cup and replaced it carefully on the saucer. Then he winked at Minogue. He sat upright. Minogue watched Corrigan labour again to look jovial when he whispered.

"British intelligence at work in Ireland, I ask you," Corrigan said. "That'd make a change, wouldn't it? They never applied any in the country before."

Minogue agreed with the thrust of the conceit, but he could only manage a smile.

"Who needs any fecking spies lurking around here, Matt? Go into any pub in Dublin and you'll know everything that's going on. The country's a bloody sieve. Here, look now. Tell me a bit about the case you're on."

Minogue knew that Corrigan was trying to get something for nothing. It took him but three minutes to give Corrigan the gist of his investigation. He did not embellish any detail.

"And you're looking for a handle?"

Minogue nodded. He felt a barrier, an invisible line running down the table between them. He knew that Pat Corrigan was preoccupied by the assassination of Ball. Minogue did not dislike Corrigan. Minogue also knew enough of the workings of the Special Branch to understand that Corrigan had to be circumspect. He looked around the cafe. Bewley's was one of his cathedrals. He recalled the phrase that he had heard on the news: "had received information." And what did that mean? Given the choice of the two most likely alternatives, Minogue guessed that someone had tipped off the INLA. They didn't maintain a network of touts, and even if they did, they'd never have gotten a man — or a woman — close enough to Ball to know for sure what he was about.

Corrigan had regained his agreeable expression. He laid a hand on the saucer and slid it to the centre of the marble table-top.

"You never know, Matt. I tell you what, though. We'll stay in touch, so we will."

Corrigan's car was next to the door to Bewley's. Corrigan smiled briefly at Minogue, then he stretched his arms over his head and groaned.

"That's what you get for being up all night. They called me and me going up the stairs to bed. The perils of being indispensable. Ah sure the holidays are coming up," Corrigan continued, grasping the door-handle. He seemed anxious to restore something which had ebbed from the conversation. Holiday, Minogue thought. *Hegel's Holiday*, the glass of water upright and poised over the umbrella.

"Pat."

Corrigan turned from the open door, the grimly benign smile still holding firm under the grey eyes. Almost like a cat, the eyes, Minogue thought.

"You know how it is with me, Pat. A bit of a crank, I suppose," Minogue began.

Corrigan tried to maintain the smile.

"Do you remember that business with the Ambassador?"

"Could I ever forget it, Matt. You've had it rough."

"To be sure. There were droves of people thought I was owed something after that. Jimmy Kilmartin included. That's why he took me under his wing, I'd say. God knows why really. I was glad to be able to pick meself up out of the bed afterwards. Even drink a pint or two and wake up safe in bed in the morning."

Corrigan snorted, but held the flinty smile. He waited.

"Plenty of people telling me that I could call in a favour any time," Minogue added in a vacant tone. "As I say, I don't know what for. I mean, I was just there by coincidence really. But you don't want to be disabusing people of their notions. Do you know what I'm saying, like?"

"I think I do," Corrigan replied bleakly.

"You were one of those people, you see, Pat. Said to call in my chips with you any time I needed."

Corrigan looked up and down Fleet Street. Minogue scrutinised his face until Corrigan met his gaze again. A double-decker bus, its full diesel roar at the curb opposite, drowned out Corrigan's voice.

"Fire away," Corrigan murmured. Minogue didn't need to hear the words after he noted the expression.

"What about Ball, Pat?"

"Well, what about him?"

"Was he really doing intelligence work here?"

Corrigan was watching each passer-by's face until they passed beyond Minogue. Then he'd shift his scrutiny to a new face so he'd not collide with Minogue's limpid stare.

"Yes, he was. We think. I just hope to God it wasn't a leak from one of ours that cost Ball his life."

Corrigan gathered cheeks full of air and then released them slowly. He looked suddenly resigned, gentle.

"Are you going back to John's Road?" he asked.

Minogue replied that he was.

"Hop in and we'll go that way with you."

Corrigan's driver was a detective, Dunne. He had a head shaped like an egg, pointy end up, upon which the divinity that shaped rural Irish people's ends had pasted elephantine ears. He stopped the car next to Kingsbridge Station. It was five minutes' walk to Minogue's office from here.

Corrigan was jittery. Minogue did not know what to do. Corrigan had explained to him that Ball had merely been the devil they knew. Why raise a fuss when they knew Ball was a tricks man, only to have him transferred and the Gardai track a new man in the job? Someone had to do it. . . . No, they had no way of knowing whether Ball had been in touch with Combs recently. When the guileless Minogue asked why, Corrigan had slapped his knee lightly in an unconvincing gesture of mirth.

"Man dear," Corrigan began, as though explaining venial sin to a child, "sure don't they have the best electronic detection and security in the business? Bar none, the Yanks included. Listen in on their phones, is it? Sure we bought most of our bells and whistles off the British firms. You can be damn sure that they wouldn't be sending the equipment to us if they thought we could be using the stuff on their embassy here without them knowing about it?"

"Uh," Minogue grunted.

"I'm not saying we don't do any of it, but they have a cast-iron system. They have bigger fish than us to worry about."

"How much work did Ball actually do, Pat?"

Corrigan made no reply but looked vacantly up at the sky as if to sight gamebirds for his rifle. Minogue noticed the slice of jug-eared driver's face in the mirror. He was studying Minogue.

"All right, Pat. One more thing though."

Corrigan leaned his head against the glass of the car door, looking down his nose at Minogue. He had a genuine, rueful smile now, as though he knew a cat was out of the bag.

"Plough ahead."

"Did that Costello fella ever spend time here in Dublin? When he was on the run from the North, I mean."

Corrigan's frown returned instantly.

"I don't remember exactly, Matt."

"Can you find out — quicker than myself, I mean — if Costello spent time in south County Dublin?"

Corrigan's panther eyes widened momentarily before narrowing.

"Are you saying what I think you're saying?"

"I suppose I am. Whatever that is."

"Like Costello is somehow linked with your fella? But sure Costello was done in years ago. His own crowd popped him, did a terrible job on him. He was a bad egg anyway, was Costello."

Corrigan bit his lower lip for several seconds, gazing out at the grey stone walls of the train station. Minogue looked to the mirror again. The driver was pretending to be deaf. Minogue yanked at the doorhandle and pushed at the door with his knee.

"Look it, Matt," Corrigan said.

Minogue was taken aback at the tone of solicitude he heard in Corrigan's voice now. He sounded more puzzled than dismissive.

"On the off chance, on the wildest off chance, I'll poke through the files. Maybe not today, but I'll get around to it. Will that do you?"

CHAPTER 11

As soon as he saw the light on the phone, Kenyon knew it would be Moore. It was eleven o'clock. The ache had found its way up his neck to the back of his head. His head pulsed as he reached for the receiver. He paused to squeeze his eyes. The light on the phone flashed again. Kenyon imagined an anonymous listener at Government Communications HQ sitting up, adjusting his headphones. Would they do that to him? He knew that GCHQ could monitor every phone line in the Irish Republic, even the new uplinks to the satellite. It wouldn't be Robertson who'd patch a tap on him for this. It was more likely a casual feature of C's bullish grip on the Service.

"Glover here," said into the phone. His palm was moist.

"Mr Glover? Edward Moore from Dublin. Returning your call."

The bugger sounded almost friendly, Kenyon thought.

"Yes, Edward," Kenyon said. How did a senior partner in a law firm talk to one of the staff?

"I wondered if perhaps you were trying to get in touch with me," Moore said with unmistakable irony.

"Yes. We heard about that incident there. It's all over the papers here. Not affecting your work, I trust." He was remembering Moore's remote manner.

"Not yet, Mr Glover."

Moore wasn't having any of it, evidently.

"How do things look on the ground?"

"I have no reliable way of knowing," replied Moore, the edge of irony still keen. "My appointments still stand. I'll be following up on them. I wondered if perhaps there was something in the works that I mightn't be aware of here."

Kenyon's headache had found its way precipitously to his forehead.

"There's been a change of plans here that you'll need to know about and follow. If you locate the material we discussed, I mean."

Kenyon looked down at his notepad, the doodles which he was drawing heavily and repetitively. He had begun by writing INLA and a question mark. He had tried to obliterate the letters with scribbles. The rest was a jumble of triangles and sharp edges.

"Because of the situation here?" asked Moore airily.

Kenyon squirmed in the chair.

"Partially, yes. You must be ready to pull out at a moment's notice. We haven't been asked to close down your visit yet, but it may be so decided."

Moore seemed to be considering Kenyon's choice of the passive form.

"And if you do find anything, you must arrange to show the material to somebody in Dublin before you come back here."

Moore said nothing.

"A Mr Murray. He has an interest in what we are working on, you'll remember from our discussion. It may have a bearing on recent events in Dublin. Murray is already in Dublin to take charge of the situation there."

"He's doing some work for our firm?" asked Moore.

Kenyon wanted to let loose with his anger.

"He's in one of our partner offices," Kenyon replied with effort. "But he has priority at the moment. It's rather important, I'm afraid."

Kenyon wondered if Moore could read the leaden tone.

"Mr Murray then," said Moore slowly, as though puzzled. "And I have his number?"

"Yes, the one I gave you. Remember, you may be called back at any time if it is decided the situation warrants it."

"All right," said Moore neutrally.

Kenyon swore as he dropped the receiver back on the cradle. He made to pound his palm on the desk but held off just as his hand came to within an inch of the desk.

The hotel restaurant was full of Americans, busloads of them. They all wore name-tags with the name of the tour operator framed on each badge. Moore was surprised to find that he was less readily scornful of them here in Dublin than mildly interested in them. What passed for a *maître d'* had sat Moore next to a couple of dinosaurs from Minnesota. He had winked at Moore as he drew out the chairs for the pair. Very busy sir, he had said. When the waitress lay down a huge mixed grill in front of him, the *maître d'* had murmured that the Yanks would soon be poking around the graveyards in Ballydehob looking for their ancestors.

Moore returned to the *Guardian* and wondered if anyone not born on this island could feel at ease with

the blend of casuistry and friendliness. He had until
mid-day. He couldn't move on the Combs' house without first seeing this Minogue. He had reserved a hire
car yesterday. It was parked by the hotel and Moore
had the key in his pocket. He fended off the gregari-
ous and nasal Minnesotans by studying his route to
Minogue's office, designated on the map by a black
box near to where train lines converged at a railway
station. The waitress called it Kingsbridge, the old
name for this rail terminus from the west of Ireland.

When he had seen the headlines about Ball, Moore's
first thought was Ball might not be the only one on
their list. In a detached but deliberate way, Moore had
spent several minutes considering whether he was in
immediate danger himself. He had then dismissed the
idea. No one could know him here, unless it was
Kenyon who had leaked it.

Moore bought the Irish newspaper and, his breakfast now strangely heavy in his stomach, returned to
his room. INLA not IRA. Had Kenyon put him into
Dublin knowing that something like this was likely?
Moore stood and looked out the window of his room.
He was three floors up. There was one sliding window
with a jam to block an attempt to slide it back more
than six inches. Below his room were trees and shrubs,
railings marking the boundaries of houses and offices
which adjoined the hotel grounds. He heard a vague
hum from the floor beneath him. A vacuum cleaner,
he guessed. He looked at the door into the hallway. It
was locked, but he had not used the safety chain.

As he left, Moore abruptly realised how wary he
had become when the lift doors opened at his floor.
Without thinking, Moore jumped to the side. There
was no one else in the lift. He changed an Irish fiver to
coin for the public telephone. Moore had felt acutely
vulnerable at the automatic plate-glass door as it

whirred open in front of him. The handle of his brief-case felt slippery in his palm. Tiny and exact pieces of information assaulted him: a drop of water in his ear from the shower, the nails on his brief-case hand slightly longer than he liked. For a split second he imagined the heavy sheets of glass shattering with a blast, slicing, spinning. Taking a limb away, spotting the walls with his blood fifty feet from the door. A dim reflection of himself was carried away to nowhere by the sliding door.

He headed to the carpark and started his car, a claustrophobic Mini Metro, whose last client had smoked cigars. He opened all the windows and drove out onto Leeson Street. He did not feel reassured when he saw a Garda squad car parked by the hotel entrance to the street. The car was empty. Clumps of aged Americans were getting onto their tour busses. Someone laughed loudly. Moore turned. The ancient Minnesotans waved at him from a gaggle of garishly-dressed fellow Americans. They looked like lizards to Moore, cartoons. Stopped by a traffic light, Moore's thoughts turned again to Kenyon. It had to be con-nected to the assassination of Ball. Murray must be Secret Service, too; with Kenyon and the rest of Five along as passengers. Combs though . . . where could it fit? The lights changed.

Minogue could not get his brain to take up the yoke of work. He really should try to see Kilmartin. He saw half of Combs' face peeping out from under an enve-lope on the desk. He edged the envelope aside to look again at the tired face. Today the face looked resigned as well as cautious. Eilis was watching him.

"You want me to know by telepathy that I should be expecting this Mr Moore. Is that it, Eilis?"

"That is it."

Minogue stood and ambled toward Eilis' desk.

"There's a messenger after dropping off stuff from Foreign Affairs and Justice with your name on it. It's plain to see that they are copies of Mr Moore's permissions to go ahead."

"Um. Can you tell Detective Murtagh that he may be asked to bring Moore to the house? He'll be good company for Mr Moore, I'm thinking," Minogue said in a conspiratorial whisper.

Eilis almost smiled, but she caught herself in time. She began clapping her ashtray noisily against the sides of a rubbish bin to make room for an afternoon's butts.

"And Eilis," Minogue remembered.

Not heard above the din, he had to raise his voice. "Eilis."

She stopped and placed the ashtray on her desk.

"Do you remember that Costello fella a few years ago? Shot dead and mutilated a few years back? Up in the North, but there was talk of him being kidnapped from here?"

"I know the name, but I think it was before my tenure here."

"I believe that the Special Branch were investigating it, too," Minogue said.

Eilis nodded slowly. Her face took on a moody cast, Claudette Colbert about to dip her feet in some aggrieved ennui because her celluloid gangster paramour was momentarily inattentive.

"I remember reading about it in the papers and the kerfuffle about it. A big feud started, fellas getting murdered every week for a while after."

"Do we have an active file on him? An unsolved, like?" asked Minogue.

"If it was more than three years ago, it won't be here in its entirety. There'd be a summary here and any updates noted in brief, too."

"Well, I'm not much interested in reading ten filing cabinets full of this stuff. Could you give yourself fifteen minutes or a half hour over the Costello files and run through them like a roaring lunatic? Not read them, mind you. Look for mention of places in south County Dublin — Stepaside, Kilternan, Glencullen, Barnacullia, Sandyford. I'm hoping that Branch Surveillance Reports on Costello are still in existence."

Minogue rubbed his eyes and returned to the copy of the telex. Arthur Combs, Customs and Excise career began in 1931, retired 1977. Combs had worked as an insurance clerk in London after leaving school. He had had a secondary school education. He had applied for Customs and Excise twice, failing a test the first time but succeeding in the following year. No other known occupations in the fifty years after that. No criminal record. He had worked in various parts of the Port of London until he retired. There were four promotions in his career, but he had hit a plateau after the last one in 1963.

Had Combs harboured any of the secret longings which Minogue imagined besetting a man entering old age without a family? Customs man, like Le Douanier, his secret life on canvasses. Not a fabulous life by any means, quietly shuffling into old age in a London suburb. Combs was not recorded as having done Army service during the war. That was odd, Minogue thought, a single man not being called up. Maybe he had been working in a protected job doing his bit for the war effort at home. Combs must have cultivated other sides of himself to hear Mrs Hartigan's account. Languages, reading, travelling perhaps — and his drawings, of course.

Minogue knew that, customarily, there were no records of British visitors to Ireland. It would be next to impossible to discover whether Combs had been on holiday here before. What would have decided him on living here, though, and why pick Kilternan? If he had known the area from past visits, then some locals must remember him from before. From before . . . he'd have to go back further with Combs, to make him less of a victim, a cipher. That'd mean Newman, the police in London for a start.

He retrieved Newman's telephone number from his notebook and dialled. Newman was in a meeting. Could she take a message? She could, Minogue said: Sergeant Minogue from Dublin (should he be saying "a disgruntled Sergeant Minogue?") in connection with Mr Arthur Combs. He needed a more detailed background on Mr Combs. Need Inspector Newman call back? Only if he needs clarification on what I'm requesting.

At half-past twelve, with his belly light and grumbling about a dinner, Minogue's day became overcomplicated. He wanted and needed a dinner. He was also very keen to get to hell out of the briefing room.

He had almost apologised to Mr Moore when he had opened the door and led him in. Minogue had been astonished to see a tall, pin-striped figure standing boldly in front of Eilis' desk at five minutes before twelve. Moore had chalky, smooth skin. He must have a very good razor, Minogue believed. Moore's tie was knotted in a manner which Minogue had never seen in real life, but only in ads for shirts and ties and suits. The tie was red and spotty and it was firm over the collar button. It worked very nicely against the white shirt. Even Eilis' face began to give way and her eyes widened at the sight of Moore.

Jesus, Mary and Joseph, Minogue said inwardly. It was as well Kathleen didn't have telepathic powers to hear Minogue's gargoyle blaspheming within. In comparison with Moore, he himself could pass for one of those men dug up from the bogs in Sweden after lying there for a thousand years, skin and eyelashes and clothes intact but now residing in glass cases in the museum. Minogue had digested a total of four and a half pages from two government departments, brief requests, all to permit Mr E. Moore every liberty that was practical in respect of looking to the effects and the estate of Mr A. Combs, decd., of Kilternan, County Dublin. It was understood that Mr Moore would in no sense be requesting special privileges in regard to the current Garda investigation into Mr Combs' death. Mr Moore was to submit copies of all documents he might generate (who wrote "generate" Minogue wondered) in the course of his duties as the legal trustee for Mr Combs' estate. No effects were to be removed from the decd.'s residence without the written authorisation of one M. McCartan in the Department of Justice. In the matter of safeguarding Mr Combs' residence and the effects therein, such authorisation could be granted by telephone in response to the relevant written request from Mr Moore . . .

At the discretion of the investigating officers (unnamed), Mr Moore could be apprised of certain details of Mr Combs' death, provided that the rights of any suspect or potential suspect were not prejudiced in receiving such information or that the investigation was impaired by disclosing such details. Life insurance, Minogue wondered. And more. The letter from Foreign Affairs noted that Mr Combs' estate might be subject to a determination by the Revenue Commissioners in the Department of Finance as to whether taxes or death duties were or would be owed from the estate of Mr Combs. Public property, now, thought Minogue. The bureaucrats had swooped.

"And good day to you, Mr Moore. We spoke on the telephone."

"Sergeant Minogue, hello."

The voice was even, incurious.

"You found your way here all right, with the traffic and everything."

"Dublin is not too big, Sergeant."

"You must have pressed the right buttons with our civil service, Mr Moore."

He shepherded Moore back by Eilis' desk and ushered him into the windowless briefing room. It smelled of ashtrays and damp socks. At least someone had wiped the blackboard and arranged the chairs around the two pitted table-tops.

"You are bona fide, authorised and up-and-running as regards officialdom here, Mr Moore. There are men labouring a lifetime to be so recognised," Minogue began.

"Fine," Moore said.

"Maybe you could let me know how you did it. So I can get the same results, you see."

Moore tried out a smile. It seemed to come from a long way away, setting only on the lower part of his face, pushing his eyebrows up momentarily. Then it was gone.

"I think I know what you mean. So it's not just the British civil service which works best in the future conditional?"

Minogue liked that.

"Well, we more often dwell in the pluperfect here. The politics and things here. Lost fortune, you understand. I gave up trying to figure it out some time ago."

There was something about Moore which reminded Minogue of a plate-glass window. It wasn't that you couldn't see through it, but more a quality of mirroring things from the outside. Minogue was passing the letters across to him when Eilis appeared in the doorway.

"Excuse me for a moment, Mr Moore," Minogue said and closed the door behind him.

"There are two messages," said Eilis. "Mrs Kilmartin phoned to say that they're not allowing any visitors to see the Inspector until tomorrow at the earliest. But that he wakes up sometimes and appears to have all his faculties," she said.

"More than I ever had, I can tell you," Minogue murmured.

"And Pat Corrigan called. I don't need to go through those boxes of files by the sound of things now. He says to phone him. It's about a surveillance report on a certain person in Glencullen several years ago. Said you'd know who he was referring to."

Minogue clicked his fingers.

"That definitely tears the arse of out things. We may be on the move, Eilis." As he turned the doorhandle, Minogue caught a light scent of aftershave from the room.

"Excuse the intrusion, Mr Moore. It's feast or famine, I think, and I don't have an appetite for feasting at the moment."

Moore nodded. He kept his legs crossed lightly. An academic, Minogue thought.

"May I ask if you are close to a resolution of this case then, Sergeant?"

He had asked in such a casual way that Minogue was half-way through an honest answer before a hint of caution slowed him.

"We may well be making some progress at last."

Moore's expression did not change.

"But it may be a complicated box of tricks entirely. You probably know yourself that these murders that don't fit into the 'known-to-the-deceased' variety are the ones that do have us flummoxed for a while at least."

"There was a robbery in progress, though?"

"Let me say first, Mr Moore, that the deceased appears to have been the class of person who liked to keep to himself. We are not entirely sure at all as to what valuables he had in the house. A robbery in progress, you ask. Well. It has all the hallmarks of it. Household effects upset. A lot of damage done. Items of value on the person missing. Wallet, you see. About forty pounds that he had in a little bowl in the kitchen, too."

Moore pursed his lips slightly. He changed legs. Minogue caught a glimpse of a white, hairy shin atop the socks as Moore shifted.

"May I ask you then, Sergeant, something else? If I'm stubbing my toes here, please tell me."

Minogue glanced at the flawless sheen on the black oxfords. They hadn't been scuffed yet.

"Was Mr Combs the victim of, shall I say, anti-British sentiment?"

Minogue tongued his lower lip.

"Now, there's an interesting question, Mr Moore. Yes, it is. I don't know. It might be a possibility, but we're not concentrating on it at the moment. Does that sound equivocal enough to you?"

Moore tried a little with his smile, but it was gone as quickly as his other efforts.

"Not wishing to be obtuse, now, Mr Moore. But we don't show our cards too soon. Now, have you had your dinner at all . . . ?"

"Later in the day, thank you. I'd greatly appreciate the chance to get to Mr Combs' house as soon as I can."

"You'll accept Detective Murtagh's assistance, won't you?"

"No need, actually — "

Minogue searched Moore's face.

"It's a matter of policy here, I'm afraid, Mr Moore. We may need to return to the house in search of further evidence. An unsupervised visitor might upset things. Inadvertently, of course. Now, would you like copies of the rules in these letters here? About notifying us as to what you might do with Mr Combs' stuff? Then I'll leave you in Detective Murtagh's very capable hands."

"Kindness indeed," Moore replied. He stood and laid his brief-case on the table.

Minogue was mildly amused by Murtagh trying to exact a handshake from Moore. It was the only clumsy moment for Moore that Minogue had noticed. He changed hands on the brief-case to take Murtagh's outstretched hand. Eilis watched them go.

"A natty dresser," she murmured. She reached for another cigarette.

"A cold fish, too, by the cut of him," she added after blowing out the match.

"Just the man for this class of work so," Minogue added. "I hope that Pat Corrigan is buying me a dinner."

"You had better phone him all right. He sounded like his trousers were catching fire."

There was no trace of smoke from Inspector Corrigan's trousers. Minogue and he sat outdoors, on the footpath in Dawson Street. The staff of the otherwise stand-up-and-eat-it-quick delicatessen had placed tables, chairs and imitation Martini umbrellas out on the sidewalk in an effort to make boulevardiers of their clientele. Cotton-wool clouds moved quickly across the sky, a breeze flapped the umbrellas in the sun.

"What's that stuff?" Corrigan declared. Meant to be a question, his words came out as an accusation when he pointed to Minogue's scrambled egg.

197

"Take it easy, Pat. It's paprika. Your palate is crying out for some training." Minogue spooned more soup.

"That's cold soup, too. I've heard about that stuff."

"Gazpacho. It's meant to be cold."

Corrigan dusted crumbs off his trousers.

"So there they were. We had a team up in Glencullen for ten days then. It was only sight stuff with a few good snapshots."

"No tap on the blower, Pat? You must be getting very slack. Don't the District Justices watch the telly and see how every other jurisdiction does it?" Minogue said.

"You're a howl, Matt. We didn't do much about it except stuff more files. Anyway, Costello stayed there for a week or so. We got word that he had just done a job up in the North. Then he cleared out of the house and we lost track of him. But sure the next thing is he's full of holes and butchered."

"But sure, indeed," Minogue echoed the Irish national phrase.

"Tell me now, Matt, how you knew the answer before I knew the question."

"I don't follow you."

Minogue was distracted by the groups of students on the sidewalks. Trinity College was down the end of the street. No Iseult among them.

"You put me up to looking into Costello's files again. Making it up like you didn't know the answer. Come on now and spill the beans."

"Beans?"

No Daithi either. A couple was kissing passionately. Minogue was shocked. It was the girl who was pinning the boy against the railings. Busses screeched. People at the next table were laughing. The girl disentangled herself slightly. The better to dive back into the kissing, Minogue thought. It was not Iseult's face, he noted with relief. The woman grasped the man around the neck again.

"Jases. They'll be peeling off their clothes and having a wear next," Corrigan grumbled.

"What beans?" Minogue asked.

"What put you onto this idea? Costello?"

The boy encircled her with his arms. That was nice. And one hand strayed to her hair. Very nice hair. Would it feel like Iseult's, the way she was always complaining about it being too dry? And stroked her hair. Lovely hair. Lustrous hair.

"Well?" Corrigan prompted again.

"Let's call it an association which, like Count Dracula, can't stand the light of day."

"Combs is English. British. Was, anyway. What was he doing living in bloody Kilternan? There, answer me that one."

"I'm not sure that I can, Pat. You tell me what he was doing going up to Glencullen for his sup of drink every evening."

"Is that a fact? Right enough, you mentioned that before. Sure it's only a bit up the road."

"It most certainly is not up the road a bit. Not if you're seventy something years of age and you have a pub around the corner from your own house."

"You think that Combs was snooping around or the like?"

"I'm exploring the outlandish possibility that Mr Combs might have been in touch with Mister Ball over an item concerning the late Mr Costello and Mr Costello's friends."

"Mr Costello's friends are mainly members of the INLA. By the leaping Jesus, Matt. Do you know what you're saying?"

Corrigan sat back in the wire chair and placed his ham hands on the armrests.

"You don't say," Minogue said.

Corrigan leaned forward suddenly.

"So the INLA killed your man?"

"No, they didn't."

"Who did, so?"

"I don't know who killed him, Pat. If I did, I would be buying you the dinner. I need to talk to someone in the embassy, though. Someone in the same line of work as Ball was. To spring something on them and see what they say."

"You can't. We're not supposed to assume that intelligence operatives work out of embassies, Matt. Rules is rules."

"A poke at one of them, Pat. One of us has to poke at him. You do it if that's the way it has to be done, but I need some finger on them."

Corrigan noted the discrepancy between Minogue's tone and his slouch in the chair. He looked like he was daydreaming, but the tone was acid.

"Come on now, Matt. There's a Second Secretary shot and killed on the streets not twenty-four hours ago. We're not even allowed near the place to interview anyone in the embassy. Damn it man, my own men are playing second fiddle to a team of Brits that landed off the plane this morning, and we're being phoned every hour from Justice. To remind us to let their 'experts,' if you please, do their investigation. 'Experts,' is it? Now how am I going to get anyone to let me do what you want? These are diplomats. This is Ireland, remember. We have this wee issue going on with the British for eight hundred years or so. They make the rules and you and I, we follow the rules. Especially at times like this. That way we don't bollocks up things."

Minogue's eyes remained out of focus. Corrigan wondered if it was the effects of that odd food he had eaten.

"Well, I bollocks things up, Pat. As a matter of routine. I have, I can and I probably will again."

"That's a different class of a game you're talking about now," Corrigan said evenly. "Don't come the heavy with me."

"What are we fighting over, yourself and myself?" Minogue said languidly. "Someone at the embassy knows something about Combs. Ball seems to have had some contact with our Combs. I want to know what they knew about Combs' murder. Not to mention me helping my friends in the Branch with this assassination last night . . . "

Corrigan leaned forward again.

"Look. I can't get at them. I told you that Ball was probably some kind of intelligence officer — "

"It's 'probably' now? But one small favour at least," Minogue said studying Corrigan's frown. "Nothing out of this world now," he added.

The frown drove a deeper crease between Corrigan's eyebrows.

"Will you arrange a tail on someone for me?"

Corrigan rocked back in his chair. He shook his head. He pushed back the chair, still not looking at Minogue's face.

"Matt, sometimes when I hear people saying that you're a bit cracked, I wonder to myself if maybe they're not right."

Corrigan made a minor ceremony of standing and buttoning his jacket. Minogue stayed seated, looking up Dawson Street.

"I might have to do it myself then, Pat. I don't think any of Jimmy Kilmartin's lads is up to doing the job properly. And I'll tell you what. If Moore is who or what I think he is, then we'll need an expert. I'd ask you for a phone tap, but I know that your blood pressure would pay the bill in the end."

Corrigan nodded once, decisively.

"Just do it for twenty-four hours."

Corrigan stood with the pained expression still wrinkling his forehead. He stroked his chin. Minogue propelled himself up from the chair. He eased the skepticism on Corrigan's face with a squeeze of Corrigan's upper arm.

"Something will give way, Pat. Don't be fretting."

"There's always the pension, isn't there?" said a resigned Corrigan. "Listen. You'll get one full day out of me. I can put a two-man team out when your Moore gets back to his hotel. More than that, bejases, and I'll have to go to the top with it. With your scalp tied to my belt, for fear they'll be wanting one."

Kenyon was half-way into a salmon sandwich when Bowers swivelled from the monitor.

"Memo for you, sir. A Code Three. Do you want a hard copy or just screen-read?"

Kenyon swallowed a mouthful of sandwich. He had never warmed to the use of terminals for internal mail, especially for any messages higher than a Code One. Despite assurances and performance evaluations of the system proving that the network was secure, despite the best efforts of simulated hostile "breakers," Kenyon retained his dislike of having something which reminded him of a television in his office. Reluctantly, he walked to the terminal and keyed in his code to retrieve the message.

"Print it, yes," he said to Bowers and returned to his chair. The jagged tearing sound of the printer lasted less than a minute.

"Second telephone inquiry on a flagged name with the LMP, sir. They've had an alert on the name since Monday, authorised by you."

"Yes, I know. Go on," Kenyon said.

"To Inspector Newman, by name, from police in Dublin re Arthur Combs. . . . Wanted more detailed bio on that party. For attention of one Sergeant Minogue, sir. The copper you wanted to know about, that's him. . . . "

Kenyon felt his heart race. The police in Dublin had twigged to something? He pressed fingers into his eyes, rubbed, then held them against his eyelids.

"That's it, sir."

Kenyon needed to clear his throat. He gently placed the remains of the sandwich on his desk. It could mean that the Irish police were just becoming frustrated and hoped that a detail missing from their previous picture of Combs might help. Yes: if they had found any bombshell left by Combs, why hadn't a real storm erupted? Had their police handed it over to their Foreign ministry and were they sitting on it, at a loss to evaluate it? The ex-head of MI5, a former minister . . . the embassy staff running intelligence ops? No, the Irish would never sit on this; they'd have looked for corroboration straightaway, gone for the jugular.

Kenyon shivered with an intuition that he was overlooking something. Was the inquiry a feint, to see what the Met would say? Kenyon's brain rejected that: the Combs character would hold up, that's why it had been picked. Newman could send a three-hundred page life story if he wanted; dental records, too. The documentation would be seamless.

But, for a few seconds, the doubt swept back, greater. He had a fleeting sense that something was moving by him, out of reach, a sluggishly moving tableau of events, inexorable, indifferent to his efforts to direct their course. Kenyon shook himself out of the drift of thoughts. He had been at work on this nearly fourteen hours. Was he losing his grasp of the events?

He picked up the print-out, folded it thoughtfully and left for Robertson's office.

"Has Moore drawn anything from the coppers over there?" Robertson asked.

"I'll be asking him that when he makes his call."

Kenyon checked his watch.

"About another twenty minutes. I just have the sense that things might unravel there rather suddenly. Part of me says the Irish haven't twigged to anything, but then I keep coming back to the killing this morning. Ball. Damn, we don't have a way of knowing what's going on there yet. That's what has me on edge."

"Anything from GCHQ on messages to their embassy in London about Combs?"

"SIGINT have heard nothing so far and they have all the codes. But their embassy here knows that their lines back to Dublin are not secure. I just have this vision of an Irish civil servant stepping off the plane at Heathrow with a diplomatic bag under his arm, full of what Combs was doing for us in Ireland. Yes, going to their embassy to plan how best to use it against us. . . . Christ, when I think of Murray, I almost think we deserve to have this cock-up thrown at us — "

Kenyon fingered where he felt the light pulse, the root of a headache in his forehead.

"James, listen," Robertson interrupted. "I know we're asked to hold our nose on this and that it troubled you from the very start. It could be a tight situation, I know."

Kenyon began pushing back his cuticles. He managed to disregard the tone of reprimand. He looked to his watch again.

"I don't want Moore at risk," Kenyon said. "He hasn't enough experience really. I want to pull him out. It's too damned volatile and we don't have reliable information about anything."

Robertson remained silent while he let his glance linger on Kenyon's rising colour.

"So you're ready to advise activating an approach at diplomatic levels then, James? Get the Irish onside before something gives way that we can't control?"

"Yes," Kenyon answered. He felt tired, deflated. "At least then I wouldn't have to worry about Murray in Dublin botching our show and endangering our people."

"Don't take it so hard, James. Our timing is not too far out of kilter. We have the Irish government slavering with reassurances about security for our embassy staff. After this assassination, I mean. You'll see to notifying Moore then?"

"I'll pass along anything he has," Kenyon replied.

He felt suddenly disengaged from the whole business. Even the physical surroundings seemed to recede. He was in a building in London, getting ready to close the bag on an operation which hadn't produced. Nothing novel about that. He had fifteen minutes on his hands, without the slightest urge to do anything except sink further into the chair. It was a long time since he had had his knuckles rapped by Hugh Robertson. In a way which he couldn't quite understand, Kenyon felt pleased to have been angry and to have drawn Robertson's plangent response. He could watch the diplomats wince at having to curry favour with the Irish. This did not displease Kenyon as much as he would have expected. He tried to will his headache further away.

CHAPTER 12

The barman reached out over the clutter of bottles and glasses for Moore's money. The pub was full of smoke. The seats were long gone, occupied since early evening. Nearly everyone in the pub appeared to be drunk or at least well on the way to being drunk. Faces glowed with the heat and the beer. Raucous laughter, a shout, more laughter; eyes closed, laughing helplessly with mouth agape, teeth showing to the gums. Everybody was pissed, Moore decided.

He sipped at the beer before swallowing. Too fizzy for bitter, but nice, malty beer. His eyes stung from the smoke. A woman brushed against him as she followed another to the Ladies. No one could hear the television and no one was watching it. Four barmen skipped, reached, smiled and poured pints of Guinness while a constant stream of shouted orders, hand signals and winks kept them busy. Moore looked at the door where he had entered. There was no sign of the man in jeans.

He hadn't noticed until he was crossing the street from the hotel. Then there was the vague speculation, the itch which made him feel vulnerable. As though the street was broader, the traffic faster. Nothing at first. Moore set up his checks. Instead of going into the first pub, he broke into a stride. He headed for the canal bridge, which he had crossed this morning, and launched into a brisk walk down Leeson Street.

He remembered that Leeson Street turned into a one-way street as it neared that park, St Stephen's Green. If there was a back-up in a car, he'd have a long block to lose them, too. The shops were closed. He couldn't take up a surveillance point off the street without attracting attention. The evening was warm. Moore slung his jacket over his shoulder. He had twenty minutes before calling Kenyon. The stream of headlights flowing along Leeson Street surprised him. He hadn't thought of Ireland as busy.

There were two pubs opposite each other at the end of Leeson Street. Moore stopped by the traffic-lights and pressed the pedestrian button. He could not distinguish the man from the groups who were walking down the street toward him. He looked to the four corners of the intersection. Moore had passed no clear alleys or pedestrian ways. If he did have a tail, then the tail would know the streets, that Moore had no place else to go. If there was tandem surveillance on foot, it would be easy to keep him in sight anyway. Five minutes before calling Kenyon and he still needed to get change for the phone.

A group gathered around him, waiting to cross the street. A half-dozen headed for one of the pubs. He fell in with them. All youths; Moore doubted if any of them were legal age. It didn't seem to matter. They were half-pissed already.

Moore was three minutes late with the call. He wondered if Kenyon would hear him over the racket. He pushed further into the booth and plugged one ear with his thumb. There was a smell of sugary perfume off the receiver. He fingered the fifty-penny pieces onto the chute and dialled.

The television news came on. A heavily made-up woman announced headlines. Moore watched an image of the Union Jack and the Irish tricolour spring onto the screen, followed by a clumsy graphic map of Ireland. A line marking the border pulsated in red and the word *security* appeared across the map. No one paid attention to the news. He pushed the receiver tighter against his ear. He swallowed more beer. The faces around him seemed foreign. He hadn't spotted anyone who set his antennae stirring yet. More people flowed into the pub. A barman nodded at the arrivals. How could they run a country with half the population out boozing every night? It was just his preconceptions about the Irish and the booze. He heard the telephone connections click through, a hissy pause, then the phone ringing in London.

Moore felt calm. He doubted that it was the beer doing its work already. The noise of the mob seemed to rise and engulf him. He strained to hear the phone ring again. It could only be that copper. Minogue. The one with the dry humour and the bit of stage-Irish. Minogue would have put a tail on him. Had he misread Minogue? He looked around at the faces again. Like potatoes, he thought, but flush and moist, talking and laughing. Kenyon picked up the phone at the fourth ring.

"Where are you?"

"In a pub."

"Can you hear me with that racket?"

"Just about," Moore answered. He was amused at the displeasure in Kenyon's voice. When he looked about the crowded pub, he noticed the couple immediately. They were in their late twenties, he guessed, and they came into the pub sober. They looked too earnest about making conversation and looking about. She carried a sweater tied around her shoulders. Her hair was in a pony-tail. She could put the sweater on and shake out the pony-tail if she had to take up pursuit outside the pub, a new face. The man had longish hair, over his ears, no more than ten years out of date. His jeans looked too well tended.

"Any moves from your side?" Kenyon repeated.

"No sign yet. I had a supervised look through the house today."

"We're going to make a pre-emptive approach to the Irish, probably tomorrow. The timing is not up to us. We just explain what's at stake and it's their party. I'd expect a backroom chat at the conference tomorrow. It gets going after lunch. You should wind up before then."

The barman did not know the couple. Nor did any customers greet them. The woman drank a Coke while the man nursed a pint of Guinness. They looked overly absorbed in each other but not flighty enough for it to be the first date.

"Did you hear me?" an irritated Kenyon asked.

"You want me clear of the place by mid-day," Moore said. "And if I have made any progress before then?"

Kenyon took a breath and held.

"Same as the previous protocol. Refer any material you find before then to Mr Murray. He's running things for the moment."

Moore heard the hostility in Kenyon's tone plain over the din of the pub. He wondered if he should bother to tell Kenyon that he was being tailed. Coppers both, the ones here, and amateurish, too. Moore watched as the man took another draught from his Guinness. Tipping it, he let his head back, his eyes almost closed. He glanced at Moore through the slit between his eyelids. Moore pretended not to notice.

He felt sure now. But how many did they have on him?

Moore hung up and looked at the television again. He tried to lip-read over the racket. Out of the corner of his eye, he noted that the couple was staying put. They hadn't looked for a seat or found a wall to lean against, out of the way of the swell thronging up to the bar. That was his own face he was seeing in the mirror behind the bar. He was here in a pub in Dublin with things giving way under his feet and Kenyon's terse voice still in his memory. He was almost certainly under surveillance. Had they found something in Combs' house and were playing it out? Maybe Kenyon was already too late to pull the switch on this. . . . But that Minogue with the eyebrows pushing up, some vague and private amusement, an appetite for mockery perhaps. It was that affable and devious Sergeant Minogue who had pinned the tail on him, Moore guessed. Taking the mickey out of the Brits, the favourite pastime here. Minogue playing a game. Moore's chest burned as he realised that Kenyon's instruction all but removed his chance of what could have been a double coup: if he had been able to recover any Combs' dossier, Moore'd be happier to pull it out from under Minogue's politely mocking nose.

Minogue poured enough Jameson whisky to colour the tumbler as far as the supporting pylons at the bottom of the Arc de Triomphe. He held the glass to eye level. The orange liquid covered the foreground nicely, easily topping the script "*Souvenir de . . .*" He had bought the tawdriest memento he could find at the Gare du Nord, just before Kathleen and he had taken the train back to Le Havre.

He replaced the bottle under the sink and returned to the living-room. Kathleen had fallen asleep in the

210

chair. The whisky was smoky, sharper than Jameson should be. Maybe he needed to drink more of it, more often, so that it wouldn't have the whack which he was shuddering after now. Good drink for a spring day at the races. Horses, vapour breath snorting in billows, galloping.

It had been more than twenty years since Minogue had run hard on the drink. He sipped at the tumbler and counted the years. Iseult was twenty-two and a half. . . . It must be over a quarter century since he had heard Kathleen's scream and her body hit the floor upstairs. The child, Eamonn, dead above in the cot. Nothing left at all then. Days no different than nights, for months on end. He had been lucky to hold onto his job. It was years before he knew that what had nearly destroyed him was anger, not grief.

Kathleen asleep looked a stranger to Minogue. He looked at the mute, blind television screen. Iseult wasn't home yet. He should wake Kathleen up and send her off to bed, lest Daithi come home half-jarred and cause a commotion. Minogue closed his eyes. Had Combs really missed so much by not having a family? He imagined Combs sitting on a rock drawing the patterns from the stones. Combs and Joyce supping whisky in his kitchen, a tinker swapping horse yarns with an Englishman. Jimmy Kilmartin's face drifted in behind Minogue's eyelids. Jimmy, the man who was so anxious to be seen doing the right thing. How did a person get like that, so anxious to please? But Jimmy was shrewd, tough as nails by times, no fawning Polonius. Showing how responsible he was . . . to whom? For what?

The phone rings erupted as pink flares into Minogue's eyelid world. It was his own phone. Kathleen stirred. The room was bright when he opened his eyes. Had he fallen asleep? A man with a genteel Limerick accent was looking for Sergeant Minogue.

"Who would you be yourself?"

"This is Sergeant Dwyer and I'm calling from Shankill Station. Would you be Sergeant Minogue?"

"I would."

"Well, I'm sorry now to be disturbing you. Very sorry, and it ten o'clock at night. I hope I'm doing the right thing now. I have your number from a colleague of yours. Detective Keating."

"Go on."

"I was put through to him after I called the Murder Squad. He thought you wouldn't mind being phoned at home under the circumstances. To make a long story short, I have a man here says he won't stir without seeing you. He knows your name and all. Not a word until he sees you."

"Who is he?"

"Man by the name of Joyce. A tinker."

"Michael Joseph Joyce?"

"The very man."

"What's he doing in Shankill station?"

"He was in a row in a pub here in Shankill and we took him in."

"Is it just drunk and disorderly with him?"

"No, it isn't," Dwyer said as if a conclusion had been reached. "Matter of fact he is up for assault and battery. A client in the pub. Joyce opened his head with a bottle. The man needs stitches all over his face. Joyce'll appear in court in the morning. It's a mighty serious business. The man could have lost an eye."

"Is he sober now, or out-and-out drunk?"

"Well, he can talk up the divil's own story, so he can't be much under the influence. Says that the client passed comments about tinkers in public houses.

Asked him who his wife was shacking up with while he was in the pub."

"So what does he want with me?"

"He says that there's something he forgot to tell you when he was talking to you the other day."

"He didn't mention that he was going to stretch someone in a pub with a bottle in the face," Minogue muttered.

"Ha, ha, I suppose he didn't at that. But he says it's terrible important and that you'd be needing to know right away. And if we didn't tell you, it'd be on our own heads, so it would. If he was really langers, I would've done nothing. But when he says Murder Squad, he got me to thinking, do you follow me?"

Minogue, a Clareman and thus not normally disposed to following any suggestion made to him by any party from the neighbouring county of Limerick, conceded that he did.

"I'll be by in a half hour," Minogue said.

Kathleen was turning out the light in the living room.

It was gone eleven when Minogue, Joyce and the Garda left Shankill station. Flahive, the Garda, chain-smoked as he drove. Joyce and Minogue sat in the back of the squad-car. Once off the Bray Road and its lights, Minogue could see that the night sky was still clear. He found The Plough well into the middle of the sky.

"There's no chance in the world, is there?" Joyce said.

"No. Not something like this. This is a serious charge, Michael Joseph. The man has stitches up and down his face."

"And him after abusing myself and Josie?" Joyce snapped.

"He didn't mean it personally."

"Do you mean to tell me that he tells everyone he meets the same thing, is it?"

This was a changed Joyce, Minogue reflected. Something had given way in him, struck out. Bitterness, a lifetime.

"And I suppose you'll be telling me that I would have been better off if I had have been as drunk as a lord, too drunk to hear him?" Joyce added scornfully.

"Or take a bottle to him."

He heard Joyce snort. Joyce was sober. He sat upright in the seat. Minogue could almost feel a heat of resentment from him. Where was the timid and wheedling Joyce of yesterday?

"What'll me wife and childer do and me locked up in the barracks?" Joyce declared.

Minogue had no pleasing answer. Flahive braked hard for the corkscrew bend at the bottom of Bride's Glen Road. Joyce's caravan was less than a mile up the hill.

"And all the help I'm giving you this evening?" Joyce tried.

"Help you should have given me straightaway yesterday," said Minogue sharply. "You were a foolish man entirely not to tell me about this letter the first time I talked to you. So don't be acting the maggot with me now."

"Didn't I have a few drinks on me and I left the letter in a jacket of mine? I would have tore up that letter and scattered it to the four winds after me finding out what happened to poor Mr Combs. To be mixed up in that class of thing, I says to myself. You can't trust any but your own, we often say, and it's true."

"But you didn't tear it up?" Minogue interrupted.

"Mr Combs might have told someone that a letter was on the way and that t'would be expected. Quick like. I wanted rid of that letter like it was the divil's cloak, let me tell you. So far as I might know it might have been a life-or-death thing, and Mickey Joyce shouldn't have any more truck with a poor man who was after getting himself murdered. . . . "

Life-or-death, Minogue's mind echoed. Talked to Joyce on Monday. Middle of the day. Ball was killed on the Tuesday, near midnight. The letter must have gone to a Dublin address.

"Not even one letter you'd remember off the words on the envelope?" Minogue tried. "An A, a B . . . any letters?"

Joyce shook his head conclusively.

"I wish I had learned a bit of . . . " his words trailed off, the head still shaking, slower now.

"When did he give it to you?"

"A week ago, I suppose. We were after having a few drinks and he had the jitters a bit, I was thinking to myself. I didn't like to be asking him what his business was, but I couldn't help noticing he wasn't in the best of fettle."

"Did he talk about anything that was bothering him?"

"No, he didn't. But he had a funny look to him. He took the letter out of his pocket, and he waved it at me with a kind of look on his face. I don't know what you'd call it — "

"Go on."

Joyce took a deep breath and sighed.

"He waved the letter around a bit and he says to me, 'Do you know what's in this?' We had a few drinks on us now, I don't mind telling you. So naturally, I tells him I didn't. 'That,' says he, 'that is like setting a pack of dogs on the loose.' Looking at the letter like it was

215

something very strange, not bits of paper at all. . . . I says nothing."

"Michael Joseph. Did Mr Combs know whether you could read and write?"

Joyce frowned his puzzlement and scratched his head.

"I don't know. . . . I suppose. He asked me once what I made of the state of the world, me being a traveller. In a nice way, you understand. I think I told him that I knew nothing about the affairs of people out in the world and that I didn't need to be concerning myself about goings-on like — "

"What did he do or say when you said that?"

"How can I remember that? He was always kind of nice, like, he wouldn't talk down to you. I suppose he didn't take much notice."

"Did he say anything else, then? When he gave you the letter?"

"I can't think of what . . . and me leaving, with the letter in me pocket. . . . He had the look on him again, like he was sober all of a sudden. To tell you the truth I had the willies a bit and me coming home, thinking about the way Mr Combs looked. He said something about boats, I don't know what. . . . He said his boat had run aground. Then says something about the holy ground to me. Like it might have been funny if he hadn't have been looking so shook. You know the tune, 'The Holy Ground?' "

"Boats?"

"Like a saying, I suppose. Then some other queer expression about a boat on fire . . . "

"Burning your boats?"

Joyce looked up abruptly. "That's it. The very thing. What does that mean at all?"

Minogue had no answer. Something, his thoughts nagged sluggishly — *something* — something Combs

did, something he had. Gave Joyce a letter to post —
but why not post it himself? Something of value;
value to whom? No. Combs had given Joyce money,
but would he really have trusted him with something
valuable, given the temptations of larceny or drink?

Minogue's thoughts tugged at a line, bobbed and
then went slack again. Nothing. "Burning your boats."
Wasn't that Homer? The Greeks stranded before the
walls of Troy . . . a last gamble. His tiredness rumbled
into irritation again.

Joyce's wife was standing in the doorway of the caravan. She pushed children in behind her. A crawling
infant escaped her, scurrying between her legs. She
noticed it an instant before the child made to go down
the step. Josie Joyce gathered the child and planted it
on her hip without taking her eyes from the squad-car.

"What have you done?" she cried out. "What have
you done tonight and you with handcuffs on you, you
big iijit?"

She began weeping. It turned to keening, then pleading. It set off a child somewhere out of Minogue's
sight, at the far end of the caravan. Joyce told his wife
to shut up. Flahive stood against the bonnet of the car
with his arms folded. The interior of the caravan was
lit by a gas lantern hissing on the kitchen table. Joyce's
wife had begun wailing again.

"Don't be carrying on, woman," Joyce hissed.

The glow of the city's lights came faintly over the
hedges to the north, obscuring the stars there. Minogue
sensed something moving under the caravan. He
looked down at the collie, which rested its front paws
just inside the shadow.

Joyce jostled by his wife. Minogue followed him in.
The inside of the caravan was tidy and crowded. It
smelled of smoke and cooking, bed-warmth, child's

piss. Joyce blundered to a built-in cupboard beside what passed for a sofa. Children scampered under clothes at the other end of the caravan.

Joyce tore out plastic bags and threw them to the floor. They seemed to be full of clothes. He reached his arms in and drew out a bridle and noseband. He stepped back, kicked the bags at his feet and thrust the straps angrily at Minogue.

Josie Joyce's jaw dropped when she saw Minogue take out his penknife. The children stood silent and gaping like their mother.

"What in the name of God is he doing with that . . . ?" she began.

"This was a present to ye from Mr Combs?" Minogue asked without looking up. The straps had been machine-stitched. The stiff leather was tight and creaking.

"And he said ye could keep it after ye took the horse back, am I right?" Minogue went on.

"I suppose," said Josie, darting glances from her husband to Minogue. "But if it's ours, it's ours. T'was a present. You can't be destroying it."

Minogue could not safely tease his knife under the stitches. He snorted with frustration.

"Damn it to hell. Have you a good sharp knife, Missus, one with a point to it?"

Josie Joyce's eyes bulged wider.

"Go on with you," Joyce muttered.

Minogue worked the point of the knife into the stitches and began slicing them. He levered the two straps open.

"That's a fierce amount of cash money for tackle the likes of that," Josie began.

A small plastic sachet escaped Minogue's palm and fell to the floor.

"What in the name of . . . " Joyce frowned. Minogue picked up the sachet. He felt his chest expanding, his

218

heart beating in a huge space. When he tried to talk, his words came out in a hoarse whisper.

"This, Michael Joseph, this little thing is what's going to put the bit between our teeth, man."

He held the sealed packet against the propane light. The negatives were stacked perhaps four deep, singly, in two groups.

"Guard, come in here, will you? Be quick, man."

Flahive appeared in the doorway, his nose wrinkled in distaste at having to enter a tinker's caravan.

"Get the station to phone the Technical Bureau. Tell 'em it's me and that I want Photographic and Video. I have black-and-white negatives to be developed and blown up."

"Negatives, sir?" said Flahive warily.

"And I'm going to leave them in their wrapping until they get them."

"And you want these things developed, is it?"

"Yep. And blown up, man. But big."

Minogue did not hear Kathleen coming down the stairs.

"I thought it was Daithi in late," she whispered. "But sure he's in bed hours already."

Her hair was down, an arm holding her dressing-gown together.

Minogue had helped himself to two sizeable glasses of Jameson. He was not tired and he did not feel drunk. He had prints of all the negatives in his lap, along with a plastic magnifying glass.

"It's three o'clock in the morning. What in the name of God are you doing? . . . What are those? Photos? Are you gone dotty? They're not photos of people at all. What is it, bits of paper?"

"It's something very unusual," Minogue began. "A very, very delicate matter entirely. And I'm not sure what to make of it at all," he began. The drink had had its effects, he realised then. It was too much to explain to Kathleen now.

"Can't you sleep on it?"

"I'm only just home from town this last fifteen minutes. I can't sleep with this stuff in me head. I don't know if I can swallow the thing as real at all. That Combs man that was murdered."

Kathleen shivered.

"Can't it wait until tomorrow?"

Minogue noted the edge to her question.

"It'll have to."

Minogue had checked the streets which Combs mentioned. If this was raving fiction about the Second World War, then Combs had gone to a lot of trouble to get his names and places right. Most were now in East Berlin. Unter den Linden he'd heard of before. Combs called Kufursten Damm the Ku-damm, something Minogue had also heard of before. The Rathausstrasse, where he claimed to have made the broadcasts from, had been levelled by bombing. And that man that was betrayed on purpose, Vogel. Combs thought that Vogel's family had lived in East Berlin. He wrote that he never met Vogel but only heard of his fate after he himself had gotten out. After "Russians" he had written "our allies!!!" and underlined the words several times. But Minogue kept returning to the name Costello. Combs had had his dates right, but he couldn't have known for sure about Costello's killing. All he could do was repeat Ball's hints about Costello and his grisly fate.

Kathleen eyed the bottle of whisky now dangerously at large, out of the safety of the sink cupboard.

"Once in the blue moon, Kathleen," he murmured.

He laboured to rise from the chair. Kathleen waited by the door. William Grimes, had he heard that name before? No, just the illusion of familiarity brought on by a few drinks.

"Are you still expecting to get up early?" Kathleen whispered at the foot of the stairs. Minogue did not miss the reproach. He scooped up the note he had left for Daithi.

"I'll have to get started on this very early tomorrow, and that's a fact," he replied, following his wife up the stairs. They tiptoed to their bedroom. Hooking his thumb into his socks, sitting on the edge of the bed, Minogue smelled the sugary sourness of his whisky breath. Maybe he should be hanging off the phone downstairs trying to get ahold of Corrigan or a Superintendent or two. Whatever about three o'clock in the morning, they'd have enough questions for him when he did tell them tomorrow.

CHAPTER 13

Corrigan sat sideways in the front passenger seat. He still looked tense, leaning around the head-rest to talk. Minogue was not disposed to being sympathetic to Corrigan. He badly wanted more coffee. Dunne, Corrigan's driver, had watched Minogue gulp down two large white coffees bought on the hoof from Bewley's in Dundrum Shopping Centre. Minogue caught him looking askance at Corrigan, as if to seek reassurance from the Inspector.

Minogue's hangover had hit him as thirst and sluggishness. The want of sleep had left his joints aching, but he had woken up with that tremulous sense in his chest, the excitement. While he had been driving in to town to meet Corrigan, he had had enough opportunities to wonder if the plan wasn't as mad as Corrigan would say it was. Corrigan was getting edgier by the minute. He looked at his watch before thumbing to transmit.

" — Chestnut Control to Chestnuts One and Two. Come in."

"What's the Chestnut bit, Pat? Did you sack Alpha and Bravo and Foxtrot?" Minogue asked.

" — Chestnut Two Over."

"Any sign of our man moving around?" Corrigan asked Dunne. Dunne was toying with the handset, the link with the photo team working the house.

"No, sir," said Dunne.

"What's the Chestnut stuff, Pat?" Minogue repeated.

Corrigan let the mike drop lightly into his lap.

"Us being the Branch, we thought we'd start using the names of trees instead of Foxtrots and Tangos."

It was the first laugh Minogue had had all day. It relieved his own unease at any rate.

" — Chestnut One to Control. In position and standing by. Over."

" — Chestnut Two to Control. Waiting for the word, Control. Over."

"It's half eleven and the bugger is still in the house. He could be burning the shagging negatives and photos for all we know," Corrigan muttered.

Corrigan's car was parked outside the Golden Ball pub in Kilternan. Two Special Branch radio-cars were deployed on the Enniskerry Road, both equipped with Motorola radio trackers for the transmitter bug attached to the inside of the back bumper of Moore's hired Mini. Corrigan had tried to explain the tracking system to Minogue, but Minogue's morning mind could not get around the detail. Both radio-tracking cars had computer terminals, which were radio-plugged into the mainframe operating out of Harcourt Terrace in the City Centre. A very simple thing, Corrigan told a disbelieving Minogue, to have the computer do the triangulation from the signals the two pursuit cars were monitoring. Minogue had stopped Corrigan's offhand tutorial when he had made the mistake of asking how much the system cost.

"This is a bit dodgy, all the same," Corrigan complained. "I'm beginning to wonder if we shouldn't have gone to the top with it already and not to be playing games out here, trying to make the cat jump the way we want...."

Beginning to wonder, Minogue reflected. He had had enough of a job persuading Corrigan not to ring the bells yet but to wait on Moore. Minogue hoped that Corrigan swore more because he was nervous than because he was losing his belief in the scheme. Dunne excused himself to go to the toilet in the pub. Did anyone want more coffee?

"If you find any real coffee, by all means," Minogue had said. "No instant anything."

There was promise of a sunny day yet. The smell of stale Guinness from the pub was not helping Minogue think any clearer.

"Are you listening to me, Matt? If this stuff is real at all, then Moore isn't worth playing. He's only a gofer, to clean up. He's solo, wait and you'll see."

"He may be part of a criminal conspiracy, I'd say, Pat," Minogue replied airily.

"All the more reason we shouldn't be keeping this to ourselves. If the embassy mob is mixed up in this, then I don't know what we'll do. The first thing we'll be asked is 'Why didn't you iijits inform the Commissioner and the Minister the minute you copped onto how big this was?'"

"To which you'll say, or I'll say for you, 'Your Honour, it was our honest belief that only by watching Mr Moore could we establish the veracity of the allegations in this document,'" Minogue said.

Corrigan shook his head.

"And me toasted on the stand if and when it comes up that I authorised a tracker on Moore's car without consulting a soul?"

"Initiative, Pat. What you're paid for. Would you have preferred to go begging for a warrant to toss his room in the hotel? As if he would keep the stuff there? We have to let him run with it."

"I can tell you this," Corrigan waved a finger in the air. "The minute he strays near the outside range of the tracker, I'll see red. No messing then, boyo. I'll pull the plug."

"What's the exact range of the thing?"

"It lists five kilometers. About three miles. Less in the city. What if he has a way of detecting it stuck to his car?"

Minogue shrugged.

"I still say it's a bit thin," Corrigan said, stretching.

"Tell them I'm Rasputin. That's how I conned you into squandering manpower and gadgetry from the Special Branch. Patience, Pat. There's time enough to tell them. Costello was murdered. Combs was murdered. This is a murder investigation — "

"Get up the yard," Corrigan broke in. "Costello was bumped in the North so far as we're concerned. Even if he was abducted from here. Let the RUC worry about that. Not that they are, I can tell you."

"Combs was murdered. Ball was murdered. Moore is nothing to us, as himself. He could just throw up his hands if we pounced now and say he hasn't a notion what's going on. It's what he does now that he has these photos. We don't need half the Gardai and the Branch to keep an eye on him," Minogue said.

"You don't think he'd just destroy the papers and be done with it?" Corrigan asked.

"No, I doubt it. He's in no danger. Even if he's a bit suspicious, he'll be keen to bring back the spoils to who-ever sent him here. His bosses would want to see it."

"Who gave you the idea of having the postman deliver this to Combs' house?"

"I got up early this morning and I decided to play this as if those papers were true. Once I had got that settled in me mind, it was easy enough to figure out some trick."

"Trick, is it? It's not a game we're playing. Unless it's me in playing a game with my job. Or at least my credibility as a senior Garda officer," said Corrigan.

"How true for you, now," Minogue said in a conciliatory whisper.

"A bad choice of words."

"Anyway. So you had Eilis phone your man and tell him there was stuff belonging to Combs coming in the post?"

"And to say that, sorry, we couldn't spare the manpower to go out and collect it for him. He fairly leaped at the chance to go out there on his own. That's a point in our favour."

"And there's always my own set of prints," Minogue reminded him. Corrigan yawned and took the photocopied pages from the seat.

"So this is what the poor divil was done in for," Corrigan murmured.

"It's not just the business about Costello. That's bad enough. But there's everything to suggest that it was Ball who had Combs killed. On orders, maybe, from his own boss. There's no name on Ball's boss, so he might still be attached to the embassy. All it says here about him is that he is a little bourgeois who likes to dress natty."

Corrigan squirmed in his seat before lapsing into silence. Minogue was as happy not to hear any more of Corrigan's doubts. If Combs was telling the truth, he didn't need Pat Corrigan to remind him that they had a bomb in their laps. Minogue had spent nearly forty minutes persuading Corrigan to have two Special Branch detectives land themselves in a ditch within sight of Combs' house, armed with telephoto lenses and a video camera. They had snapped Moore going into the house at a quarter to eleven, but he had been out of sight somewhere in the house ever since. The two Branch radio-cars had been waiting an hour and a half to take up pursuit of Moore's Mini.

"It'll take him time to read the stuff, Pat," Minogue said, more in answer to his own interior conversation than to Corrigan. "They're photos of handwritten notes, written under his real name, William Grimes, don't forget."

Corrigan looked up from the prints, perplexed.

"He started out planning to get his own story out about what happened forty odd years ago?"

"At the beginning, yes. He probably put it as an ultimatum to Ball, but Ball suspected the worst. That he'd shop him for setting up Costello. And maybe even taking part in the killing."

Dunne elbowed out the door of the pub. He had no coffees with him. He checked in with the photo-surveillance team. Moore was still in the house.

"Damn it to hell," said Corrigan from under a contorted forehead. "If this stuff is at all true, this Combs man should have had the hero treatment. The Russians were part of the bloody Allies, no matter what anyone says. Give the man a medal and a dinner at Buck Palace, thanks very much, that was great work you did for us, more champagne," Corrigan argued.

Minogue liked the indignant tone. He was pleased that Corrigan had been caught up in the drama, an advocate.

"There's the rub, Pat," Minogue sighed. "But later on you find poor Combs wondering if it was more than just the fact that he shared information with the Soviets."

He searched through the prints and handed one to Corrigan.

"See there. There he is speculating that it was being gay did him in again as well. That they'd never trust him again because of it. Bitter. 'The sin of being a sodomite outweighed the virtue of saving what remains of civilisation from people like Hilter.'"

Corrigan looked up from the photo.

"Did you memorise that?" whispered Corrigan.

"No, it just stuck in me mind. There it is," Minogue's finger found the line.

"God, but he was a bitter man to be talking like that."

"It's around this part, too, I think ... where he says that even if he had agreed to work for the Americans or the British in East Germany, they would have sold him out if the right opportunity had arisen. Like with Vogel, that poor divil he mentions, sold out to get something else going."

"So they gave Combs a new name, a few shillings and told him to get lost and stay lost."

Minogue nodded.

"Because he wouldn't do the dirty on the Russians. He talks about how the Russians lost over twenty million of their people in the war. Do you know, but I think he must have had great feeling for people he probably never even met in real life."

"What do you mean?"

"Maybe he was a bit romantic about a Russian soul. I don't know. That they had been so badly done by with the so-called civilised races. Those Teutonic warrior-lunatics. Siding with victims, I wonder, this old man. That might have turned his head a bit here, too, I was thinking...." Minogue's thoughts broke away from his words. Words tumbled from his mind like dice from a hand: *victim, soul, Ireland, empire, Reich, Russia*.

"What are you saying?"

"It's just an impression. The remarks that Mrs Hartigan remembers. The drawings of the old stones he did, his — "

"Do you think he became a convert, is it?" said Corrigan with a skeptical frown.

Minogue suddenly remembered Mrs Hartigan's remark about the song on the radio — the Red Army Choir singing "It's a Long Way to Tipperary" — how Combs, or Grimes, had been amused by it.

Minogue shrugged. Corrigan's eyes flicked up to Minogue. Minogue felt leaden and cramped in the seat.

"So you guessed that the Brits could say all this stuff was rubbish?" said Corrigan.

Minogue now knew that it was more than the hangover which was sapping his energy.

" 'Course they could."

Corrigan pulled at an eyebrow. Minogue wondered if he'd ask him to go through the story again. The car swayed slightly as Dunne shifted his weight on the bonnet. The sun was out now. He heard Corrigan sucking in air through whistle lips. Corrigan gathered the pages and clapped them on their edges against his knee. Seagulls screeched overhead, heading inland. There'll be rain before the day is out, Minogue thought vacantly.

"This waiting," Corrigan groaned. "Madness. He might be flushing those negatives down the jacks."

The levity was too strained for Minogue. He tried to divert Corrigan.

"So your two followed Moore to a pub last night, you said?"

"And he made a phone call there. He had a pint of beer and went back to the hotel. They don't know if the call was long-distance or not, but Morrissey — he was one of the tails — says there's more to Moore than meets the eye. Thinks that Moore knew he was under surveillance. Moore made a few checks on his way to the pub. 'Trained,' says Morrissey, 'stinks of it.' "

"Eilis phoned him at half nine with the yarn."

"Volunteered to go and get it himself, did he?"

"Cool customer. He said he'd look after it if he was out at the house today, thanks very much," replied Minogue.

"*If*. I like that. He was on the road at a quarter to ten, the bugger, so he was," Corrigan remarked acidly.

"So that was round one to convince you," Minogue said, unwilling to let the chance of a dig escape him now.

"Sure amn't I in, Matt? They'll not look good trying to say it's all rubbish if Moore treats it like the crown jewels, now that he has it. Only I wish he'd get a bloody move-on. I don't like this slow-motion stuff."

"Time and patience," Minogue said. "Patience and time. This is what Moore came to find. And then we can get onto the big business, won't we?"

Corrigan raised an interrogative eyebrow at Minogue. The grey eyes fixed Minogue with a stare.

"Who Moore's boss is, who Ball's boss is at the embassy . . . "

Corrigan rolled his eyes and turned to stare out the window.

Moore hesitated by the phone again. He had found tape and was ready to reseal the envelope. The postmark was smudged. He could not tell whether the handwritten address in block letters was from Combs' hand. He had put his suspicions on hold while he scrutinised the photos. Although the tally of negatives matched the number of photographs, he could not match each negative to the prints until he had a means of magnifying them.

Moore noticed the envelope shaking in his hand. Ball had played for keeps, it seemed. But he had underestimated Arthur Combs by a long shot. When Combs thought it was kill or be killed, he had set the INLA on Ball. And Kenyon, for all his dusty manner, had had the right instincts, too: Combs didn't lack for determination when push came to shove, booze or no booze.

What would Kenyon do when they found out that Ball had been carrying on a private war, to the extent of ripping Costello's throat out? Moore tried to stay the trembling. He realised that he didn't know what to do.

There had been no other letters delivered. He looked about the hallway. The house unnerved him with the shambles and the sense that it would soon be closed, like a tomb. It smelled like stale bread, moulding, and Moore felt a sense of something he could not put one word on, despair maybe, loss, abandon. The contractor had said that he couldn't send the lorry with the shutters and the tradesmen to nail the windows until this afternoon at the earliest. A tap dripped somewhere. Even the birdsong from the hedges didn't lift the gloom. Moore almost wished that that garrulous detective, Murtagh, was with him again today.

He looked down at the envelope again. The manila was a garish colour now, almost luminescent. It felt oddly heavier, too. He grasped it tighter between his fingers as if to control the information it contained. Seven photographs with four pages on each photo. The negatives had been cut singly, stacked wrapped in plastic. Each page on each photograph was almost completely legible without magnification.

Moore thought of Kenyon's description of Combs and what he had done forty years ago. But had Kenyon wilfully kept him in ignorance about what Combs had been up to here in Ireland? Following a strict need-to-know, using one Edward Moore as a pick-up man?

Damn, Moore's thoughts fled: to be used like this. But did Kenyon know about Ball's sorties? Costello? But the irony of that, Combs' protest that it was not because he had much sympathy for Costello or his likes. At least Kenyon had read Combs pretty accurately. So what was Moore doing in the house with this, safe in his grasp? Safe? It was like someone had handed it to him.

Moore found matches in a kitchen drawer. He brought the papers to the sink and took a match out. He looked out the window at the hedges and fields beyond. He did not strike the match but stepped over the chalked outline on the floor and went upstairs. He kept back from each window as he surveyed the fields and the lane leading up to the house. Nothing. His car alone looked out of place.

He took the photographs and negatives downstairs, put them back in the envelope and sealed it. He glanced at the telephone but dismissed the idea. His heart started to beat stronger when he paused in front of the hall door. Again he thought about the matches in the kitchen. He imagined the charred photos peeling away from one another as they burned, the negatives melting. He turned abruptly on his heel and opened the door.

Outside, Moore pulled the door closed behind him and walked down the lane. He heard no sounds save the sighing of trees caught with the first breeze of the day. The air smelled of honeysuckle. Moore started the engine and drove toward the city.

Corrigan called the second car immediately.

" — Did you copy, Chestnut Two? Our man is out of the house and looks to be headed into the city. What's your signal strength on it? Over."

" — Well within range. Over."

Corrigan turned wary eyes on Minogue. Then he tapped on the back of Dunne's seat.

"Wait 'til both of them are by us," he said. "They have the know-how as regards staying with Moore."

Dunne nodded vigorously.

" — Coming onto the Dundrum Road, Control. Over," a broad Kerry accent intoned from the radio-speaker.

" — Copy, Chestnut One. Signal still good?"

" — Clear as a bell. Over."

" — Chestnut Two?" Corrigan said.

Minogue eased back in his seat and looked up at Two Rock Mountain while the roadside hedges skimmed by. They drew into Stepaside and slowed for the bends which marked the centre of the Village.

" — In sight, four cars ahead. Over," said the Kerry accent.

Moore seemed to be taking the same route back into the city. Corrigan's car stayed ahead until Dundrum. Corrigan told Dunne to pull over into a petrol station. The three policemen watched Moore's yellow Mini pass and, five cars back, the first of the pursuit cars, a blue Nissan.

"The hotel, five to four on," Corrigan murmured. "Just the way he went out. Like a yo-yo."

Dunne leaned an elbow on the door, waiting for a direction. The three policemen watched the second pursuit car go by, less than a minute behind the first.

"Away, so," Corrigan said.

"What's with the bloody traffic this heavy now?" Dunne muttered as he worked through the gears.

Moore had not noticed the blue car until after he had gone through a half-dozen bends. The second time he spotted it, he felt his stomach tighten. He heard his breath whistle in his nostrils. The cars snaking and turning behind him always had the blue Nissan at least three cars back. Coincidence? He had caught a glimpse of the silhouettes of two men. The Nissan let in cars twice to fill any changing tally between itself and his Mini. He recognised the villages which he had passed on the way out. The roads were too narrow for the traffic at any time of the day. Cars and lorries had overrun the streets and clogged them. These suburbs, with their once-separate villages now fused into a monotonous alley for motoring commuters, were little different from the tawdry outer suburbs of London. Moore began to look for the junction he'd need if he had to make a move, a crossroads with heavy traffic and traffic-lights.

He found what he required just beyond a sprawl which bore the sign "Dundrum Shopping Centre." The phone-box was on the far side of the crossroads. Moore did not signal until the last minute. As he waited for a gap in the oncoming traffic, he saw the Nissan drift by, carried along on the inside lane of city-bound traffic. When he turned the wheel at last, he was suddenly aware that his jaws were clenched tight.

He parked, blocking two cars which had themselves taken over the footpath next to the phone. Inside the phone-box, Moore felt the tug of doubt drawing at his stomach again. Minogue: that odd mixture of irony and indulgence in his manner.

" — He's stopping," came the Kerry accent on the radio.

"Stopped. Crossroads with Taney Road. Just beyond the Shopping Centre. Oh-oh . . . "

" — What's up there?" Corrigan said.

The three heard the roar of a bus passing close to the detectives at the other end.

" — We're through the . . . we had to go through with the lights. . . . Pulling in on the city side. Over."

" — All right, all right. One. Give him lots of room. Chestnut Two, are you copying this?" Corrigan said.

" — We are. In sight of the crossroads now. We have visual with Chestnut One."

Corrigan frowned. The first car was badly placed if Moore decided to double back, but the second should be able to take over easily. Corrigan's own car was within a mile of the junction, he guessed. He told Dunne to hurry it up. Minogue watched Corrigan's pulse tick in his neck as he waited for the transmission to resume.

" — May be checking for a tail. Over."

The words had rushed out before the abrupt click of the transmission out. Corrigan waited, his thumb wavering over the button. The two in the car might have to go by Moore.

" — Still in the car. Over."

Still Corrigan said nothing. Dunne had edged himself sideways in his seat. He was looking from Corrigan to Minogue.

" — He's out of the car. Heading for a telephone-box. I'm getting out, hold on — "

" — Making a call, by the looks of things . . . "

The Kerry accent sounded winded. Minogue guessed he had run through the traffic to keep Moore in sight.

Corrigan nodded to Dunne.

"Move it, Dunner. Quick, man. What's the go-slow here?"

Moore placed two ten-penny pieces on the chute and dialled. The insistent beeping told him that he had guessed right, a non-existent telephone number. He began talking into the receiver and nodded his head several times for effect.

He let his gaze drift over the crowded intersection. He couldn't see any blue Nissan now. When Moore caught sight of the man looking into a shop window some hundred feet down from the booth, a tremor burst abruptly in his chest and parachuted slowly into his belly. He felt the air leaving his lungs. One car for sure, a voice said within. He gripped the phone tighter, while his thoughts raced uncontrolled for several moments.

He watched the traffic-lights and began counting. If the timing was right, he could do it handily enough. Thirty-seven seconds on full green, no right-turn lights either. It was cut-and-dried; all he had to do was time himself. Each time the lights for the city-bound traffic changed to red, the heavy traffic bottle-necked almost immediately. Count five, say, into their red light and any back-up car on the other side of the junction would be blocked for a count of thirty.

He searched for the name of the road which led uphill to his left. Taney Road. Moore thumbed the index and fingered open the page. He could not stop his whole hand from shaking. He followed through the map on the next page, tracing a route from Goatstown through to the university and toward Ballsbridge, close by the embassy. If they lost him, they might wait for him to try an entry there, though, Moore reflected.

His heart was hammering now. He swallowed and looked out over the traffic again. The streets on the map didn't allow parallel pursuits, so he could take the first turnoff on the city side and just boot it, running laterally from the pursuit. But for now, stay to the speed limit, move promptly. If the traffic stayed thick, he had a better than even chance of losing them. He put down the phone and checked the map again. The window-shopper was now interested in electrical appliances, closer to the phone-booth. Moore was startled to realise then that he wasn't frightened now. He was excited.

Again he considered a drop for the envelope. Textbook, but he'd have to pick one on the hoof while he was driving and hope to find something secure enough until Murray sent out someone to get it. Under a hedge somewhere, wrapped in plastic in a ditch? Messy. An embassy man groping about in some laneway, trying to find them. Moore bit his lip. He could try losing them long enough to destroy the material. Give an oral report on it. He'd have to read it again, though, go through it for essential details, and hope to hell his short-term memory held up long enough to get it all. Either that or read it out over the damned phone?

Moore searched his pocket for more change. He would have to contact Murray anyway, no matter what he decided he had to do with the envelope. Slip the surveillance and he'd have options, time — and so would Murray. Murray could take it off his hands. Kenyon might piss and moan, but it wasn't Kenyon who had to make decisions here and now. Moore pocketed the map, open on the page he had chosen for his route.

CHAPTER 14

Corrigan turned to Minogue.

"Smart enough not to touch the phone back at the house."

Minogue managed a smile. Corrigan had the face of a man whose horse had unexpectedly gained ground toward the end of the race. His eyes glittered.

"Well, he'll find us when we want him to, the little shite," Corrigan whispered with a weak smile starting below his nostrils.

" — Talking into the phone . . . looking around," said the Kerry accent.

Dunne piloted the car around a curve in the road. Minogue saw the Shopping Centre ahead.

" — Get clear for to take up any slack, Car Two," Corrigan barked.

" — Will do, Control. Just need a minute to . . . "

"Pull over here," Corrigan muttered. "Yeah, here. I'm not entirely sure I like the look of this."

The warning tone in Corrigan's voice registered on Minogue. He, too, began straining to see across the junction ahead. A double-decker bus slowed to a stop in the traffic-lane next to the car.

"Fuck sakes, get us out of this!" Corrigan hissed.

Minogue returned the gaze of schoolchildren looking down from the bus. They were laughing. Minogue felt like a zoo animal. The bus edged by the three policemen. Dunne was sweating heavily, turning the wheel uselessly. Corrigan sat paralysed, concentrating on the voice from the radio.

" — Reading something. He's opened it up. Some book . . . "

Dunne began swearing now, quiet, sincere, rural obscenities.

" — He's off. He's turning around. Over."

" — Who's on him?" Corrigan said into the mike.

" — Repeat, Chestnut One," Corrigan's shout erupted through Minogue's trance, "who's clear on pursuit?"

Corrigan sprang forward in the seat, his cheek jammed against the head-rest. Dunne licked the insides of his lips and flicked glances at the wing mirror. The bus stopped finally beside them. They were blocked. It was perfect timing for Moore, Minogue realised.

" — Chestnut Two to Control. We're jammed — "

" — He's gone. Gone up Taney Road," cawed the Kerry accent.

Corrigan's mouth hung open. For a moment he became completely still. Then he hammered the seatback with the edge of his fist. He leaped from the seat and began waving his photocard at motorists to clear a way. Dunne began edging the car into a space being cleared ahead. The lights changed. Dunne had the car moving as Corrigan fell heavily back into the seat, grasping at the doorhandle.

" — Chestnut One to Control. Signal's converging, there's some fade . . . "

Other cars turned up Taney Road ahead of them. Moore had plenty of padding if he wanted to lose them. Dunne bullied the car across the junction. From the far side of the junction, Minogue caught a glimpse of the other radio-car, a blue Nissan, with full head-lamps on, stuck half-way up on the curb. Tires howled somewhere.

Corrigan was livid. He tried to smother his breath-ing, but it came out of his nostrils in harsh, wheezy whistles. Dunne leaned over the wheel as if to spur the car on through the unengineered limits of second gear. Then Corrigan took a deep breath and let it out of his mouth, all the while glaring at Minogue.

"I might have guessed we shouldn't have been diddling around with a small unit for this. That kind of stunt he just pulled doesn't happen by accident, Matt. He's a pro. Here we are, flopping around. If we don't spot him ahead of the junction up ahead, what do you call it?"

"Goatstown."

"Right. He can go any of three ways he likes. And we'll be sitting there, holding our mickeys."

Corrigan's anger faded into a bitter inflexion. The car lurched back over the white line, greeted by a horn behind. Minogue was flung onto an elbow in the back seat. The car dived and rose as Dunne stamped at the brake, then clutched into second and pulled out to pass. Minogue fell back against the seat. He de-cided to stay put.

" — Control to Chestnuts One and Two. Give me a situation in order."

There was no hesitation this time.

" — We're through onto Taney Road," the Kerry accent replied reluctantly.

"Meaning ye're well behind us, ye morons," Corrigan hissed off-air.

" — In sight of Chestnut One, sir. Coming through the junction now. Two over."

" — Well we're ahead of ye both on Taney," Corrigan spat into the mike. "So get a move-on for the love of . . . "

Both radio-cars confirmed.

" — What's the signal look like? Over."

" — Intermittent . . . fading in spots."

Corrigan rolled his eyes.

" — Same with Two."

Corrigan thumbed savagely to transmit.

" — Central this is Control for Operation Melody. I want in on the South Dublin frequency. Confirm you'll link me. Over."

" — Confirming your request, Inspector," came the cautious reply. "But you'll have to wait a minute or two, sir. There's a lag now that we're trying to sort out the new equipment . . . "

"Maybe a squad-car'll pick him up, sir," said Dunne.

"Squad-car my Aunt Fanny's fat agricultural arse," Corrigan retorted. "Moore will go to ground for a while at least. But at least we can keep him away from the embassy, if he has ideas in that line."

Minogue believed that the snap was meant for him, not Dunne. Neither Minogue nor Dunne dared to speak. They listened while Corrigan directed one of the radio-cars toward the British Embassy on Merrion Road. Still waiting for the link, Corrigan swore with impatience and glared out the back window at the grille of a labouring lorry. Somewhere in the line of traffic struggling behind the lorry was the other radio-car.

"*Dum spiro, spero,*" Minogue soothed. Neither man asked for an explanation.

Minogue wanted to lie down, empty his head. He'd mucked it up. He had second prints of Combs' stuff, but they might never get to the accessory, Ball's accomplice — his boss. Moore had turned out not to be a pin-striped dope after all. And now, Pat Corrigan un-ravelling there in the front seat, too, giving himself a heart attack. He had read Moore wrong. The same Moore could be laughing up his sleeve now.

Minogue yawned long, the tears gathering at the outer edges of his eyelids. He opened his eyes into a bleary world and listened while Corrigan issued in-structions brusquely into the car radio for the uni-formed Gardai on the network. Corrigan dissembled fluently to the Gardai in the squad-cars, telling what he knew would be attentive policemen that it was a Special Branch matter and that the driver was to be detained on the spot.

Then Corrigan's face appeared between the seats as he looked down at Minogue. The soft grey eyes stared, eyelashes sweeping twice, and he looked back over the dash.

"Nice work, Pat," Minogue risked.

"In case you didn't overhear me, I'm going to grab this Moore any way I can. That's my way and that's the way we should have attacked this bloody opera-tion in the first place."

"But we had to be sure the photos were worth something, Pat. Now we know; we have the bit be-tween our teeth, don't we?" Minogue said, as sin-cerely as he could.

Dunne worked at seizing the gearbox again. Corri-gan gave Minogue a searching look. Minogue saw Corrigan's fretful tongue run around inside his lips, upper and lower in turn. He now felt reasonably sure that Pat had very good dentures indeed.

Moore stepped out of the car and drew in the heavy, languid sea air. He had parked next to a lorry, which concealed his Mini from the coast road, a good couple of hundred yards back up the lane from the railway station. Bootstown? No, Booterstown. He found the public phone attached to the stone wall which made up the back of the station-house. So far Moore had seen nobody moving around the building. Mid-day, slack.

Moore dialled and waited. He heard the switch-board clicks before the phone began ringing.

"Yes?"

Had Kenyon given him the right number?

"Mr Murray please."

"Hold, please."

They didn't even ask, Moore reflected.

"Please phone at the alternate number."

Irritated by the security, Moore struggled to remember the six digits. He took out a fifty-penny piece, all the change he had left, and dialled again. He heard two rings before the receiver was lifted abruptly.

"Murray here."

"I'm calling about some material I've located."

There was a long pause before Murray spoke.

"Mr Moore? You can be specific on this line," he heard Murray say slowly. "The line is continuously encoded, incoming and outgoing."

Moore hesitated, distracted by the hissy quiet from Murray's end.

"I have some extremely sensitive material here," Moore said. Still silence from Murray's end. Moore felt that obscure agitation again. It had lain buried beneath the tension which had gripped him when he had first spotted the blue car. Even now, confident that he had lost any pursuit car, the burrowing doubt gnawed at him again. Stupid, he thought, the damn place had him on edge: looks like Britain, but completely alien.

"Are you still there?" Murray said.

"What?" asked Moore.

"You had a look at the material, did you?" Murray said again.

"Yes, yes. But look, I don't want to go into detail here now — " he began.

"I told you, the line's clean," Murray broke in angrily. Moore held his breath again, feeling the pounding begin at the base of his skull. Tell Murray?

"Are you still there, Moore? How did you locate the material?"

"Self-addressed envelope," Moore managed to say. "Thirty-five mil negatives, black-and-white, and photographic prints. The numbers match, but I can't read the negatives ... "

"Prints of what?"

"Seems like the original was handwritten notes. Twenty-eight pages, I estimate."

"And you read the prints?"

"Yes. But — "

"Anything or anybody local in jeopardy?" Murray cut in.

Moore hesitated. He'd have to tell Murray about the pursuit.

"There are allegations about an embassy man."

"Who?"

"Mervyn Ball, the one who was assass — "

"Only party identified?"

"There's mention of another person, somebody working with Ball. Unnamed."

"Have you made contact with your firm about this yet?" Murray asked.

"No. That's partly why I'm calling you. I'm in a phone-booth here in the south suburbs. . . . I think I had some company."

"Had? Repeat that," Murray said.

"At least one car. There may have been more on foot."

"The local law?"

"Something special, I think," said Moore. "Plain clothes."

"But you shook them for certain?"

Moore thought again of Minogue's grave clown's face.

"I'm pretty sure. But I don't like my chances for too long. I'm still out in the open here. There's no way I'm going back to the hotel — "

"Don't even consider it, no," Murray interrupted.

"There was a tail on me yesterday," Moore added. "They were fishing, general observation. They might even put out an All Points to pick me up. . . . I mean, if they knew I had this material . . . "

Then Moore heard the savage undertone which Murray didn't try to suppress.

"What do you mean, 'if they knew'? Have you been set up, Moore?"

Moore recalled a moment in Minogue's office when he had looked up from his briefcase to find Minogue staring under his eyebrows at him.

"I'd be out of commission by now, if I had."

"We need an RDV," Murray said after several seconds' silence.

"You don't think I could — " Moore began.

"Listen for a moment, Moore. You've had your instructions on this. We need that material. Forget your guesswork here. Your job is to get out of the area and to clear anything you have with me."

"But I haven't even had a chance to let my superiors know. . . . In a matter this serious — "

"Don't put a foot wrong now. Don't let these people make you jittery. You can't stay out in the open and you know that. We're all on the same side here, remember. I can get your material out, understood? Now, where are you, and how long can you maintain that position securely?"

"There's a suburban train station. Bootstown — no, wait, Booterstown. South suburbs, on the coast."

"Booterstown?"

"Yes. There's a carpark next to some wasteland, right by the sea. It's down off the main road. You can't see me from the road."

"Wait a minute while I locate . . . "

Moore heard pages turning at Murray's end.

"Okay. I have you. You're out the coast road, Merrion Road. You're quite close."

"I'm not going to take the chance of getting on a main road again."

"I'm well aware of contingencies," Murray snapped. "Can you hold there for ten, fifteen minutes? Pass the material to me there. It'll be in London by five this evening."

Moore hesitated.

"I'll have a dip. car," Murray continued. "The law won't touch me even if they have a nose for me."

Moore knew that he couldn't hold onto the envelope and expect to get on the plane with it. He felt a mounting anger at Murray's tone, his insinuations, his rudeness. No wonder Kenyon had been curt on the subject of Murray taking charge. He wondered about trying to place a call to Kenyon, direct.

"I can get to you inside fifteen minutes," Murray was saying. "Then you're on your way, clean. Understood?"

He had shaken off the coppers too: the need to do something right away with the dossier had receded. Murray had to see the material anyway. He might as well wait for him here.

"O.K.," said Moore finally.

"Fine. Think about afterwards, after I have this material. Head back into the city. Go about your business as if everything's just so."

"I'll be bumping into the law one way or the other. There's this copper, I don't quite know what to make of him, Minogue — "

"The worst they can do to you is pick you up and ask you a few questions. They may give you the once-over on some pretext but, just remember, they can't press you on anything. If they get stroppy, I can let them know here. You're covered all ways, just remember that. These are bluffers here, these coppers. Amateurs. Take my word for it."

Moore thought again of how easily he had jettisoned the surveillance. Textbook simple — with the help of a chaotic and crowded road system.

"All right," said Moore in a flat tone.

"A carpark, you say?"

"A yellow Mini Metro. You'll have to drive right around to the far end of the carpark to see me. Just find a red lorry, I'm tucked in next to it."

Moore hung up. A train drummed and squealed into the station. He walked back to the car and got in. Two schoolgirls in uniform walked out of the station carrying heavy sports bags. Moore let down the window and checked his watch. The smells of low tide swept in from the strand, displacing some of the stench of stale cigar smoke from the Mini's interior.

Another train rattled into Booterstown station. More schoolchildren came out and walked up toward the coast road. Moore checked his watch. Murray would be here within minutes.

He wondered if he should move out from behind the lorry so that Murray could spot him quicker. He abruptly realised that this made no sense. He must be getting rattled. If Murray could spot him easier, so could the law. He felt claustrophobic next to the lorry. If it fell over . . . ? Spooked: no, of course it couldn't move. Moore listened to the hum of traffic from the coast road some two hundred yards beyond where he sat. He looked down at the envelope again, wanting to open it and read more.

A witch-hunt, he thought, and Kenyon hadn't hinted one iota about what Ball had been running right here in Dublin. Did that mean that Kenyon was in on the scheme? Was Kenyon part and parcel of a joint assassination squad worked by his own Service and MI6? The boss that Combs alluded to?

Moore visualised a debriefing with Kenyon. A wry smile from the otherwise dry Kenyon, a caution about need-to-know. A well-rehearsed homily on the duties of field-officers, with a few bromides about the Defence of the Realm. . . . But Combs' plainly sincere disgust at the Costello killing, that he was sure Ball had actually taken part in the killing personally. Surely . . .

Moore's thoughts drifted astray, the unease still hovering, as he watched two schoolchildren dragging their school-bags along the footpath from the station entrance. One of the boys had been crying recently. His knee was grazed. The other idly swung his bag to and fro, resigned to the slow progress of his mate, as if the older boy was wise to the ways of bullies, that his mate would live to see another day. Combs' exclamation marks after his mention of Costello's death: "pure and simple sadism!!!" Would he, Moore, be expected to sit quietly through the debriefing while the contents of Combs' material was passed over? Maybe Kenyon would simply take off the gloves and tell him that it was none of his business what the intelligence services had to do in a war with terrorists. Still Moore's doubts lingered. There must have been Army involvement in the snatch to get Costello across the border. And Kenyon knew all this, he had to.

" — Chestnut Two to Control. We have a navy blue Rover at the gates. Over."

Corrigan's eyes bulged. He snatched the mike from his lap. They had separated from the first radio-car, which was trolling vainly in the suburbs south of them. The radio signal from Moore's Mini had disappeared nearly ten minutes ago. There had been no sightings from the regular patrols of Garda squad-cars yet.

Minogue had opened the window to evade the sour, penetrating smell of Dunne's sweat.

" — Repeat, Chestnut Two. Control over."

Dunne's foot lightened on the accelerator. Minogue rolled up the window to hear the transmission. They were driving down through Seafield toward the coast road.

" — Navy blue Rover with embassy plates coming through check-point."

" — How many on board?"

" — Just one, sir. Male, forties, suit . . . "

" — Who is he?" Corrigan asked, his eyes out of focus.

" — We don't know, sir. No. Doesn't match our photo-file for current staff . . . "

Dunne turned to share a wink of excitement with Minogue. Minogue felt the surprise tingle in his fingertips. A good smoke would be just the ticket now, he thought.

" — He's through the gates now. Gone right, heading south toward Blackrock."

" — Copy here. Stand by, Two," said Corrigan.

Corrigan seemed to be staring at the back of Dunne's head. Then he turned abruptly to Minogue.

"Damn and blast it, I'm going to go the whole hog," he whispered. Before Minogue could say anything, Corrigan was talking into the mike.

" — Yes, Two? Take it up and locate for us. Chestnut One, make your way to coast road to take up slack. Copy."

Dispatch intervened before the reply from the radio-cars.

" — Central to Operation Melody Control."

" — Yes," said Corrigan resignedly. "Standing by."

" — Er, sir . . . Standing orders posted prohibit your request. . . . Can refer you to, em, requisite officer. If you have his telephone number already . . . "

Corrigan seemed to smile, but when Minogue looked closely it was a sneer which remained.

" — Override the directive for this. Chestnut Two, proceed. I don't want him so much as dreaming you're on his tail, do you hear?"

The radio-car managed to beat dispatch to the button. Minogue believed he could read a smile in the detective's voice who replied.

" — Copy, Control. Chestnut Two on track. South on coast road."

" — Central to Operation Melody Control."

" — Go ahead, Delaney."

" — Sir, are you receiving clear? Repeat: directive to avoid any surveillance of embassy staff; to be accompanied only if requested for security details."

" — We copy here. I'm still overriding it, Delaney. I'll fill in the card for it. I copy your notification. Out."

There was an unsettling silence from the radio. Minogue caught Corrigan's eyes. Corrigan's sneer was gone now. He eyeballed Minogue steadily for a moment.

"You best keep your tongue in your head, Matt Minogue. I'm not in the humour of any guff."

Murray hadn't expected heavy traffic. Stuck far back in a row by lazily-timed traffic-lights, he studied the map again. There were no short-cuts. The train station was well out of the way of the main road — if the scale was accurate, that is. He swallowed again, his throat dry. Would he ever have started this with Ball if he had known that he, Murray, might be here today, on his way to meet a man he'd probably have to kill?

Murray missed second gear, grinding it before he wrenched the stick into the gate proper. Stupid academic question. Hindsight . . . but could he even try to get this Moore onside, have him come in? Moore seemed so damned reluctant to hand over the photos without having okayed it with Kenyon. Loyal: due procedure. Christ, the man was trained as a barrister; he'd want chapter and verse. Unlike Murray, this man had never seen Belfast at street level, every building concealing a potential bomb, a sniper, an ambush. No, Murray realised with a hollow ache in his stomach, he couldn't hope to turn Moore in a matter of ten minutes' persuading. Couldn't hope to motivate a man with no real stake in a campaign against terrorists.

Murray passed a large hotel before he saw the overgrown marshland which lay between the road and the matte silver sand which the tide of Dublin Bay had exposed. A salt marsh, a bird sanctuary, he glimpsed from a passing sign. Just over the low parapet which formed the boundary of the marsh, Murray saw the roofs of parked cars. Among them was a red lorry. The building further down could only be the railway station.

He tucked his elbow into his side and felt the prickly heat of panic start in his armpit. The dull, solid weight of the automatic tugged at his jacket pocket. A train emerged from the station, city-bound, moving slowly against the greys and purples of the bay.

" — Chestnut One to Control. Over."

Corrigan acknowledged.

" — We're getting a signal, sir. It's steady enough, on the outer edge of the range. It shows to the city side of us."

" — Where are you, One?"

" — Coming through Blackrock, Control. Five minutes and we'll be on you — "

The other tracking car broke in before Corrigan could reply.

" — Car Two to Control. We're reading a very spotty signal, too, sir. Just this minute."

" — Wait a minute, wait a minute," Corrigan's voice began to rise. He turned to Minogue.

"Now we're talking. Moore's out there somewhere close to us. Between Blackrock and town."

"And that embassy car is headed out from town, too," said Dunne. He stroked one of his mammoth, gristly ears. Minogue's mind lost traction. Dunne piloted the car through an amber light. His brain fogged, Minogue's eyes indolently took in details of the roads they were passing. They were within a mile of the coast road. Corrigan pinched his lip.

" — Passing Merrion Gates. Signal clear. Two, over."

"This is Trimelston, sir," said Dunne. "He'll be gone by us when we hit the coast road."

Dunne's anxious glance brought Corrigan to.

"Get out onto the coast road anyhow, would you," he said.

" — Wait, wait. He's turning into Booterstown station. Chestnut Two, over."

Corrigan sat up in his seat and barked into the mike.

" — Copy that, One?"

" — Copy, Control. Signal is stationary, sir. It looks to be within a mile of us. The Punch Bowl, say . . . or the train station."

Dunne accelerated by two cars. The three policemen were now in sight of the coast road. They were a mile to the city side of Booterstown.

"Decoy?" Dunne tried.

"Me bollocks," said Corrigan, wide-eyed with antic-ipation now. "Moore is close by. The smart money says they have something arranged at the station. Damn and damn again."

"They're trained, Pat," Minogue said quietly. Dunne's eyes flickered to Minogue's in the mirror.

"It'd be a lovely set-up they'd have if they use the train," Minogue added. "We'd not get to them at all and they know it. We should pull the plug on them fast. Get the patrols on it."

Corrigan snorted. He licked his lips before talking into the mike.

" — Central, this is Control for Operation Melody. Delaney, are you still on here?"

" — Yes, sir."

" — Delaney, I need a lot of stuff now, the whole shooting gallery. Are you listening to me?"

" — Sir . . . "

" — All Dublin Garda frequencies, all right? If you have to wait for air, get South Dublin first. I need Gardai at all suburban rail stations. All stations, from Bray to Howth. For immediate apprehension and de-tention of male passenger or passengers, possibly two, repeat, two males. Individually or together. Every sta-tion, do you follow?"

" — I copy."

" — First possible suspect, male, aged mid-thirties. English, name Moore, Edward Moore. I'll give you a description now in a minute. Second suspect, proba-bly English, driving a navy blue Rover. It's a diplo-matic plate."

" — Two Englishmen, sir?"

" — Yep. Two. Either or both suspects will be carry-ing envelope containing photographic material. Im-mediate detention subject to my arrival. Sit them in the car and don't let anyone near 'em."

" — Dip? Or consular staff, sir?" Delaney asked cautiously.

The three policemen knew that Delaney wanted it on the tape.

" — Immediate detention. Gardai can cite descriptions of two suspects wanted in a bank robbery on south side. I'll settle it when I get there. Over."

"Be creative for the love of Jases, Delaney," Corrigan muttered with his thumb off. Dunne laughed aloud.

" — Read you, Melody control. Descriptions please. Over."

" — Here's one. Both may be travelling together for one stop and no more. Hold."

Corrigan turned to Minogue. The grey eyes were bigger now. Minogue saw the sweat gathering under Corrigan's thinning hair.

"Give them something to ID Moore, Matt."

Minogue took the mike. The radio cawed before he thumbed to transmit.

" — He's going down the station road. . . . Slowing . . . seems to want to park. It's tight for us to just follow him right down, Control . . . "

Corrigan responded immediately.

" — One of you out with a brief-case and a handset. Go down on foot and be ready to get on a train after them. We're coming up to Booterstown ourselves. Give us a minute. Car One is about three minutes back. Hold position, observe and wait for me. And don't forget that Moore character is probably stuck in there somewhere in the carpark. Over."

" — Copy."

Corrigan thrust the mike back to Minogue.

" — This is Central, standing by for description from Melody Control. Over."

" — Here I am. Melody Control, that is," said Minogue. He didn't know where to begin.

" — Moore's close on six feet. Well-dressed . . . very well-dressed. Suit, dark. Driving a hired Mini, yellow. . . . Moore is thirty-five or six, I'd say. Pasty-faced. Sort of distinguished, you might say. Doesn't have much of a sense of humour. Pronounced accent. . . . Let me see, what else . . . "

CHAPTER 15

Murray let the Rover freewheel down the gentle in-
cline toward the station. Save for two schoolchildren
already stepping onto the footpath, the station seemed
to be deserted. One boy's face was streaked from
crying, his school-bag dragging along the path. Murray
saw the panels of the red lorry over the rows of parked
cars. Coke, the ubiquitous banner of American civilisation standing out against the pastels of sea and sky.
Moore was to the sea-side of the lorry.

Murray braked and turned the Rover into the
carpark. As he turned, he noticed a car turn in off the
coast road behind him. A bolt of alarm ran down his
back. He stopped just inside the carpark and waited.
The car pulled into the curb. A casually-dressed man
stepped out from the passenger side. He carried a
soft-sided briefcase and a newspaper. He smiled at
the driver, seemed to crack a joke, and strode on
toward the station. Murray watched the car in his
mirror as it turned back onto the coast road.

Murray waited until he saw the passenger pass the
entrance to the carpark. Then he reversed the Rover
to the end of a cluster of cars. Out of sight of the

station now, he could get to the lorry, walk to Moore's car from behind. Murray's fingers slipped as he leaned across to unlock the passenger door. His hands were moist and they trembled. He placed the keys under the front seat and wiped his hands with his handkerchief. He couldn't keep his hands steady. He took the silencer out of his pocket and matched it to the muzzle of the automatic. Sure he had a purchase on the thread then, he rolled the silencer with his palm. The cylinder fell off and landed between the seats. Murray swore. He reached down and tried again. He tightened it this time, using the handkerchief for grip.

Murray stepped out of the car. He felt he was entering a different world. Small polka dots sailed down in his vision and burst. He held the door from slamming and braced his knees to banish the feeling of feebleness in his legs. Have to do it, his mind was shouting furiously. He felt vulnerable as he started walking. He stared intently at cars, expecting some to be occupied but none were. The grilles of the cars seemed to be animate presences, vague threats as if they'd spring into motion. The lorry was about ten cars down from where Murray had parked. The pistol scratched his thigh, the five inches of silencer jammed under his belt to secure the gun. Murray looked down at his fly to see if the outline of the silencer was visible as he walked. He approached the car next to the red lorry and paused. He looked around. Nobody.

Christ, he thought, Moore is in too deep: he'd never come over. Not a chance. If only he could have ten minutes, though, he could . . . Useless, couldn't think like that now: he must commit himself to action. Murray stopped again by the back of the lorry and edged out to take a look down toward the station.

Over the car roofs he could see the white roof of the Ford, still by the station entrance. A puff of smoke escaped from the driver's window. He heard fragments of pop music. The newspaper flapped, page turned. It dawned on him that he'd have to kill Moore right in his car.

Murray thumbed the safety off and walked around the back of the lorry. *Make it quick, in and out.* He felt the ice-pack grip him tighter around the chest and hold. Moore spotted the movement in the mirror right away. Murray saw the head turn to look through the back window. He heard a car engine from the carpark behind. Too late now to back around the damned lorry to check, he knew. Murray kept walking instead and grasped the passenger door handle of the Mini. Locked. Moore's face appeared in the window as he leaned across the passenger seat to unlock the door. Murray tried hard to smile but his face felt set, frozen. Moore's puzzled gaze searched Murray's face.

"Hello, Moore," Murray managed to say in a choked voice. Moore blinked. His eyes darted down from Murray's face as his fingers closed on the golf-tee stalk for the lock. Murray saw the manila envelope on the seat below him, half-covered by the stretching Moore. He tried the door again, but too soon: Moore's fingers had slipped. Moore suddenly froze, his fingers tight on the lock now. Murray wondered what he was staring at.

Murray looked down. A wrenching tremor seized at his heart when he saw that the grip of the automatic had slipped sideways in his belt. Moore had seen it. Both men stayed perfectly stiff for several seconds.

Murray broke the spell first. He grasped the automatic, drawing it cleanly from under his belt. Moore was turning the ignition key. Murray yanked at the doorhandle in one last try. The Mini's engine came to life, the roar of the small engine's revs rattling the tappets. Murray let off a shot as the Mini lurched forward. The glass whitened in the rear passenger window, but the Mini was still squealing away, engine screaming. Murray crouched and fired through the back window. The Mini turned sharply but still accelerated, shedding pellets of glass. Murray stood, uncertain. He thought about his own car and turned to run around the rear of the lorry. Rounding the lorry, Murray heard the squeal of tires, the crash of metal and glass.

"Mother of the Divine Jesus!" Corrigan shouted.

The yellow Mini rocketed out from behind a lorry. The driver of the Mini almost lost control as he swerved. Minogue believed that he saw two wheels of the Mini lift off the ground.

"Box him!" Corrigan roared.

Dunne shouted too and swung the car back toward the road. The Mini did not brake. The impact threw Minogue against the front seat and then dumped him across the back seat on the rebound. Dizzy, he heard Corrigan kicking at his door. Dunne was out first. Corrigan lay back on Dunne's seat then, gave a shout and landed a tremendous flat-footed kick on his door. It flew open and Corrigan was up and scrambling to get out. Minogue saw that Corrigan's forehead had been cut. Corrigan's hand was clutching for his pistol as he levered himself out of the door.

Minogue stepped unsteadily out of the car. A man was running up from the station. One of us, Minogue thought indolently. He rubbed his eyes. His head was still buzzing. Corrigan was pulling on the door of the yellow Mini. Minogue couldn't see anyone in the car. Dunne saw the gunman first.

"Gun!" Dunne screamed.

Corrigan looked over the roof of the Mini. Minogue looked down at the running man. He was zig-zagging around the cars, banging their panels with his arms and hand as he charged through. As he ran he was tugging at a pistol under his arm. The pistol out, he began shouting, the gun jabbing the air with each piston stab of his arm.

The gunman hesitated. A gorgeous brown suit, Minogue observed dreamily from somewhere behind the enormous, numbing nose. Incongruous, silly. A gun? Minogue looked to the slip-on shoes. A hundred quid, easy. Minogue's nose was pulsing slowly now. It felt like a slowly inflating balloon. The elegant gunman darted a look toward cars then, thumping panels heavily to slow himself as he ducked. Who was doing all that shouting now? Dunne, yes. Shouting at me, Minogue realised. Guns? *Kathleen'll be livid with me . . .*

Corrigan had the heels of his hands resting on the roof, aiming the Walther. Dunne screamed at Minogue again.

"You!" shouted Corrigan. "Put down that gun! Put it down or we'll shoot. Drop it now! Police!"

The gunman frowned, his arm wavering. Looked shocked, Minogue thought. So he should be. . . . Maybe he was hurt? Well-dressed, but . . .

"Drop it now!" Corrigan roared. "Drop the gun now!"

Minogue heard the car radio come to life. The gunman's face eased then he raised his arm.

Corrigan shot him once. The man fell backwards with a surprised shout. The detective crouched by the car stood up and ran on tiptoe toward the fallen man. Standing near him, his gun pointed down, it seemed like a party game to Minogue. The detective moved to the side and gently toed something metallic, sending it skittering a few feet across the tarmac. Not smart,

Minogue's faraway brain tut-tutted. An automatic with a single-action could go off if you so much as open a box of Rice Krispies in the same room. . . . Everybody's scared, aren't they? The man on the ground drew up his legs and groaned. The suit, the suit: it'll be ruined, Minogue's thoughts fluttered about nearby. That's blood, that is, Minogue's eyes began arguing with his brain. Concussed, the brain sneered back. You're concussed, my dear man . . .

A blue Nissan came tearing down the road and slewed to a stop, the driver's door flying open. Minogue stood up slowly from his crouch. He felt dizzy and pleasantly limp. He saw that one of the man's slip-on shoes was off. Dunne grabbed at the radio and began talking. While he waited for a reply, he pointed to Minogue and gestured toward his own nose. Minogue looked down at the blood on his own shirt. He touched the bridge of his nose and felt a resonant throb, not yet painful but vaguely warm. He walked slowly to the driver's side of the Mini.

Moore's window was open. The door was jammed, the front wing of the car crumpled and pushed up near the door-hinge. Moore was lying sideways across the front seats.

"Moore, are you all right there?" said Minogue. His voice vibrated in the lumpy blockage which was his nose. He saw liquid gleam, oily, on the seat-back.

"Can you hear me, Moore? Are you . . . ?" Minogue wheezed out.

"Something in my back, I don't know," Moore said in a quiet, level voice. He did not try to move. "It's kind of numb there now . . . "

Minogue saw Moore's fingers moving slowly then, the eyelashes fluttering. The fingers clenched and loosened. A runnel of dark liquid crept out on the rubber matting of the floor, met a rubber vein on the

261

pattern of the mat and spidered around it. Blood, Minogue saw. He turned to Corrigan's ashen face now framed in the window opposite.

"Tell 'em to get a move-on, Pat," he heard the nose say. "Two."

Corrigan's eyes bulged as he stared at Minogue. Then he nodded and shouted Dunne's name. Another car skidded to a stop next to him. Two detectives jumped around the open doors as they bounced back on their hinges. Minogue wondered if it really was a police siren he was hearing in the distance.

"I didn't know this . . . " Minogue began to say. His voice was completely trapped in his head, somewhere behind his face. "We'll look after you, don't — "

"He would have killed me, you know," said Moore. The voice carried a tone of fearful, lucid warning, at once earnest and pleading. Minogue would later remember the strained tenor in Moore's plea, as from his children's fevers or as they woke from nightmares, still pursued into their waking worlds.

CHAPTER 16

"I told the Commissioner I'd be happier with the other thing," Minogue murmured. He was trying not to stare at Kilmartin again. He had barely recognised Kilmartin on first entering the room. Jimmy Kilmartin's face glowed against the pillow.

"You mean that fella Pat Corrigan shot?"

"Him, yes. He was way senior to Ball. Ball was only the pot-boy really. That Murray character was the wild card. He had the power to pave the way and cover it up."

Kilmartin studied Minogue's nose and the two black eyes.

"Do you mind me saying that you sound like Donald Duck? No offence now."

"I've heard them all, Jimmy."

"You look like you were in a shocking row."

"I was. Moore's car hit us a good wallop. I was concussed and I didn't know it. I hit the lip of the seat, the metal frame where there's not enough sponge."

"A real hero," Kilmartin murmured.

"Kathleen says different. More like an iijit."

Minogue found himself staring at Kilmartin's face again. What was it about Kilmartin that was so different? Was it just the bed-rest and being forcibly kept away from his job that had cleared his face of cares?

"Not much hope of getting them to turn the fella over to us," Kilmartin added. "But you had the pig-iron to ask them."

"The embassy? I tried. Didn't get that far. But how do you know all this?" Pleased with his intelligence, Kilmartin winked.

"Ha ha. A little bird. Here, I'll tell you anyway. God Almighty was in visiting last night. Himself and the new Assistant Commissioner, Tynan, after he took his life in his hands and vetted you. To see if I was in the land of the living. Now I don't much like Tynan, but you know how it is with the man himself. Larger than life."

Minogue knew. God Almighty a.k.a. Thomas Martin Lally, the Garda Commissioner, was a porcine brute of a farmer's son from Longford. He was shrewd and overbearing, with a tongue like a rasp and a bottomless fund of fulsome *bonhomie* which he parlayed as charm. He repelled Minogue. Tynan he rather liked. Tynan had studied several years for the Jesuits before becoming a Garda.

"Oh yes. Himself has his own little copy of what you dug up, Matt. But that's between yourself and meself."

"And Pat Corrigan and half the world."

"Not a bit of it. The Minister put it all under wraps, the one copy. Or so he thinks."

"The prints I made, you mean?" Minogue said.

"Ah, no matter. Don't be upsetting yourself. Himself says to me he might have known it was a homo at the bottom of all this."

Minogue rose abruptly from the chair. "Look it, Jimmy — "

"Sit down, Matt. Sit down. There's people that don't have your delicate touch. I was just testing you. I wasn't trying to get a rise out of you."

"My eye, you weren't. Lally's a boor. He shouldn't be in the job. It's as well he didn't talk like that to me."

Kilmartin raised a supplicant hand.

"Easy, man. Don't be deserting a sick man's bedside. Come on now."

Minogue felt something give way in his chest. He sat down.

"Oh, but there was great crack and sport to do with the names that were in this notebook thing. Pillars of Tory Britain. One of them was head of MI5 after the war, even. Another one was a Home Secretary and he's still a big wind there, cocked up in the House of Lords like mutton dressed up as lamb. Aren't you glad when you wake up every morning to find you're living in a republic? None of this Lord and Lady Muck stuff. This King and Queen stuff is for children. Or gobshites."

Minogue stroked his chin. Forgot to shave this morning. Saturday senility.

"But sure the crunch is we have no way of ascertaining whether the stuff from this notebook is true at all. The business that happened to him after the war and so on. There's no mileage in that for us. But the Costello racket — and that fella in the embassy, God rest him. I'm sure it's ninety-nine percent true. They must have been mad entirely. All grist for the mill here, though, I needn't tell you. Couldn't have happened at a better time, hah?"

"Costello," Minogue murmured.

"Ah, but this poor Combs divil overplayed his hand with that ultimatum. And he was right to be wary of that Ball character; I mean to say, look what Ball seems to have gone and done to Combs in the end. I'm

265

not for a minute saying that Combs wasn't hard done by in Britain, mind you."

"Wasn't the only one hard done by," said Minogue.

"War's war, Matt. Are you thinking of that fella they sold down the river just to keep Combs looking clean wherever he was then, Berlin? That would have sold a lot of Sunday papers if that had come out."

"Um. Vogel. Means bird. Yes . . . "

"I didn't get through the full bit about them throwing Vogel to the wolves," Kilmartin prodded.

Minogue ignored the hint. He was thinking of the hour he had spent earlier this Saturday morning, sitting in his car at Sandymount. A lone horse and rider had been cantering back and forth, far out on the strand.

"This Vogel back in the war, Matt? That trickery?" Kilmartin said again.

"Combs said that he didn't realise what had happened to Vogel until after he got out of Berlin himself. He doesn't go into specifics, but he says that Vogel was betrayed in such a way as to have the credit for uncovering an Allied spy reflected on Combs himself. All he knew was that the Germans weren't so suspicious of him after they got their maulers on Vogel. He says he was sure that he was about to be arrested. He was warned that some people suspected him of being a double agent. That bit. That was in 1943 and very few of his pals were around to look after him in Berlin."

"That was a real eye-opener about how Combs got his info back to the Allies. The codes," Kilmartin said.

"He used to use specific words in his broadcasts, he says," said Minogue. "The words being codes for different cities where he had found out that, say, troop trains were being assembled or that they were working on new armaments."

"Then the Allies would bomb those cities and get the most for their money," Minogue added.

"I have no knowledge of that sort of stuff, the history and the moves during the war," Kilmartin reflected aloud.

"Apparently those bombings drove a lot of armaments production underground or at least dispersed it and gave the Allies time to set up something else during the delays."

"Anyway, they gave Vogel away to keep Combs looking good," said Kilmartin. "Yes. When Combs got to Lisbon and asked what had happened to Vogel, he heard that he had been picked up. He didn't know anything except what he had heard from the Nazis about a big coup, finding an agent and knowing his code-name and all. The officer who he talked to in Lisbon — he's the one who went on to be head of their MI5 — told Combs that they had hoped to get more mileage out of Vogel but that Combs had chickened out early. 'A poor return on our investment,' he said to Combs, if I remember reading it right."

"God that was a terrible thing to say to him. Dirt and treachery," Kilmartin murmured.

"And then they wouldn't touch him with a forty-foot pole after the war."

"Indeed," said Minogue. "While they sorted out what they wanted to do with him. They tried to slot him into the Russian zone to do spying for them again; he turned them down flat. That might have been Combs' biggest mistake. And the thing is, who's to say the Russians would have welcomed him with open arms anyway, even if he passed on info to them as well as back to London?"

"Um," said Kilmartin. "They'd be just as suspicious as the Brits and the Yanks, I suppose. They'd be thinking the same as the Brits were thinking, that

Combs was being planted as a double by the other side. Jases. Allies, it it? The ins and outs of it all. The man was left with no ground to stand on."

"They kept on putting him off over the years," Minogue continued. "When he asked to be allowed to live back in England, I mean. Then they wanted some innocuous gaffer to look in on some goings-on here. Quid pro quo, I suppose. He doesn't talk about details of what they offered him, but they must have promised him that he would be, what's the word ... rehabilitated. After he did a bit of work for them in Ireland. The rest you have to guess at," Minogue said.

"Then Ball gave him the chop?"

"Looks very like it to me. Combs miscalculated."

"While he was thinking and bellyaching about what they did to him years ago, they thought he was going to do the dirty on them in their efforts here."

"Now you have it," Minogue concluded. "He said that Ball was continually boasting about Costello being looked after. Not alone that, but Ball dropped heavy hints that suggested he was present at the Costello murder. There was some torture and mutilation carried on, if you remember. Maybe it was just to let Combs know that he was a tough nut, so not to be getting ideas himself ... "

Minogue lost the thread of the conversation when Kilmartin started talking again. Minutes later, he became aware that Jimmy had finally stopped talking. Now he, too, was staring out the window.

"I want me dinner," Kilmartin said solemnly. "And I'm not going to sit here in the bed waiting for them to plonk some muck in front of me, stuff you could drink out of a shagging straw. I want me meat and me two veg. Will you come down to the cafeteria with me?"

Kilmartin shuffled down the hallways, eying the nurses and avoiding the doctors.

"God but that was a wicked dinner. Healthy, I suppose," Kilmartin said, shaking his head. "Ah, but you should have seen the two of them, Matt. Tynan and Himself. Himself sticks his big snoot in the door and tiptoes into the room first. 'Matty Minogue isn't here is he, Jimmy?' says he. Putting it on, of course. But there was something to it. And do you know what I said to myself when I saw that?"

"I don't."

"I says to myself, well I wish that I could inspire such fear as Matt Minogue, such as would cause him to do that."

Kilmartin paused in the hallway to stare at a nurse. Minogue took in the compound smells of the hospital, struck again at how powerful a sense the nose housed. Time to take a swipe at that Proust chap again, maybe.

"Oh yes. He was much as told me you were a pain in the neck about it all. His neck like, too."

"I hope I was," Minogue observed. "He has plenty of it to pain, let me tell you."

"Didn't he explain the ramifications to you?"

"The ones he thought were important, I suppose. After he reminded me of the Garda oath to keep my trap shut."

"Tough enough job for a Clareman."

"He spent a lot of time telling me that I could never expect the British secret service to fork over one of their, what did he call them, some antiseptic name . . . operatives, yes. That Murray fella. I couldn't expect them to hand me one. He wasn't overly excited about the conspiracy to murder charge I wanted issued."

Kilmartin laughed light-heartedly and slowed his promenade to peep into the rooms they passed.

Minogue remembered God Almighty starting with the flattery, soothing. He had made a great show of welcoming him into his office. It was the greater,

Minogue knew, because the Minister's Secretary was waiting there, too. Minogue instantly read Lally's gesture as a territorial display for the civil servant.

"Heard a great account of you, Matt, as did Mr O'Reilly here and indeed the Minister," the Commissioner began.

"And what with Jimmy Kilmartin laid up for a while and him forever singing your praises, sure the promotion is long overdue. Mr O'Reilly brings the Minister's commendations."

Not a word from O'Reilly, just a watchful interest. Minogue knew O'Reilly from two telephone calls and a curt letter received the morning after the shooting. It was O'Reilly who was to do the lecturing, apparently.

" . . . Goes without saying that this was a shocking crime, Sergeant. But as the Commissioner had pointed out, we are fully behind you and the Special Branch officers who assisted you in this matter. The Minister has expressed his whole-hearted commendation and a recommendation for your promotion."

God Almighty's jovial expression faltered but slightly when Minogue finally balked.

"It's very likely that the State could charge and convict Murray on first-degree murder in the deaths of Arthur Combs and Tim Costello," Minogue said mildly.

To his credit, O'Reilly didn't duck.

"If your assumptions are accurate, yes."

"But how close are you, Matt?" the Commissioner asked blithely to drive home what O'Reilly would be delivering presently.

"Well, we're stuck. They're holding to the business about Combs. They've sent dental records and everything. The package looks watertight. They insist the fella we're talking about was drowned in Lisbon under mysterious circumstances in 1946," replied Minogue.

"It was all a long time ago to be sure," said the Commissioner. "God knows what kind of tricks and twists they got up to during the war, that crowd. That's how they treat their own, I suppose. A great argument for Irish neutrality, wouldn't you say, Mr O'Reilly?"

O'Reilly ignored the mild jibe. Minogue was not ready to give in yet.

"And Costello?" he said.

"Oh, right, him," said the Commissioner. O'Reilly looked quizzically at Minogue.

"I don't need to remind you that we're all bound by the rules of disclosure and confidentiality we signed when we became public servants. Let me put it to you like this, Sergeant. Costello was killed by unknown assailants — "

" — a known professional assailant, you mean," Minogue interrupted.

"That's not clear at all, Sergeant. Costello had made a lot of enemies, it's safe to say. Oddly, Costello has become useful to the cause of peace and security here. And you're forgetting that Costello was killed outside the jurisdiction of the State. A productive outcome, I think," O'Reilly continued.

"Anyone ask Costello if he wanted to be such an altruist, posthumously?"

"Costello was rabid, Sergeant. He lived and died by the gun. I'm surprised to hear you taking his part so steadfastly after your experiences with his ilk," O'Reilly replied without any reprimand that Minogue could detect. O'Reilly wasn't to be baited without showing some of his own sharp tongue, apparently.

Minogue saw God Almighty rub a knuckle to his nose and nod once. Tidy, ironic, almost funny about Costello: more use to us dead than he ever was alive. And Combs? Minogue returned O'Reilly's unblinking gaze. He wanted to inquire as to how the British had reacted when the photocopies of Combs' notes were laid on the table. He would not give the two men the satisfaction of asking.

"Both you and Inspector Corrigan demonstrated great foresight," O'Reilly said.

Both you and Inspector Corrigan, Minogue repeated within. Pat Corrigan running with the envelope, looking for the highest rank he could find from the dozens of policemen converging on the train station. Like a grenade he wanted to rid of.

"And another thing, Matt," the Commissioner broke in. "Nobody walks around the streets in this country waving a gun about. Not a fancy embassy attaché or whatever they want to call this Murray. Not the Queen of England, for that matter. This is a democracy. I can tell you in all candour that it wouldn't have caused a stir here if Pat Corrigan had popped him for good."

He looked for bloodthirsty corroboration to O'Reilly.

"And like I said to Mr O'Reilly, I want the embassy and their bosses back in London to take note of your promotion, that we have nothing to be ashamed about. We held our end up here, so we did."

O'Reilly nodded once at that. Minogue almost gave up then. He didn't care to know how much of an edge the dossier had given anyone at the security conference.

"Definitely," O'Reilly added. "Not alone that, but your good work allowed the Taoiseach to send a strongly worded statement to the British Prime Minister."

"But what could he say to her, Mr O'Reilly?"

"I can disclose that he said he fully expected her to ensure that the embassy in Dublin was not to be used as a base for any covert operations of any description in this country."

In this country . . . the phrase echoed for several moments.

"In the Combs' case, one of theirs went astray — "

"One of ours," Minogue said. "Combs lived here. This was his home. People liked him. Did ye look at his drawings? Then tell me he was 'one of theirs.'"

"Ah now, Matt," the Commissioner interceded. "It's just phraseology. In a manner of speaking, like. Let's say that this wasn't Combs' home turf."

"But Tim Costello was one of ours?" Minogue had said then.

Kilmartin roused Minogue from his brooding when he began laughing at some recollection.

"Didn't the pair of them persuade you how much you had done for the greater good of the country, Matt? I heard the phrase uttered in this very room."

Minogue didn't answer.

"Here, we should have something to be celebrating your lad's exams. Cheer up, man."

"He's not certain until the results come out, Jimmy. He just said that he did great because the questions he had studied had come up."

"Sure that's life itself, isn't it, Matt? You answer the questions that come up, not the blather that the philosophers do be cooking up in their heads and all the rest of it. Iijits. . . . Grandstanding a bit, aren't you, Matt? Wearing your morals on your sleeve. Take the bloody promotion and don't be so damned upright."

Minogue was astonished. Jimmy Kilmartin being so pointed? Quite without warning, Minogue began to laugh himself. The sourness which had occupied his thoughts began to ease. Kilmartin was eying him with cautious amusement.

"You might have something there," Minogue allowed. "Bumptious. Still, the nerve of you to be talking to me like that. What's come over you?"

"Well, for one thing I don't have to get a twist in me gut every time I see you and think to myself that Matt Minogue should have my rank. You're over-moral, man dear. You'd be surprised how clear things get and you lying here on your back all day. All the things you should have done, could have said. You know yourself, I suppose. They'll never admit to having Costello bumped off. Poor Combs either — Grimes, I mean."

"But couldn't we have demanded Murray? He committed crimes in our jurisdiction. Even the chance to question him. He was on the plane and in a London hospital before tea-time."

Kilmartin snorted dismissively.

" 'Diplomat' my arse. I agree with you. In the abstract, of course. It was all part of a trade. You know that. They were on the blower very rapid after news of the escapade hit London. They say he's still on the critical list, Murray — "

"He was shot through the lung and that was the worst of it," Minogue protested. "Moore was the worse off with being shot in the back, but did you hear him complaining? They just want us to forget we ever had a chance to talk to Murray."

"All right, Matt. But don't be a gobshite. The deal is done. Go home and tell your wife that she's married to a man who routinely scares the wits out of his superiors."

Hugh Robertson was smoking one of his rare cigarettes in the restaurant. Kenyon watched the ceremony vacantly. Robertson searching as though he had forgotten which pocket held the cigarette case. Drawing one out, tapping both ends of the plain

cigarette on the tablecloth. Searching for minute pieces
of the dark tobacco before brushing them off the table.
He offered Kenyon one, then lit his own and inhaled.
The cigarette smelled of Turkish tobacco. Kenyon
guessed they were hand-rolled in a specialty shop in
the City.

"Yes, I told him that in my view Moore did excellent
work. Everything according to instructions and more
besides. We hadn't counted on Murray running amok,
I reminded him. 'Moore displayed initiative and should
be commended for that,' I said. I didn't tell him that I
have three years to retirement and that he could . . . "

Kenyon was still drifting in the trough of relief after
what Robertson had told him during the dinner.

" . . . fuck off with himself, don't you know."

Robertson smiled and batted his eyes. He looked
about the restaurant before turning to the wine again.

"As if we are to be held to account for Six making a
royal balls-up. 'Let them get together with the Foreign
Office to put the egg back together,' I told him. Not in
so many words, of course. After all, they loaned the
problem to us. Never wanted it in the first place, did
we?"

Kenyon tried to smile in return. He couldn't manage the sultry, silent-movie smile which Robertson
seemed to produce effortlessly.

"I told him that James Kenyon had read Combs
accurately, had evaluated the problem accurately and
had moved at the first opportunity to try and pull the
damn thing out of the fire. You can imagine that he
was recording it all, because I was called in as a
speech-writer for him to report to Maggie with. I can
see him parrotting it all. 'Well ma'am, Mr Kenyon read
the Combs business accurately and moved at the . . . ' "

Kenyon was moved to express some gratitude, but
he feared he'd be maudlin.

"Thank you, Hugh. You don't know what it means to — "

"Don't be overpowered, James. I told him the truth. He can gild the lily if he wants to later. I also mentioned, by way of a polite reminder, that when he needs a lamb for the ritual slaughter, we'll be going for Murray's neck."

"When do we get our hands on Murray?"

"Christ, don't ask, James," said Robertson languidly. "Six claims that he can't be interviewed yet. . . . Means they're doing it right now, probably, before they pitch him over to us. . . . "

"You see, James," Robertson eased himself against the chair better to expound, "C is a man whose disposition leads him inevitably to find villains. Villains and heroes. For a man in his position it's an extraordinarily simplistic way to see the world. But it has its advantages from my point of view here with this. Moore is a hero. Moore nearly lost his life in the service of national security, um? He'll be fine in a matter of months, but he'll need to watch his kidneys for the rest of his life, poor chap. We're giving him the option of a good disability out or a switch to other work. Once I explained to the old man that Moore is a hero, he copped on. All this consultation . . . I far preferred the old days, didn't you? Scandals and moles aside, of course. Consult the old man after an op. Drop an ambiguous memo, and let him go back to his greenhouse or Sanskrit."

Kenyon smiled tightly.

"But our present Duce was parachuted in to clean house. He's not, er, you know . . . "

"One of us," Kenyon completed the hackneyed Service joke.

"Just so, James," Robertson went on archly. "There's really no need for him to be running about preparing lengthy defences for the business in Dublin. He'll find out for himself. *Qui s'excuse, s'accuse.* Not our problem at all, at all. Even a layman can see that. What we had was a circus: Murray and Ball and their vendetta, running an alcoholic tout, one Mr Combs, through the embassy. A dicey enough proposal in Ireland even without Combs being a bloody Trojan horse. Where it would have stopped with Ball's rough-and-tumble tactics, I don't know. There's a case to be made for sending in proper tricks boys to do for what's-his-face and his ilk right on their home turf in the Republic. We could aerate more like . . . what's his . . . ?"

"Costello."

"Yes. Naturally, Mad Murray has to prevaricate when it crossed your desk . . . and we're supposed to be the good fairy and fix up everything, good as new?"

"I wish C held that — "

"Ah, but I told him this, James. That part he can stomach, because he's mainly concerned for his own arse. PMO called him in the morning after, into committee, and the PM was doing her Sphinx bit at the end of the table. Not happy at all. 'Looked like the first tank must have looked to the first soldier who saw it coming over the trenches at him,' C said to me. *La belle dame* stuck the prod in deep apparently. Told them what it meant for border security negotiations. Didn't divulge to anyone what they had to give away to even keep the Irish at the damn table and still get Murray and Moore and that garbled dossier here. . . . Didn't tell them what it did for her re-election plans if she didn't score a nice coup here either, mind you."

Robertson poured more wine. He snorted before sipping.

"Shopkeeper's daughter she may be, but she's twice the man of any around that table. There's only so much the Irish can mine with the papers, of course. If they ask too much for sitting on it we can retaliate in some other arena. If they went public or leaked it, they'd suffer in the long run. Their opposition parties and the lunatic fringe there could do a slash and burn on them, too, I expect. Scream bloody murder about the government giving into perfidious Albion again. Bloody-minded people there. What would they do if they didn't have us to complain about?"

Kenyon didn't fend off Robertson's roving bottle this time. He felt the wine working now. Robertson blinked several times. His eyes were soft and glassy from the wine. The waiter brought coffee. Kenyon alone drank some. Robertson drained his glass.

"Canny bastard, that copper, though," Robertson murmured. "Having the copy and baiting poor Moore . . . "

"Moore was on the plane two hours after the shooting. He didn't get to talk to the copper again," Kenyon said.

"Too bad he opened his mouth to the Irish security on the scene at all. The bit about the copper, Minogue, saving his bacon. I don't like to hear that sort of remark. Before our mob got out from the embassy and threw a blanket on the stuff."

"Shock, maybe," Kenyon answered. "Human after all. Murray was ready to kill him, he says."

"Oh-oh, James. I thought we could have a dinner and get half-sloshed without you going moral on me," Robertson chided.

Kenyon didn't mind the riposte. He believed that Robertson drew the remarks from him, a proxy conscience for himself.

"I would have felt the same way as Moore," said Kenyon.

Robertson fixed him with an indulgent and skeptical eye. Kenyon felt he could match Hugh Robertson's jaundiced eye this time.

"And I think you would have too, Hugh."

Robertson made no reply.

CHAPTER 17

A traffic accident near Milltown put idle-time upon Minogue. He switched off the engine and leafed through the postcards. RTE was playing Ravel. In honour of the weather, Minogue surmised. He had the tail end of a hangover from the party for promotions. He let down the window. The drops flicked onto his face.

He leafed through the postcards again. Minogue had bought the last three copies of the Magritte postcard which his daughter had discovered in the bookshop. He had bargained for an envelope for each. As usual, when he was faced by pen and paper, Minogue could think of nothing sensible to write. Nothing mawkish, though, that was for certain. He caught a motorist staring at him and remembered that his face was still that of a Halloween caller. Minogue then hastily wrote on Daithi's card. He stuffed the card into the envelope before he decided to change his mind about what he had written. Beside the card he inserted five crisp ten-pound notes and the business card for the travel agent in Abbey Street, the one that would give him a special deal. It'd probably be to the States, if he knew his son at all.

He was still examining the puffy-white clouds of the Magritte postcards when the horns started behind. He turned the ignition, but the engine didn't catch for several seconds. The road ahead was clearing.

Bestselling Crime

Prices and other details are liable to change

ARROW BOOKS, BOOKSERVICE BY POST, PO BOX 29, DOUGLAS, ISLE
OF MAN, BRITISH ISLES

NAME..

ADDRESS...

....

....

Please enclose a cheque or postal order made out to Arrow Books Ltd. for the amount
due and allow the following for postage and packing.

U.K. CUSTOMERS: Please allow 22p per book to a maximum of £3.00.

B.F.P.O. & EIRE: Please allow 22p per book to a maximum of £3.00.

OVERSEAS CUSTOMERS: Please allow 22p per book.

Whilst every effort is made to keep prices low it is sometimes necessary to increase cover
prices at short notice. Arrow Books reserve the right to show new retail prices on covers
which may differ from those previously advertised in the text or elsewhere.